BORN TOUGH: JACK

A RANCH ROMANTIC SUSPENSE

JULIET BRILEE

BORN TOUGH: JACK

A RANCH ROMANTIC SUSPENSE

JULIET BRILEE

ACKNOWLEDGMENTS

I couldn't write my books without the amazing team of friends, family, and paid professionals who offer their observations. Special thanks go to the veterans and law enforcement officers who have offered guidance. And thanks go to Joshua for his input about navigating the world as a visually impaired individual.

ACKNOWLEDGMENTS

Thank You

I couldn't write my books without the amazing team of friends, family, and paid professionals who offer their expertise and observations. Special thanks go to the people in law enforcement and ranchers who have advised me. Thanks go to Joshua for his input about navigating the world while visually impaired.

For more information about the five love languages and the book by Gary Chapman https://5lovelanguages.com

1

*J*ack Stone counted his steps as he covered the length of the horse barn. He sucked in a breath, found his cool head, and strode back to the three men standing at the opposite end. He'd hoped this would go more smoothly.

Brick, their cowboy, shifted his gaze from one man to the next, unwilling to take a stand. Smart guy, Brick.

Striker rubbed his chin thoughtfully, like he was the boss. That was the previous ranch owner's fault. As ranch foreman for nearly two decades, Striker had been given free rein and understood the cattle, horses, and land better than the rest of them. He was an excellent resource. That didn't make him in charge.

Jack's half-brother, Luke, all chill, rested an arm on a stall. "Horses? For real? You're serious about breeding horses?"

"It's always been a cattle operation at the Tall Pines," Striker said. "Always— Until the minis. They were Louise's thing."

Besides cattle, a dozen miniature horses had transferred with the sale when the Stone family bought the south Florida ranch last year.

"I'm not saying get rid of the cattle." Jack lifted his hands and gestured like an attorney laying out a closing argument. "I'm talking about expanding. Start small. I talked to the owner of the S bar C in Ocala. I'm driving up to check out some horses. Dad's new caregiver said she'd stay through dinner."

Striker's brows cleaved together, and his gaze flicked to Luke.

Jack growled inwardly. Why was Striker checking with Luke for confirmation? He was the manager. Him. Not Luke.

"You already made an appointment to see them?" Luke asked.

"That's what I said," Jack bit out.

Luke scowled. "Without running it by anyone else?"

He clenched his jaw, caught himself, and intentionally relaxed. "I'm saying it now. And I told you last week I was thinking about it."

Luke opened his phone and tapped it, then looked up impatiently. "People say stuff. That doesn't mean they're gonna do it."

Striker nodded and exchanged a glance with Luke.

Of course, he'd side with Luke.

Last year, while Jack had been sitting in jail, Luke had traveled from Montana to Florida in his place. Luke had convinced the old rancher they were the best buyers. Because of Jack's half-brother, their family owned the Tall Pines. But Luke was wrapped up in his tech business and had no interest in running the ranch.

Jack fought back the urge to grind the enamel off of his teeth. "Sometimes people mean what they say." Luke's share of the ranch was slightly bigger than his, but he wasn't asking permission. "These horses came up for sale unexpectedly. I need to jump right on it."

"Did you mention it to Garrick?" Luke pocketed his phone.

"He thought it sounded good." That was a stretch, but as usual, Garrick wasn't at their meeting. Since separating from the Army, their younger brother was a wild card, as likely as not to attend the meetings, missing even the more formal ones.

"You've seen him today?" Luke asked.

"No, but he marked off his chores," Jack answered. There was a task clipboard they signed when they finished ranch duties. Old school. More of a ghost than a slacker, Garrick preferred working alone. He was up earlier than the rest of them, got his tasks done, signed the log, and disappeared.

Jack held Luke's gaze, and they exchanged a brief, meaningful look. At least they agreed on giving Garrick space.

"I don't know," Luke said. "Can we talk—"

"—I've got to act today. There's room here to get started, and we can build another barn." He'd been riding since before he could walk. It was about time he made his dream come true. He wasn't backing down.

He held Luke's gaze.

A text pinged from the phone in his pocket. He ignored it.

Yellow flashed outside the door behind Luke, in the corral attached to the barn. Jack's breath caught in his throat.

Dani. Luke's sister-in-law must've come out early to brush the mini horses. The side of his mouth lifted. Who wears a dress to do ranch chores? Not that he was complaining. He could watch her in a dress all day, but her hand was on her hip, and she seemed frustrated. "Brick, can you go check on Dani? I think she's having a problem out there."

"Sure thing." Brick hustled outside.

The ringtone sounded, and Jack answered his phone, in case it was someone at the S bar C.

"I texted." The irate woman on the other end came through the speaker. "You didn't answer."

"Who..." Awareness broke over him. It was the woman at

the house with his dad. "What do you need? Is everything all right?"

"No," she huffed. "I'm leaving. Your father fired me."

Jack pinched the bridge of his nose and tried to speak calmly. "He can't fire you. I hired you."

"He fired me. And he said ... Well, I don't generally use that language. He's sitting in his chair. I'm leaving. Now."

"Wait. Can you just—" The call ended. *No! Not today.* He exhaled hard and stared at the phone for a beat. Tension threaded through his neck. "Dad fired the woman they sent out this morning. I thought she was tough enough to handle him. She used to drive a school bus."

"Is he okay?" Luke asked.

"Yes." Jack was so angry he could spit nails. "He's sitting on his La-Z-Boy throne. Hey, can you deal with him this afternoon?"

"No can do. I changed my flight. I leave for the airport in an hour." Luke glanced at the door. He divided his time between his tech start-up in Bozeman and the Tall Pines. But lately, he'd been traveling more than usual.

"Great." Jack walked to the nearest stall and gripped the door, wanting to yank the thing off its hinges. Whiskey Rocks, one of the few horses still in the barn, nickered, moved closer, and nudged him. He lowered his head to the gelding's soft muzzle and breathed in the scent of his favorite horse.

"I wrote it on the task board a while ago," Luke continued. "Signed out for the next few days. I'll check on Dad, but I can't stay."

Right. Figures. Jack's chest deflated. There was always some reason his father's care fell on his shoulders.

The ranch was already shorthanded, and they had a of couple day-worker cowboys coming out to work cattle. He couldn't ask Brick or Striker for help. It looked like he'd have to postpone his trip to Ocala.

The meeting broke up.

Jack stalked to the office at the end of the barn to finish cleaning out the old desk, aggravation making it easier to hurl things into the trash. The task was tedious, but he'd postponed it for too long, and it was necessary to make the area usable.

With only a short time until Luke left, there wasn't much else he could do. He dropped to the swivel chair and called Adam at the S bar C. There was no way he'd be able to get there if he had to take care of his dad.

"That's a shame," Adam said. "We have another interested party..."

"Can you give me a few days?"

"Afraid not. But I'll keep an ear out since I know what you're looking for."

"Thanks." He shoved aside his frustration and managed a courteous tone. Adam had influence in the Ocala equine community.

"Hey. A buddy of mine has an opening coming up for a ranch manager. Horses. They need to know their stuff. Got a man retiring next year. We're accepting applications, but this is on the down low, word of mouth only. We only want the best to apply."

Outside the window, Luke and Striker huddled in conversation. Those two were thick as thieves. "I might know someone," Jack said. It'd be foolish to release Striker from his contract, but he wouldn't mind having a second in command who looked to him rather than his half-brother.

They ended the call, and the landline rang. Few people besides the veterinarians still used it, but on this ranch, with spotty cell service, it was the most reliable phone. Someone was usually near the barn.

"Jack?" It was the veterinarian they used for the minis.

"What's up, Doc?"

She groaned. "Listen. This is serious. I have five minis I'm trying to re-home, but it has to be a special place. They were in bad shape. One was ... well, the details are in their files."

He balked. They had no extra room in the mini wing of the barn. "And?" He was going to make her say it while he figured out how to politely decline. He didn't want more miniature horses. Until he built his new barn, they'd have to use the extra stalls for the standard-size horses he planned to buy.

"Can you take them?"

He rubbed his forehead and swallowed his impulse to say no, choosing a more diplomatic response. "I don't think so. Can't you send them to Sacred Haven in Valencia Cove?"

"They took six. Another six went to Tender Hearts Rescue. I wouldn't ask if we had other options. I can still work on finding them homes if you'd at least foster them. Otherwise, we may have to consider euthanasia...."

He released a long, resigned breath. They'd be expensive and need a lot of attention. And Dani would have more work.

"Please?"

He scowled. Damned if he didn't have a soft spot for women needing help. His plan to breed horses was slipping through his fingers.

"Can I take your silence for a yes?"

"Alright." He rubbed the space above his nose. "When can I expect them?"

"Soon."

He ended the call, shaking his head. This day kept getting better and better.

———

Jack held his breath while Serena, the employee at Helping Hands Services, checked her computer. "I'm sure a woman as sharp as you can come up with something." One way or another, he'd find someone to take care of his father. After three days without help, he was down to his last nerve. "It should only be for a few more months. My dad's just seventy-four. He's gettin' better." That might be wishful thinking, but Bud Stone had worked hard on the Double B back in Montana, before his hip replacement and the stroke. Before Jack's mom died.

"Nothing's changed since we spoke on the phone." The attractive redhead bit her lip. "There's nobody else available."

Jack studied the bleak, off-white walls of the office and fought the frustration threatening to wash over him and drag him under. Then he leaned in and gave Serena his friendliest smile. It usually worked on the ladies. "You sure you've got no one sooner?"

A door to the side opened and a gray-haired woman appeared. She spotted Jack and shot him a glare. She was the second woman his old man had fired. What was her name? He gave her a friendly nod. The woman frowned and pushed through the exit. There was no telling what she'd told the other employees.

Gathering what remained of his charm, he returned his focus to Serena. "Absolutely no one you can call?"

She winced and gestured to the door. "You've run through our best people."

"We'll pay one and a half times the regular rate."

"No. I'm sorry." She lowered her voice. "Unless a client dies and frees someone up."

He leaned in conspiratorially. "Are you suggesting we kill someone?"

"No!" Serena said, aghast. "Sometimes our customers are very ill and ... you know." Her brows lifted toward her hairline. "You could check Clark's Caring Helpers in Heron Park."

Jack rubbed his chin. No. He could not. Last summer, when

he was new to the area, he'd gone out with Clark's daughter and allegedly broke her heart. Clark had threatened to punch him in the face if he ever darkened their doorway. "We've already tried them, and this place is much better."

Serena winced. "Sorry. But your father ...."

Resigned, he forced a pleasant tone. "No worries. It's all good. I can handle it until you have someone. I just have other things to do."

"I get it. Lots of people need support at times like this."

Caregiving was not what he'd signed up for when he'd agreed to move south and run the new ranch. He was supposed to be the cattle boss, the rancher. Not spend his days cleaning, cooking, and helping his father bathe and dress. If you asked him, this entire arrangement was bait and switch, and it was too late to return to his old life. So here he was, begging.

To top it off, the five new miniature horses they'd accepted two days ago had monopolized what little free time he had. It was like owning a pack of very expensive Great Danes, only more needy.

Serena stacked the papers on her desk and powered down her computer. "I'm afraid you wasted your time coming in. Anyway, you're on the waiting list. We'll contact you when we have availability." Her gaze met his and held. She glanced at the clock. "I get off in ten minutes. If you want to ... discuss our services."

A jolt of something moved through him. "That is a kind offer," he drawled, holding her gaze a beat. She was hot and probably in her early twenties. For a moment, the devil on his right shoulder threatened to beat the good sense out of him.

He'd recently passed his forty-second birthday. But when he shaved, his face looked kind of younger. The few strands of gray were hardly noticeable in his dark blond hair, and he stayed fit. He'd aged well. This meant he'd gotten to the stage where some of the most tempting women were around the age his daughter would've been if she'd lived.

"I'm afraid I'll have to pass. I have another appointment." He lifted his felt Stetson from where he'd set it.

Serena's age was an issue but not the only one. Living down his reputation from back home, and those wild weeks when he'd first moved to southwest Florida, proved challenging. But he'd vowed to reform. There was something bigger at stake here. He needed to prove his competence to his dad and brothers, to earn the ranch manager title. Then his dad would even up the shares. And he might be able to convince his brother Garrick to sell him his shares.

Last year, back in Montana, his dad and his uncle split the family ranch. When their side of the family acquired Tall Pines, his father divided the business unequally, giving his half-brother controlling interest because he had the coolest head. It still chaffed Jack's chaps. How could he be an effective manager when Luke held the bigger share?

Serena's expression shuttered. "Someone will contact you when a caregiver is available. We're about to close for the day." She gestured toward the exit across the room.

"Alright then." He tipped his hat.

As he showed himself out, he heard her mutter, *"Don't hold your breath."*

Pulling his brim down to shield the late afternoon sun, Jack climbed into his pickup truck and slammed the door. He rubbed his hands over his face and groaned. Being nice, polite, and charming hadn't gotten him a damned thing.

He needed to hit something. Now.

"Use your tools," Dr. Dave's voice played in his head. *"What tactic will help you achieve your goal?"*

After eight months of court-ordered weekly meetings, he now carried his counselor's voice in his head. He'd met the conditions for his mandated counseling when his probation ended two months earlier. But he'd agreed to the tapering-off approach and had a few more appointments. If pressed, he'd admit they weren't that bad. Introspective. Self-aware. Behavior patterns. Emotional intelligence. Those new terms had crept into his vocabulary. And it didn't suck to have a sharp man to talk to, because he sure as hell never had a normal conversation with his dad. The psychotherapist was a former Navy SEAL who'd grown up on a ranch. The guy was tough and knew a few things.

He inhaled deeply and let it out slowly. *I can keep myself calm.*

He tried again.

And again.

Yeah. He huffed. That wasn't enough. He still needed to hit something.

Avery, his seventeen-year-old niece, and her friend were staying with his father, and he ought to be getting home. But he couldn't face his old man filled with this much frustration. It would be like two angry bulls locking horns. And he'd vowed to change his ways. Feeling one degree calmer from the deep breathing, he put his Ram 2500 in gear and headed toward the Cedar Bay Boxing Club.

Jack dragged his sweaty body to his truck, and the boxing club receded in the rear-view mirror as he drove east. Turner's Tap, a popular bar featuring live country music and line dancing, sat on an open stretch of road on the way to Pine Crossing. He'd spent a few nights sampling the craft beers and local women when he'd first moved down. Right about now, that didn't sound half bad, and the mix of Cedar Bay locals and tourists who frequented Turner's worked in his favor.

After parking his truck, he got his swagger on and took a place at the bar next to a hot blonde. "Hey there."

"Hi yourself." She seemed friendly enough.

"Looks like you have something good." He inclined his head toward her drink. Something frozen, probably a margarita based on the salt. "Can I buy you another one?" Her first one was half-full, but after three days of catering to his father's demands, and an hour of pounding the bag, he was fresh out of decent lines. Something that never would've happened to his old self.

"Um." Her brows jumped together. A burly guy in biker garb, with sleeves of tattoos up his massive arms, sidled up to the woman's right and scowled.

Jack thought fast. He'd sworn off fighting, and the hulking dude was built like a semi-truck. These two probably belonged to the Harley outside. Jack plunked down some cash. "Their round's on me."

The biker's expression relaxed a few degrees. "Thanks."

Jack backed away and found a table by the wall. He sipped a craft brew and scrolled through text messages from his friends in Montana.

In his hometown outside Bozeman, he had plenty of drinking buddies, including a couple of women who enjoyed a little no-strings fun. Moving to a ranch two thousand miles from the Double B meant meeting new people. At this phase of life, it was more difficult making connections. Joining the Florida Cattlemen's Association hadn't helped since he couldn't leave his dad for long, and he'd only met a few Pine Crossing locals.

A photo appeared on his phone screen. His friends, Mia and Scott, were throwing darts at Duke's back home. He tapped the *like* icon. Something pinched in his chest. They were a thing now. He wasn't exactly jealous, but his friends were all pairing off. The divorced ones were remarrying, and his long-time unmarried bros had even found women.

Everything was changing. He'd received two wedding invitations in the past month. They could have it. People were like fireflies—beautiful in the wild, but catch them and put them in a jar, and they were just bugs. That was marriage for you. Jack wasn't going there again. Still, heaviness settled over him as he studied the photo. He swallowed hard.

Nothing that a second draft wouldn't cure.

2

The aromas of coffee, cinnamon-apple baked goods, and tonight's meatloaf special filled the diner, but Danielle Tremont found the scent of men's cologne and their clothing carrying the odors of a hard day of work more interesting. Blind since birth, her favorite pastime was bantering at the diner while enjoying a slice of their delicious pie. She leaned toward the man on her right and laid a hand on his arm. "Chet, your stories are hilarious. I'll have to come over and see those piglets."

His arm tensed briefly beneath her hand. "Sure, come over anytime, Dani. But I thought—"

"It's just an expression, honey. I have what they call visual vocabulary. Most people say *see* when they mean meet up or understand."

"That makes sense," Chet said warmly. "Come out in a couple of weeks. We're expecting kittens any day. Maryjane will show you around."

"I'll get to hold a piglet and a kitten? Now I must visit." She pulled her hand away. Flirting with the men at Mac's Diner or

Lone Star Pete's, the tavern next door, was good sport, but she didn't expect it to spill over into the rest of her life. Actual dating never seemed to go well, but these people were becoming her friends.

Someone sat on the stool to her left. He carried the fragrance of bath soap, grease, and perspiration. A working man who cared about being clean. And it sounded like he was alone. She perked up.

"One order of apple pie for Miss Danielle." Amber, the counter worker, approached, and the thunk of the plate on the counter was followed by the scrumptious scent of her hot apple pie.

"This smells divine." She tasted a small bite. Warm chunks of apple melted on her tongue in the perfect filling, not too sweet, and with a touch of cinnamon and lemon. "Oh, my ... mmm mm. I've gone to heaven. Y'all make the best pies."

The man to her left ordered. "I'll try a slice of apple pie, too."

He had a pleasant, smooth voice.

She leaned over. "You won't regret it. You might even wind up buying yourself a pie to take home."

"There you go again," Amber said lightly. "We'll have to start paying you a commission."

The truth was, almost every time she ate a piece of pie, one of the customers she spoke to wound up ordering a slice, or an entire pie, to go. If only she could monetize it.

"Will you be here Saturday morning, Danielle?" Chet stood and moved behind her, heading toward the register.

"If Brick drives to town for feed, you can bet I will." She hitched a ride whenever someone from the Tall Pines Ranch came into town. Today she was later than usual on account of her sister having a meeting online and doing her grocery shopping closer to dinner time. Happily, it turned out that this was the time to come. Midafternoons were too dang slow. While better for eavesdropping, there were fewer people to chat up at the counter.

A couple of cowboys, whose voices she recognized as being from Parson's Ranch, strolled in and filled the now-vacant spaces to her right.

"Hey, Danielle," Tanner said from the counter seat beside her. "You look beautiful today."

"Why, thank you. You're not so bad yourself." That always threw them. They knew she was blind, but she had yet to find a man who didn't appreciate being called handsome.

"Him? Now how do you know he's nice-looking? He might be hideous," Roy, the older cowboy to the right of Tanner, asked.

"You know I can tell attractiveness by voice, right? It's a thing." A thing she'd made up but most people bought it.

"It is, huh?" Roy sounded skeptical.

"Sure is." Tanner jumped right on the compliment. "She can tell I'm good lookin'." A smug smile filled his tone.

"For real," Dani went on. "And Roy, I can tell you're very handsome too, quite a catch. Even though you were a lady killer in your youth, you still have it. And I like the woodsy scent you wear. Is that my favorite? Knotting Hill?"

"You nailed it, pretty lady." Roy chuckled.

"Did you wear that for me?" She fanned her smoothly polished fingertips and placed them on the bare skin at the base of her throat. It paid to get regular manicures and wear sun dresses, even if late March was a bit chilly.

"It was a Christmas present from my wife. But I'm glad you like it," Roy said, probably puffing up a little.

"How does she do that?" someone in the booth behind her asked.

Dani allowed a small, satisfied smile to curve her lips. Both she and her sister were born with unusually sensitive olfactory systems. But she practiced mindfulness training every day, constantly working to improve both her hearing and smell. High sensory clarity was crucial for visually impaired people, even more so now that she was working with essential oils and healing herbs.

"You been working in the garden today?" Tanner asked. "You've got dirt under those nails. Like a real farmer."

"Why, yes." Heat flooded her face. She pulled her hands together in her lap and groaned inwardly. She'd washed up after gardening but must not have gotten all the dirt. This is why pulling weeds was a bad idea. The garden gloves blunted her ability to feel the weeds, and digging in the garden bare-handed got her dirty. Dang. It stunk being at the mercy of people telling her these things.

"Now you've embarrassed her," Roy said.

"Sorry, Danielle." Tanner's voice softened. "I meant it as a compliment."

"Tanner, you need to get off the ranch more," Amber said.

Dani put cheer in her voice. "Don't be silly. Tanner, you have wonderful powers of detection."

"I heard you're working the herbs with Thea," Roy chimed in.

"That's true." She sat a little taller. The esteem of working with the old woman herbalist at the ranch erased some of the shame of being caught with dirty fingernails. But her apprenticeship with Thea wasn't something she typically bragged about.

Roy continued, "That cream she sold me really improved my bursitis. Tell her it worked, and it smells good, too."

She lifted with pride. "Thank you. I helped create the formula." Her first solo recipe, the special blend, contained capsaicin, CBD, and wintergreen oil.

"With talents like that, I might have to marry you," Tanner said.

"Are you finished with the pie?" Amber asked. "You've hardly eaten any."

"Can you put it in a to-go container?" she said. "I should eat something with more protein."

"Put it on my check," Tanner said. "Get whatever you want, sweetheart. Dinner's on me."

Dani laid a hand on his muscular forearm. "Why, thank you."

And once again, she was eating out for free. She released a small, contented sigh. If one of these men were actually her date, this evening would be even better. But she didn't have to make her own dinner, and she'd happily take the delicious meal with a side of male attention.

By the time Jack polished off his second draft, the surrounding tables had filled with couples. People were out having fun, not watching TV with their father and getting him ready for bed, which was what he had to look forward to.

His stomach growled. It was dinner time, and he needed to get a move on. Cooking for his old man was getting tiresome, but greasy potato skins, wings, and other bar fare wouldn't suit his dad. There'd be hell to pay if his father's stomach acted up. Mac's diner, on the way home, had decent food, and he could pick up a home-style meal. Pleased with his plan, he marched to his truck and headed toward Pine Crossing.

As usual, the parking lot for Mac's was jammed with vehicles, mostly pickup trucks. While he'd eaten lunch at the popular diner, he was rarely there come dinner time. Rumor had it people drove from Cedar Bay for the meatloaf and desserts.

Amber, the older woman working the counter, greeted him, "Well, look what the cat dragged in."

"Hey, beautiful. It's busy here tonight."

"Meatloaf night. Always is."

"Then it's high time I tried it. Can I get two meals to go? And throw in a couple slices of apple pie. But only if it's sweet as you."

"I'm more spicy than sweet." Amber winked and rang up his order.

While returning his credit card to his wallet, he froze and swung his gaze toward familiar laughter. Unmistakable, familiar laughter. His pulse sped up.

What was she doing here at this time of day?

Dani Tremont sat at a stool about halfway down the counter, leaning toward the man to her right, laughing at something he said. To her left, the mechanic with a ponytail, who'd worked on his truck, was trying to get in on the conversation. His niece, Avery, called Dani the *queen of the diner*, and she could be found holding court most any time she could get a ride into town.

On the plus side, Dani couldn't see him. But it'd be a jerk move to take advantage of her blindness. Should he walk down and speak to her? Did he have to? Despite living on the same ranch, he'd done well avoiding her. Danielle Tremont was forbidden fruit.

Dani's hair fell over her bare shoulder. Unless you called that thin wisp of fabric a sleeve. Wasn't she cold? Even though the dinner rush had started, he could make out her sweet Georgia accent as she told the man beside her, "You are so smart."

Ponytail leaned in and said something that made Dani laugh. Jack's hands tightened. He stretched his fingers to avoid making a fist. She wasn't in trouble. He didn't need to intervene. But the man was too close. And being blind, she probably couldn't tell. His sister-in-law's younger sister had no way of knowing that the loser was leering at her.

When she laid a delicate hand on the jerk's arm, Jack's teeth clamped together. He stood only twenty feet from the woman, but she had no idea he was there. No matter. He kept a close eye on her. Those men would have to get through him if they gave her a hard time. Which was precisely the kind of thinking that'd landed him in jail for a month.

"Well, hey there." Someone poked his side.

"Ellie. What brings you out this time of day?" Typically, his sister-in-law would be home making dinner. Luke loved home-cooked meals and considered dinnertime sacred.

"I've been grocery shopping. I'm picking up Dani. I know." She lifted a palm. "It's late. I had a meeting that ran over. But it'll be worth it if I get the account."

"I'm surprised you're not home cooking," he casually remarked.

"Oh. I was supposed to tell you. Luke's staying in Bozeman another day. Something about a new platform they're launching."

Of course he was. His half-brother always had something to keep him from doing ranch work.

Ellie took a step forward. "C'mon, Dani, we need to go. Didn't you get my text? The ice cream's turning to soup as I speak."

"What? No. I have a tuna melt and fries coming. Tanner's buying me dinner."

"That's nice for you. Get it to go."

Conversations quieted as people listened in.

"You know that sort of thing won't keep," Dani said firmly. "It's meant to be eaten right away."

Ellie's face screwed up in frustration. She moved a little closer to Dani. "I have two half gallons of ice cream in the car, which won't keep. We need to head home."

"I can't just up and leave. It'd be rude. And Roy here was

telling me all about his goats. It's fascinating." Dani's voice oozed southern charm.

Ellie looked Jack's way and rolled her eyes.

Glad to be on the sidelines, he studied the volley between the sisters. He had two brothers and a sister, and they didn't always get along.

He glanced toward the kitchen. What was taking so long? Judging by the number of people waiting, he'd be here a while. He should've gone home and cooked.

"You go on," Dani said firmly. "I'll walk home. I brought my cane."

Jack whipped his gaze to Dani. Did she just say she was walking all the way to the ranch?

"You're not walking home." Ellie folded her arms across her chest and tapped her foot. "It's almost seven miles, and there're no sidewalks."

"Well, I'm sure one of these gentlemen here will give me a ride."

The mechanic to Dani's left perked up. Several cowboys in booths to the side glanced over with interest.

Ellie frowned and approached him. "Jack, you're waiting on food, and I need to go. Can you give her a ride?"

"I would. But Avery and her friend are staying with my dad, and she said something about homework." And his dad was probably all kinds of hangry by now.

"I'll handle the girls. Thanks." Ellie called over to her sister, "I'll see you later, Dani. Jack's here."

Ellie backed out of the diner.

Hold up! He hadn't said yes. Was she leaving him to drive Dani? After months of successfully managing not to be alone with her?

"I'll give you a lift, sweetheart," one of the nearby cowboys called over.

Alarmed, Jack stepped forward to tell Dani he was her ride.

Then he halted, hearing Dr. Dave's voice in his mind. *Chill.* He needed to rein in his impulses. Choose a different tactic. What was his role? A year ago, you couldn't have stopped him from taking charge of the situation. But Dani wasn't a kid. She was thirty-two.

"I'm driving Danielle." Ponytail smirked as though it was settled.

"We can give her a ride." The ranch hand on the right side of Dani sneered at the mechanic.

Ah, hell. No way would he stand by while some random guy gave Dani a ride.

"Not necessary." Jack strode over and stood behind ponytail. "I'll be giving my ..." He was about to say sister-in-law, but she wasn't really that. "I'll be giving Dani a ride. She lives on our ranch." That was the best he could come up with, and it seemed to shut the guys up.

Ponytail slid off the stool and headed for the register to pay his check.

Amber came around and cleared the dirty dishes. "You change your mind about eating here?" She winked.

"Looks that way. Can you make only one of the meatloaf specials to go?" He took the seat to Dani's left.

Dani shifted toward him. "Jack. I would've been fine. You don't have to stay on my account. I know how busy you are."

"No problem." A lie. His dad got cranky when dinner was late.

"I didn't get the name of the gentleman sitting there before you."

"Gentleman?" He scoffed. That jerk overcharged him for a new fuel pump last month. "That's not the word I'd use. He's a regular at Turner's and a real ... never mind." Every time Jack stopped in for a drink, that horn dog mechanic was in the hall by the bathrooms with a different woman. He was probably headed there now.

"If you see him," Dani said, "you must be there too."

He snorted. "Right. But I'm not married. And I respect women too much to ... forget it."

"He's married?"

"Yes," he bit out, growing uncomfortable with the topic. "Most of these guys you're talking to are probably married."

Her smile slipped into a pout. "Tanner's not."

Jack slid his gaze to Tanner, sizing him up. He worked on Parson's spread, probably late twenties, early thirties, age-appropriate for Dani. But not good enough.

Dani swung sideways on her stool, putting her back to him. "Tanner, tell me what a big cowboy like you eats to stay so strong. It smells wonderful." She continued flirting with Tanner and Roy, despite him sitting right beside her. He shouldn't care. But it messed with his thinking. Her soft hair tumbled down her back, and her smooth shoulders were pink from working outside. And the fragrance she wore ... damn. He was way too close for comfort. As one of her self-assigned protectors, he had no business thinking about kissing her right there, on the soft skin of her shoulder.

"Here you go, honey." Amber set their meals on the counter.

"Eat up, Dani. I have to get back." Jack dug into the meatloaf special. It was every bit as good as it looked. He added two more meatloaf dinners to his carry-out order.

Dani picked at her tuna melt and spoke softly. "You don't have to be so ... grumpy. Lighten up. I may as well have ridden home with my sister."

He ignored her and finished eating.

Dani turned away and talked to the men on her right. If he wasn't irked before, this sealed it.

Jack stood. "I'll take her check."

"Tanner was paying for mine." Dani had only eaten half her meal.

"I've already got it." No way was that ranch hand thinking he had any rights to Dani.

"I'll catch you next time, Danielle." Tanner reached over, clasped Dani's fingertips, and squeezed. "Don't work too hard in that garden."

Jack scowled. "What she does is none of your business."

"Who are you—" Tanner stood.

Roy pulled Tanner back. "Let it go."

Dani reached into her tote. "Can someone help me with my sweater?"

Tanner moved.

Jack jumped right on it. "I've got you." He grasped the soft sweater, and his hands brushed against Dani as he helped her into the sleeves. Chills raced over his skin. It happened every time they touched, which was why he made a point of keeping his distance. Being close to her was kryptonite to his willpower. Up until now, it'd worked pretty well. But here he was, giving her a ride home. The big man upstairs must be having a good laugh on his account.

"Jack, will you carry my pie and my tote for me?" she asked in her honey-like accent. "It's crowded, and it'd be better if I held your arm and walked sighted guide."

Right. Dani had to hold on to him. It didn't mean anything. But when she wrapped her delicate hand around his upper arm and squeezed, something in him came to life. Something that better settle down, because Ellie's younger sister was off limits, and he'd do well to remember that.

Preoccupied, he crashed Dani right into a customer eating at the counter.

"Excuse me," Dani said.

"No problem, sweetheart," a male voice answered.

"Well, hey, Pete." Dani turned on the charm like a faucet.

Jack whipped his gaze around. It was the bartender from the Lone Star.

"Why are you eating here tonight?" Dani asked. "Y'all have the best chicken wings at the bar."

"Can't beat Mac's meatloaf." Pete shifted a curious gaze from Dani's face to her hand on Jack's arm and up to Jack's face. "How are you doing, Jack?"

"All good." It didn't mean anything that Dani held onto him, but he drew her closer as though it did. Pete didn't need to be getting any ideas. She was friendly to everyone. It was one of the things he loved about her.

"I haven't seen you in a while. You need to stop in. I got two new dart boards." Pete's eyes held a question as they swung from Dani to him again.

"Sounds great." If someone would watch his dad. "I've gotta go. Later, Pete." Jack stepped away, pulling Dani with him.

"See you," Pete said.

"Not if I see you first," Dani quipped, then lowered her voice. "Pete's a good guy. He gives me free cocktails."

"Wonderful," Jack said, wishing he could unhear that. He had enough on his plate without worrying about Dani drinking too much at the local watering hole. He paid and lifted the bag holding his three carryout meals and pie, and a smaller, separate bag, Dani's pie.

The customers waiting at the entrance parted, and Jack held the door, their bags, and Dani's tote, and guided her into the cool night air.

She clutched his arm more firmly. When her fingertips brushed the side of his chest, he tensed and moved his arm. And forgot to tell her when they reached the steps.

Dani missed the first step. Stumbled. Fell into him.

He caught her, almost dropping the food bags, and held her arms to keep her upright.

"Are you trying to kill me?" She tightened her grip on his arm and pressed a hand on the center of his chest.

"Sorry," he said roughly. "Are you okay?"

"I'm fine. A little shaken up is all."

He dragged in a breath, settling his thundering heart. She needed to move those pretty polished fingers from his chest.

A funny expression came over her face.

Did she feel it too? How could she be attracted to him? She couldn't see him, never had. And she had no idea how he looked at her.

She withdrew her hand. "If I ever need more excitement in my life, I'll ask you to lead me somewhere."

"I'll be more careful." He led her to his truck.

After sliding the to-go bags onto the middle of the bench seat, he helped her in.

"What were you doing in town?" Dani asked as they rode toward the Tall Pines Ranch.

Her floral scent filled the cab. Would her hair smell like that? Her neck? Every nerve ending inside him sparked, aware of her proximity. "Looking for help. My dad ...."

"Did he fire another caregiver?" Dani asked, oblivious to his interest in her.

"The last one didn't make it through the morning."

"He's a grumbly old thing. But he's pretty nice to me. Did you find someone?"

"No." He groaned inwardly. "It's not looking good."

"Can I help?"

Could she? Silence filled the space while he tried to come up with an excuse. A reason to refuse her help without making her blindness an issue. It was an issue. But not the only one. If she were in his house assisting his dad, it'd defeat his efforts to keep her at a distance.

From the moment he'd first seen her, a switch inside him had flipped. And Danielle Tremont was absolutely not available. In addition to being blind, she was ten years younger than him and Luke's sister-in-law. Not that he minded sparring with his half-brother, but this issue was a bigger deal than most.

He needed to let her down gently. "You could hang out with him and call me if he needs something. But he needs help in the bath and toilet, help dressing, there's cooking ...."

"What about Thea? She's a good cook and knows a lot about helping people."

"She's old."

"And strong."

"And busy." The elderly woman, who lived on the ranch, might get hurt trying to help his father. "Thea can't handle him."

"You'd be surprised. I've been working with her. If I take over more of the garden, she might be willing to help with Bud until you find someone. It's worth asking."

Yes, he could ask the ancient herbalist. But he didn't want to. Would it be worth the risk of entangling her in his family issues?

Jack drove the truck through the electric gate and past the old Florida ranch house where he lived with his father and younger brother. He rolled by Thea's cottage and enormous garden and parked between the live oaks and cabbage palms in front of Dani's small house. His half-brother, Luke, lived with Ellie and Avery another quarter mile up the drive. "Hold up. I'll walk you to your door."

"That would be lovely."

He came around, and her loose hair brushed him as he helped her out. *Just get her inside and leave.*

Dani gripped his elbow. "You're quite the gentleman despite —"

"What?"

"Nothing."

"Not nothing." The nuclear power plant inside him came online and brought him to a stop. "What'd you hear?"

"Just ... you being in jail and all."

Anger tightened his jaw. What had Luke told her? "Only a month. Well, followed by a month of house arrest."

"Didn't you ... hurt someone?" she asked softly.

He bit back the growl rising in his throat. "Not a woman. Never a woman. What I did was illegal, but it was justified. I'd never hurt you. And I'm different now. Have I ever given you cause to be afraid of me?"

"No." She laid her other hand on top of his arm, circling it completely. "To be honest, I've hardly seen you since moving here." She squeezed his upper arm.

Hardly seen him? Odd word choice. That didn't keep him from enjoying her hands on his arm. "I've been busy with my dad ... ranch stuff ...."

"Do you have time for a favor?" Dani asked tentatively.

He glanced toward his house. Bud would be hungry and likely a pain in the butt. He needed to relieve his niece. "What do you need?"

"Can you come in and adjust my thermostat?"

She wanted him to follow her inside? Bad idea. And he was running late. But how could he say no? "Sure." He accompanied her into the cottage. "It's freezing in here."

"And that, Sherlock, is why I need you. I tried fixing it, but I can't make it work." She patted her leg, and her yellow lab ran over, all wagging tail and licks. "How's my Lucky?" She scratched his ruff.

Outside, the ranch dogs barked, and Lucky growled softly in reply.

The overhead light was on. Jack shoved a hand through his hair, confused. "You use the lights?"

"For security. People think someone's here. It's safer."

"Good choice. You can tell they're on?" Lucky approached and sniffed up and down his leg.

Dani pulled herself taller. "I can feel the switch. I'm blind, not stupid."

The dog paused his sniffing and looked from Dani to him, alert to the stress in his owner's voice.

"I'm surprised you didn't move into the new house with Ellie and Luke." He gave the dog a scratch to prove he was a friend.

She huffed. "The newlyweds? I passed on that. They don't need me hanging around. It's enough that they have Avery. Besides, I want to live on my own. I'm independent. Lucky, come."

When she bent over to pet her dog, her dress hiked up, exposing a nice stretch of leg. He felt like a perv for staring. She didn't know. Couldn't know. And he wasn't about to announce it.

"You're okay here on your own?" He eyed her. His father's goal was to regain independence, take care of himself, and return to ranch work. What did independence mean for Dani, who was so vulnerable?

"I had a lot of training in independent living skills at the school for the blind. It's about time I put them to use."

"Just now, when you're in your thirties?" That was insensitive, even to his ears. If he was trying to keep her distant, he was off to a good start.

"I've always had roommates. Until recently...although ... never mind."

He scanned the area for the thermostat. The sparsely furnished cottage echoed as though nobody lived there. A crock pot sat on the kitchen counter to the left of the microwave, a single-serve coffee maker, a couple of bottles of wine with screw-on caps, and nothing else. In the living room to his right, a lamp with a crooked shade occupied the end table between the uncomfortable sofa his brother had bought and a swivel rocker. Plain mini blinds were lowered at the windows, and a dusty TV hung on the wall. At least she had a laptop on a small computer desk at the end of the room. But there was no art. No throws. No vases of flowers, knick-knacks, or the usual stuff his ex-wives had liked to put around.

He'd used this cottage for a few nights when he first came down from Bozeman. Bare bones, then. It was emptier now. The jail cell he'd stayed in flashed across his mind. Luke and Ellie let her live like this? "It's different. Minimalist. Where's your stuff?"

"I've ... lived with other people the past several years, so I didn't need much. There wasn't a lot to start with, but Ellie and Avery took some things to their new place. Ellie will take me shopping."

"When? It's been over a month since they moved."

"She's busy with her job. And she's had more to do since Luke's been working in Bozeman. We'll go when their schedules settle down."

"It smells ... interesting in here."

"Do you like it?"

That wasn't the word he'd choose. "Sure."

Dani grinned. "That's my essential oils. I keep them in the other room. I like the fragrance of them all mixed together. Kind of spicy citrus, minty, floral, lavender. I've started adding them to Thea's herbal creams. Roy, he's one of the men at Mac's diner. He said it really helped him."

Jack adjusted the thermostat in the hall. "What temperature do you want?"

"Can you put it on air at seventy-five?"

He set the temperature. The thermostat was digital, probably impossible for her to operate. He rubbed his chin. This situation wasn't right.

"Would you like something to drink?" She moved to the kitchen with surprising ease and opened the fridge, revealing meager contents: protein powder, fruit and vegetables from Thea's garden.

He opened and shut a couple of cabinets. At least they'd left dishware. The pantry held soup, a wide variety of canned beans, and at least a dozen cans of pineapple. "I guess you don't want to be caught short on pineapple."

"You know what they say ... when the mood strikes. Seriously, I love it fresh. But if it's in the fridge cold, I'll eat it all up." She set the bottle of tea on the counter. "If you're looking for a glass, they're to the right of the sink."

His brows drew together. "Do you do much cooking?"

"I use the microwave."

"Did Ellie pick up food for you at the store?"

"No. I'm fine."

"You don't have many groceries."

"I mostly eat bean salad or make green smoothies, but I can eat at Ellie's whenever I want. Sometimes I eat with Thea. Why?"

"Just wondering." Unlike the other men in his family, he was an excellent cook. Despite his cowboy lifestyle, he'd prepared many a meal alongside his mother. It seemed to cheer her up and had paid off in the end.

This was a sorry excuse for a kitchen, and there was hardly enough food to put together a meal. He was supposed to be in charge of this ranch, yet here was this blind woman who barely had what she needed to get by. On his watch. No wonder she wanted to eat out.

She hooked her index finger over the rim of a glass and poured, stopping when it reached her fingertip.

"None for me, thanks. I need to get over to my dad, but ... say ... do you like meatloaf?"

"Sure. Do you?"

"Yeah, but ... hold on a sec. Let me get you a dinner. I have an extra."

"And grab my pie. I didn't bring it in."

He went to the truck and found the bag from the diner on the seat where he'd left it. No small bag with her slice of pie.

And there were only two dinners in the carry-out bag. Not three. And his pie was missing. Had they shorted him? He could swear he'd seen three containers in the bag when he'd paid.

Jack checked the floor, looked under the seat, and scratched his head. Giving up, he removed one of the dinners and carried it in. All he really needed was one for his dad. But he'd been looking forward to having meatloaf again tomorrow.

"Dani?" he announced himself as he entered and set the packaged meal on the kitchen counter. "Your pie wasn't there. I'm putting the meatloaf dinner by the microwave."

"Thank you." She was at the sink scrubbing her hands. "That's weird about the pie. Are you sure you got it from the diner?"

"I did. But it wasn't in the truck." He scanned the room again. No bag with pie. Huh. "I'm leaving now."

"Wait. Before you go. Will you check my hands?" She fanned her wet fingers.

"Okay. Why?"

"Is there dirt under my nails? Tanner said there was."

Now why would Tanner tell her that? Even if she did. He moved closer and took her hands in his, examining them, pushing aside the urge to lift those delicate fingertips to his lips.

The moment stilled.

"They look fine to me."

"Thank you."

He studied her lips, her pretty, unfocused greenish-brown eyes, and the smooth skin of her neck. He refused to give in to this attraction sparking inside him. Kryptonite. He needed to leave.

The ranch dogs began barking again, then settled. Jack cleared his throat. "I'm going now. Will you be okay?"

"Of course." She chuckled softly, drying her hands. "I'm good. Thanks for your help."

He strolled out and was about to climb into his truck when something caught his eye.

Was that movement at the side of the house? It seemed large.

The dogs had been barking.

Was something out there?

He strained to hear.

Between the electric fencing that ran the length behind the cottages, the guard donkeys, and the cattle dogs, coyotes and deer typically stayed clear. He grabbed a small tree limb from the ground and moved forward, circling Dani's cottage. The moonlight was barely sufficient, and he didn't see anything.

Branches cracked in the distance.

He stood very still, listening.

The front door to the cottage opened and closed. When he rounded the corner, Dani was outside, on the steppingstone path, with her dog.

"Jack? Is that you?" she asked.

"Yes. I thought I heard something. It was probably a raccoon."

He climbed in the truck and drove back to the house nearest the entrance. This was home now. A Florida cracker house, wooden, with a wide front porch, an unused old fireplace, and air conditioning they had to run in the winter. Go figure.

While he walked from the paved driveway to the walkway made of shells, the nagging sensation and disquiet eating at the back of his mind didn't let up. Something had been outside Dani's house, and he was sure there'd been three dinners. And what about the pie? Amber had handed him that small bag.

An animal couldn't open the truck, and there'd been no sign of a person. Did he drop it when Dani stumbled on the steps? The wooden porch steps creaked as he hustled inside with the remaining meatloaf dinner.

He shook his head. There wasn't something on the property. He must've left part of the food at the diner. He was simply stressed from running late. That's why his heart was beating so hard.

It wasn't Dani. She was Luke's kin, and he was only being helpful. He'd done a good deed. Racking up points with the cattle boss in the sky. It was done. Mission accomplished. And he'd been a perfect gentleman. He was tough enough to resist a pretty woman. He was her protector. And he'd remember that.

3

*B*ud Stone threw the box of tissues across the bedroom, knocking over the water glass on the dresser. "Wh-what took you so long?"

"What the hell, Dad?" Jack retrieved the items from the floor and wiped the spill. Thankfully, the glass was mostly empty and didn't break. He took a moment facing the wall and squeezed his lids shut, wincing. That was no way to talk to his father. He could do better. "Your arm's gettin' stronger. Aim's pretty good too."

"Humph. I'm hungry. Where were you?" Long rays of morning sun streamed through the window and lit the crevasses in his father's frowning seventy-four-year-old face.

"I was working in the barn. You were sleeping. Garrick was supposed to check on you. Why does your room reek of menthol?" Jack peeled back the covers and found the sheet covered with something sticky and smelly. "Is this that cream I bought you? All over the place?"

"It fell ... in the bed with me. I lost the cap. Damned stuff doesn't work anyway. Are you gonna help? Or just stand there?"

"What do you need first?" He counted silently. Bud had

come a long way since his stroke, but getting his dad ready in the morning was challenging.

"Need my boots. I'm done with slippers." Bud's voice was scratchy.

"Slippers might be more comfortable." He surveyed the room. The slippers weren't in their usual place by the bed.

"I'm not geriatric," Bud continued.

"Right, Dad. You're as young as you feel. Can you wear your slippers until after you've eaten breakfast?"

"Nope. I threw them away." A triumphant, lopsided grin curved the corner of his dad's mouth.

Jack growled softly, helped his dad into his jeans, and plunked the old leather Ariats beside his dad's feet. Tension crept up his neck, threatening a headache, and it wasn't even eight-thirty.

Garrick stuck his head in the bedroom doorway. "I'm outta here. I made fresh coffee. Bye, Dad." His brother, five years younger, had separated from the Army last fall and was always disappearing or going to some meeting.

"At least someone's done something useful." Bud rubbed a gnarled hand over his forehead. "I need coffee."

"After we get you dressed." Jack helped his dad with his socks and positioned a boot beside each of his father's feet, lifting one for him.

"Stop. I'll do it myself." Bud struggled to push his foot into the boot. "Dammit. You brought me the wrong boots. These are too small."

Jack angled the boot differently. His father's foot slid in.

Now that speech was coming easier to Bud, Jack longed for those early months of silence following his father's stroke.

"I feel good." Bud gazed at his feet. "I'm going out to the barn today. Might go for a ride."

His father hadn't been on a horse in a year and a half and

hadn't walked as far as the barn since they'd arrived. "Let's focus on getting you breakfast first."

"If you could keep a woman," his father narrowed his gaze, "this wouldn't be an issue. I'd have a daughter-in-law to help."

"If you didn't fire your helpers, things would go much more smoothly," Jack muttered. His dad fired them as fast as Jack hired them, even though he told them he was their boss. As the oldest son, by all rights, he should be running the ranch, not acting as the primary caregiver for his dad. But Garrick was rarely around, and golden-boy Luke was in Bozeman half the time. Until they found help, someone who'd tolerate Bud's crotchety attitude and foul mouth, it was on him.

"We should get Ellie over here."

"Wouldn't that be nice?" Jack said dryly. "Ellie's busy with her own work. She's started teaching online, and her business is taking off. She's even cutting back on helping with the minis. We'll get you situated, and then Thea's coming over. I was in the middle of repairing the tractor. Then I've got stalls to—"

"I'll come out and help you."

"You can't shovel stalls, Dad. You can't—" He stopped himself. Why be cruel? His father, a former rodeo star, had worked hard all his life and probably felt as useless as he did. They had that much in common. Since the ranch came with a competent foreman, Jack found himself doing more grunt work than he preferred. Turned out Florida ranch operations differed from ranching in Montana, and he was always playing catch-up.

"Tell Striker we'll meet here today. In the dining room. I need to know what's going on." Bud's jaw set. His dad was grasping at threads of power, but there were already too many bosses and not enough cowboys on this ranch. And now his dad wanted in on running the place?

"Striker's in the west pasture, and Brick's feeding the horses. We're meeting in an hour."

"I'm coming."

"We can meet in the dining room if you want. I'll text him after breakfast." He pulled the walker into place.

"I'm using the cane today."

"You haven't been cleared to go off the walker."

"You think you're my boss now?" Bud glared.

"Suit yourself." He got his dad the cane. His brothers might give him hell, but they didn't have to put up with Bud.

He helped his father stand.

"Ouch." Bud placed a hand on his lower back. "Arthritis ... is ... bad."

They made their way to the dining room, Jack shuffling behind, ready to catch his father. Although he was tough enough to cowboy all day, caring for Bud was another story and was stretching Jack's last nerve. He ground his teeth, biting back the urge to hurry his dad up.

The voice of Dr. Dave played in his head. *"Use your tools."*

Jack practiced his calming breath and channeled his frustration into beating the tar out of the eggs before pouring them into sizzling butter. *I can keep myself calm ... I can keep myself calm.* He slammed the toast down in the toaster, causing the thing to upend like a rearing horse.

Bud sat at the table, watching hockey highlights on the iPad.

There was a knock, and the door opened. "Are you ready for me?" It was Thea, on time.

Yesterday, in an act of desperation, he'd met with the old woman in the cottage next door, and she'd agreed to spend the day with Bud.

"Oh, no," his dad growled. "She can't stay."

"I brought you some tea, Bud." Thea, a thin woman with a determined set to her chin, whooshed into the kitchen, her silver hair pulled into a short ponytail, sticking straight out like a whisk broom. Her sharp eyes sparkled. "It's a neuro-booster. And it gives you pep."

"Thanks for coming." Jack slid scrambled eggs onto a plate with toast and set it in front of his dad. He glanced from the spry woman in her late seventies to the shell of a man his father had become. Whatever this woman used, his dad needed a double dose.

"Don't think a thing about it. I'm happy to help." Her brows lowered as she scanned the room. "Where's your walker, Bud?"

"I'm done with that thing." Jam dripped off the toast as Bud brought a shaking slice to his mouth.

"I'll fetch it." Jack parked the walker in the corner and lifted his hands apologetically. "The coffee's fresh."

Thea waved him away. "Go work. I'll handle this old grouch." She got herself a cup of coffee and opened the jar she'd brought.

"I'm not drinking that nasty stuff." Bud wrinkled his nose.

Thea poured her pungent concoction into a cup. "We'll see."

Jack offered Bud a rueful smile. Served his dad right for firing everyone the agencies sent out. "I'll check in with you later." He scooted out before Thea got it in her head he should try the tea.

The herbalist was old but feisty and seemed strong. Her help wasn't a perfect solution, but he'd take it for now.

Dani traced her fingers up Toffee's neck, kissed the tip of his ear, and inhaled his unique scent. A year ago, if anyone had told her she'd find the odor of a horse relaxing, she'd have scoffed. But something tense inside her released when she was with the miniature horses.

She cleaned the brush she'd been using, then smoothed the front of her clothes, checking for wayward clumps of hair. Sometimes Ellie helped care for the minis, but her sister had been tied up in online meetings the last several mornings. Working solo took a bit longer, simply wandering around the corral, finding all the horses herself. Typically, the minis were eating in their outdoor stalls, which helped. She kept close to the fencing to avoid startling them, but they seemed to understand she was blind. Once they'd gotten to know her, they'd stopped trying to bite or kick.

Even though Brick, the youngest of the ranch employees, tended the recent arrivals, grooming the other twelve horses on her own took up most of her mornings. Soon the new horses would be her responsibility and further cut into her time working with the herbs and helping in the garden. Nobody had asked her if she wanted to care for five additional horses.

With the new minis, her help would be missed all the more when she left. Once she gained a level of competence in making herbal teas and remedies, she planned to return to the city where she had more opportunities.

Her phone pinged with a text.

Jessica: *Hey Dani! Did you hear? Mark and Sandi broke up.*

She replied with a voice text of her own: *No. I want details.* She called Jessica.

Jessica answered, "Sandi left Mark."

"For real? Why?" *Serves him right!* A bubble of happiness formed inside her. She'd lived with Mark for two years in her twenties. He was visually impaired but nothing like Dani. Mark cheated on her with Sandi, another girl with low vision. Then he'd had the nerve to marry her. Dani didn't want Mark, the cheater. But it had stung.

"I don't know for sure," Jessica said. "But I hear Mark was talking about you."

"Well, bless his cheating, two-timing, rotten, minuscule heart. Let him find another Sandi."

"That's not all. I found out Parker is single again...."

Dani scowled. Was this old boyfriend update day? Parker worked at the same bank as Jessica, who'd been the one to introduce them. He was sighted. "Spare me the Parker report."

"Really?" Jessica's tone was heavy with meaning.

"I'm serious. Don't even mention me to him." If anyone understood the ups and downs of her love life, Jessica, her former roommate and best friend, ought to.

"He was asking if you're coming back. Maybe he's changed. He had such big, sad eyes."

Dani scoffed harshly. "His sad eyes mean nothing to me. She probably dumped him for cheating. Have you ever noticed how many men are liars? People don't change." She'd dated Parker on and off for four years, and she'd thought it was going somewhere. It stung when she'd found out the rat had been stringing her along, using her as a back-burner girlfriend while he continued dating sighted women.

"Awe, honey. There's got to be good ones out there. Anyway. The real reason I reached out. Melanie is moving at the end of the summer. If you want your old room back, I need a roommate."

"That's a tempting offer. I've been thinking about moving back to Jacksonville, but I wouldn't go out with Parker again. I'm sticking to it this time."

"Are you back on the singles sites?"

"I'm taking a break," Dani laughed. "No more one-hit-wonder dates."

"They might've gone better if you'd told them ahead of time you were blind."

Jessica was well aware of her antics and had been there for her when she'd quit the call center, broken up with Parker, and moved to St. Augustine to help Ellie with Avery. And tried dating apps.

"Almost all of them were skin-crawling disasters. I'm still recovering."

"There're no men in your life?" Jessica asked. "Not even hot cowboys?"

"There are lots of hot cowboys. But no dating. Ellie says we're one big family here, and I should keep my paws off the ranch workers. I understand her point, but it limits my options."

"Darn. Well, there are plenty of men here. If you decide to come."

"Make sure to tell the good ones to wait for me. I've got to go. Love you."

"You too. Happy farming, ranch girl." Jessica ended the call.

That's what she was now? A farmer? Ranch girl? No. This was her *herbalist-in-training* phase. She simply happened to spend a large portion of each day grooming horses and working in a garden. It was right to pitch in while she was here. After all, she wasn't paying rent.

She voice-commanded the phone to send Jess a horse emoji, stuck her cell in the pocket of her sundress, and sighed wistfully, an ache forming in her chest. Ranch chores, followed by empty hours when she'd listen to podcasts, read, or chat online, made her long for the friends, swimming pools, and workout facilities at the condo where she'd lived. She even missed the call center job she'd left. Not that she liked fielding complaints, but at least there'd been more people. She'd go to lunch, flirt, and occasionally date.

She was trapped here at Tall Pines, with no public transportation and too far out for affordable ride shares. Even if she had friends in town, she couldn't get there on her own. And everyone around here was busy. Ellie said they were short-handed and had difficulty finding permanent workers.

While she wouldn't turn down the attention of the people she befriended at the diner, it didn't fill the stirring deep inside her. The longing for something more. Something meaningful. Something that helping Thea was supposed to fill but didn't.

Tanner's attention crossed her mind. He seemed interested. Next time she ran into him, she'd give him her number. Having an actual boyfriend while she was here might cure her doldrums.

Dani trailed her hand along the wooden rail until she came to the gate where her dog was tied down. "C'mon boy, let's go."

Lucky's wet nose nudged her hand, and his tail slapped the fence. She slipped the harness over his head and oriented herself. If she squared off at the gate, about forty steps across the drive, she'd find the steppingstone path to the garden.

Blossoms, grasses, hay, and horses perfumed the cool morning breeze. And cattle. The odor of livestock permeated everything around here. Concentrating, Dani sniffed the west wind and detected the scents of peppermint, rosemary, and other herbs growing with the vegetables. Today she'd harvest beans and peppermint and pack the dried herbs. Her mentor had never trusted her to work alone before, and they'd gone over her tasks the previous evening. This was her chance to show independence and prove she'd been paying attention.

The thudding sound of rubber farm boots approached from inside the barn. "How's it going Dani?" asked Brick. "You find all the horses, okay?"

"Hey, handsome. I'm all done. What are you up to?"

He chuckled. "I'm finishing up here, then riding out to the northeast pasture. Do you need help getting back to your cottage?"

Brick was kind and, according to Ellie, a nice-looking man. And around her own age. But Ellie had warned her to scale back the banter.

"No, thanks. I'm fine. Thea's with Bud this morning, and I'm heading to the garden."

A fresh set of boots, cowboy boots this time, clomped along

the aisle from the far end of the barn. Her heart skipped a beat. The stride and footfalls sounded like Jack. She'd been crushing on Ellie's brother-in-law since she'd met him last summer. An older man, the jail time he'd served made him even more intriguing and dangerous. Even if he claimed to be safe, there was excitement in the atmosphere when he was around. However, they didn't cross paths often.

She might not see him because she was blind, but she was fairly sure Jack couldn't see her either. She was ... insignificant. As shown by him barely speaking to her since the other night when he'd adjusted her thermostat.

"What are you guys up to?" Jack's drawl held an amused smile.

"It's been nonstop thrills out here," she replied.

"Seriously?" Jack sounded concerned. "Is there an issue?"

"No. Everything is the same as pretty much every day." Now she wanted to kick herself. How dull did she sound?

"We have a meeting in half an hour," Jack said. "Up at the house. I'll be in the office. You done in the horse barn?" He was talking to Brick.

"Almost," Brick answered.

"Where's Striker?"

"North pasture."

"You got the tack room organized?" Jack asked.

She ought to go instead of listening to their conversation. But, like eating a slice of hot apple pie, Jack's voice made her all warm inside. She could listen to him all day. Their ride home from the diner had replayed in her head several times, especially when she stumbled, and he'd caught her in his arms.

"Hey Dani, you sure you don't want to help condition the tack?" Brick asked.

"I'm sorry," she said lightly. "My calendar is positively groaning with thrilling engagements. I do need to get over to the garden."

"Want an escort?" Jack offered.

Brick spoke up, "I already asked—"

"No thanks," she replied. Lucky would walk her.

"You sure? There are branches on the ground from the thunderstorm the other night."

Apparently, Jack wouldn't take no for an answer. She had Lucky to steer her around debris, but holding Jack's arm was tempting. "That would be very kind."

"Brick, help Dani, would you? I'll meet you at the house shortly." Jack clomped away.

Her chest dropped. Had she misunderstood? Why would Jack offer to take her, practically insist, then hand her over to Brick? He'd been downright nice when he'd brought her home the other night. He'd even given her a meatloaf dinner.

"You ... want help?" Brick asked, coming closer.

"Sure, why not?" She reached out, and he offered her his elbow. Shorter than Jack and solid like the other men around here, Brick carried the scents of hay, leather, and horses. "Why don't you tell me all about the new songs you've been working on?"

"They're nothing much." Brick played the guitar. When the weather was nice, soft strands of his music drifted across the grounds and through her open window. It was like having her very own concert.

"You're too modest. Someday I'll say I knew Brick way back when."

He huffed a soft laugh and led her to the back of the cottage, where Thea had left a bucket for collecting vegetables on the concrete bench.

"Are you sure you'll be alright here on your own?" Brick asked.

"Of course, silly. You go on and do your work."

Brick's soft footfalls moved away through the grass.

Once she'd secured Lucky in the shady spot by the bench,

she found the plastic bucket. With the bench at her back, she counted five steps to the row of beans and stooped down to begin her harvest. She ran her hand over the plant. Leaves. Stems. No beans.

Where were the beans?

Once again, she moved her hands over the soft leaves of the green bean plant.

No beans.

Her forehead tensed as she checked a third time. Was she missing something? This plant was covered with ripe green beans yesterday.

Dani moved to the next plant. The same. Nothing. What in the world? Did Thea pick them already? Didn't she trust her to get the job done? She walked between the rows of beans to the other end of the garden and checked those plants. No beans. Huh. Something was off. Wait a minute. Avery! This was her niece's doing.

More like a younger sister than a niece, Avery was the one person who'd play a joke like this on her. Well, not funny. But would Avery pick all the beans? Avery hated to garden. Why would she go to that much trouble?

This was one of those half days when kids got out of school early, and Avery should be home by now. Dani growled softly. They'd have a talk. And somehow, she'd get even. Perhaps put vinegar in Avery's chocolate milk to make it sour.

"Hey Dani," Avery called out, startling her from plans of revenge. Twigs snapped as her niece approached, and Scout, Avery's border collie puppy, ran over and licked her shin.

"Did you come down here to gloat? Ha ha. Very funny. I was about to call you. Where are the beans?"

"What are you talking about?" Avery sounded indignant. "I don't even like beans."

"That doesn't mean you didn't pick them. There're no beans on these plants. I came out to pick the beans, and they're gone."

"A deer probably got them."

"No. The dogs and the electric fence keep the deer away."

"Thea probably picked the beans," Avery said dismissively.

"Why would she do that? She's the one who told me to pick them."

"Because she's old? She probably forgot."

"She's not that old, and she's sharper than a lot of people much younger."

"Whatever. Ellie wanted me to tell you she's meeting a client at the coffee shop and wants to know if you want to ride into town. She's leaving in a few minutes. Why didn't you answer her text?"

She patted her pocket. Dang. The cell phone was there a little while ago. "Hey, Avery, do you see my phone anywhere?"

"No. I'll call you."

A moment later, ringing sounded in the distance. "Got it!" Avery said. "It was in the grass by Lucky. I'll set it on the bench."

"Thanks. I thought Ellie was meeting her client tomorrow."

"It got changed. She said to hurry."

Hurry was not a word in her vocabulary. She needed time to make herself beautiful. After all, she might run into Tanner again. But she'd promised Thea she'd gather herbs and pack the dried ones for Wren's produce stand. She clenched her teeth. The herbs would be here later, and she'd never get a date working on the ranch. But this was an opportunity to demonstrate commitment to her training. Dang. Dang. Double dang. "I can't go. I have too much work today."

"Okay. I've got to go. Emma's mom is taking us to the beach on Starfish Key and out for dinner."

"All right. Later alligator."

"After a while, crocodile. C'mon, Scout." Branches snapped under Avery's feet as she moved away.

Dani released a long breath. So much for harvesting the

beans. They were a mystery she'd worry about later. She wasn't wholly convinced Avery hadn't picked them. For now, she'd collect the herbs.

Lucky growled softly.

Her senses went on alert. "What's wrong, boy?"

He let out a low "Woof!"

She stood still and listened hard.

Quiet.

Lucky rarely barked at squirrels and rabbits. He was trained not to do that.

He continued growling softly.

Was there something out there? A coyote or a wild hog? Those boars were dangerous. One had charged a man last year.

Lucky woofed again.

She ought to get her phone and call someone to check it out, or better yet, go inside and package the dried herbs. Dani extended her hands and hurried toward the end of the garden.

Snap!

She stepped on a branch, twisting her ankle, and tumbled forward, hitting her head on the corner of the bench.

Pain pierced her forehead like a dagger. "Ouch, ouch."

She lay in the grass, touching where it hurt. Her hand came back wet. Blood. How badly was she injured? She tried sitting up but dizziness nearly overcame her.

"Hey, ma'am. Are you okay?" an unfamiliar voice asked.

"I ... I don't know."

The stranger's hand supported her shoulder.

If there hadn't been a note of sincerity in his voice, she'd be afraid of this man showing up out of nowhere. But between her throbbing ankle and the pounding in her head, she couldn't muster up enough energy.

"Here." He pressed a cloth into her hand. "Hold this on that cut. It's bleeding pretty bad. But face wounds tend to do that."

She held the cloth to her head and, with his assistance, sat fully upright. "I think I'm okay. But, dang, my ankle hurts."

"Yeah. It's swelling. You ought to get ice on it. Elevate."

"I'm not sure I can walk. I need to text someone to help. Will you hand me my phone from the bench?"

"Loop your arm over my shoulder. I'll help. You can text when you get some ice on it."

"I'll text now."

"Uh ... No. We need to move you."

Why was he arguing? Unless. Was he planning to hurt her? "I should call my sister." But Ellie was meeting a client and may have already left.

"Not now."

"I'm not alone here. There are lots of other people around. I can scream."

He exhaled hard. "If I wanted to hurt you, I'd have done it already. Listen, ma'am. I sprained my ankle on a Boy Scout camping trip. They stressed immediate first aid. Come on. Let me help."

"I'm blind."

"No kidding." He huffed a laugh. "I've seen you around."

"I need my dog."

"Hold on." He left, then returned and placed the end of Lucky's leash in her hand. "Come on. You can put your weight on me."

"Give me my cell."

"It's in my pocket. Let's get you standing."

"This isn't my cottage."

"Right. You're in the next one."

Chills prickled over her skin. "How do you know that?"

"Like I said, I've seen you around."

"Do you work here?"

"Something like that."

"What's your name?"

"Wyatt. Get ready. On the count of three, we'll stand you up."

The pain ricocheting through her body interfered with her concentration. With the stranger's tight grip around her waist, she placed a hand on his back and struggled to her feet. He was tall, narrower than Brick, sounded younger, and had to be strong. Wyatt was practically carrying her, and it didn't seem to bother him at all.

With her arm over his shoulder and a trickle of blood running down the side of her face, she held Lucky's leash tight and hobbled to her cottage.

Dani chewed the inside of her lip, her stomach clutching with unease. The ibuprofen Wyatt had given her kicked in, reducing the throbbing in her head to a dull ache and clearing the fog in her brain. Now she felt well enough to be concerned. Who was Wyatt, and how did he just appear in the garden?

"Here. Lift your leg, and we'll put this pillow under your ankle." Wyatt adjusted her foot on the seat of the swivel rocker and replaced the sock full of ice, numbing her ankle.

"Where'd you get that pillow?"

"Your bedroom."

She groaned. Now he was rummaging around her bedroom? "You shouldn't be in here. I don't know you. And just so you know, I don't have anything of value for you to steal."

"No joke," he scoffed. "That's what you're going with? I already said I wouldn't hurt you. I'm not stealing from a blind woman." It sounded like he was unzipping something. "Can I bandage the cut on your face?"

"Were you really a Boy Scout?"

"Not for long. But I learned to carry a first aid kit in my pack."

She fingered the damp washcloth he'd brought for her face. Truth be told, he'd probably do a better job than her. "I guess."

She heard paper tearing, and an antiseptic odor filled her nostrils. Wyatt dabbed at her face.

"Ouch." She gritted her teeth.

"Sorry." His touch became tender. After a moment, he backed away. "That should do it."

She ran her fingertip over a little strip covering the wound. "That's good. Are you one of the day workers?" They occasionally hired temporary cowboys, but Brick said they'd moved on.

"No."

"If you're not going to hurt me, why won't you give me my phone?"

A moment of silence stretched between them, and she scratched Lucky's ears, taking comfort from her big dog. He liked Wyatt, which was a good sign. But she'd feel a lot better if she had her cell phone.

Wyatt sighed deeply. "I'm not a violent person. I'll give you your phone. But ... will you promise not to tell anyone I'm here?"

"Why?"

He made a frustrated sound. "There are people out there who want to hurt me. I've been hiding."

"From whom? People here?"

"Not here. Out east, where I was staying."

"Why do they want to hurt you? Should I be worried?"

"It's a long story. It's me they want. For a couple months, I worked for them. It was time to go."

"And now you're here."

"Right. Well, I'm camping close by."

After a lifetime of listening to people hedge, bend the truth, and outright lie, she'd developed a talent for assessing honesty, listening to what wasn't said. Listening to the spaces between the words. Then Parker had deceived her with his smooth lies, and now she questioned her judgement.

Should she make Wyatt leave? He seemed to be telling the truth. An odd stench, like chemicals on top of body odor, hovered around him. Certainly, wherever he was staying, he wasn't bathing or washing his clothes. "You're camping nearby, trespass on our property, and just happened to be by the garden?"

"That's one way to put it."

"Did you steal our beans?"

He chuckled. "Yeah. And romaine. I've been hungry and trying to save money. And it's too dangerous for me to go into town."

"How old are you?"

Long pause. "I'm ... eighteen now."

That sounded like a lie. Even if it was true, he was young. A little older than Avery. And hungry. "Wyatt, there's half a meat-loaf dinner in the freezer. If you're hungry, heat it up."

"Meatloaf? Is it the good meatloaf from that diner?"

Before she said another word, the sound of the freezer opening and closing was followed by the microwave whirring.

"And there's potatoes in the bottom drawer of the fridge and ready-made salads."

Wyatt shut off the water. "Are you hungry?"

"I suppose I should eat. There's soup in the pantry. I wouldn't mind split pea."

"Can I have a of couple cans from your pantry?"

"Really?"

"I haven't eaten much lately."

"Help yourself to my gourmet selections." She laid her head back, listening as Wyatt opened and shut cabinets and prepared food. This kid was in trouble. He needed her, and today she needed him. She owed him. For now, she'd keep his secret.

Luke gently pressed Dani's leg and flexed her foot.

"Ouch!" She winced. "I thought y'all were here to help."

"Sorry." He gave her toe a light squeeze. Her sister sat beside her on the couch. Luke had pulled over the old wooden chair she kept in the kitchen.

Since Avery was still with Emma, she'd had to call Ellie for help with Lucky, which turned into this big production. Ellie had told Luke and called Thea. The Tall Pines telegraph worked better than fiber optics.

Which meant she needed to come up with a story —quickly.

"Just take care of Lucky. I'll be fine," Dani said.

"No. It was right to call us over to check your ankle," Luke said.

"I only called Ellie to feed Lucky and take him out. I didn't need both of you to come at dinnertime. You're making too much of this." The longer they were here, the harder it would be to keep them from asking questions—from finding out about Wyatt. After spending the afternoon waiting on her, treating her like a princess, Wyatt had done the dishes and left, saying he'd be back to check on her and help with breakfast. She'd given him her spare key, and the house had seemed empty when he'd left. "I'm okay, really."

"No. It needs to be wrapped," Luke said with authority. "You say you tripped in the yard?"

"I stepped on a branch."

Guilt practically vibrated off Ellie when she touched the back of Dani's hand. "I brought an elastic bandage. I'm sorry, sis. We should've checked all over for branches."

"I'll try to refrain from suing you." Dani squeezed her hand in return. "Seriously. Quit taking the blame. Thea cleaned up the yard after that storm. A branch can fall at any time. Life is random like that."

"I've seen worse sprains." Luke rested his large hand on her foot. "But you should still take it easy."

The front door opened, and Jack burst in. "What the hell? You're hurt?"

Dani tensed. He made it sound like an accusation.

Jack whooshed into the space beside her. "Are you okay?" Concern edged out the anger in Jack's voice.

"She's had ice on it," Luke answered. "We'll wrap it, and Dani, you need to keep icing it, keep it elevated." Luke positioned her foot.

"Be careful," Jack said.

"I've taped more than a few of these." Luke had that put-upon tone he often had with Jack.

"I trust Luke," she said. Her brother-in-law had been injured many times while performing in the rodeo. If anyone understood sprains, he ought to.

"How did this happen?" Jack asked sharply.

"She stepped on a branch," Ellie said.

"Dammit. Someone should've checked the yard after that storm." Jack laid a hand on her arm. "This shouldn't have happened."

Dani dragged her attention away from his warm hand. "Thea already moved a bunch of branches. She says the tree guy needs to come."

"I'll call someone first thing tomorrow." Jack punctuated that by giving her arm a little squeeze.

"Hold your foot still while I tape it," Luke said.

Jack growled. "Just ... be careful."

Luke scoffed softly.

"And your face." Ellie's fingertips brushed back Dani's hair. "You sure got it cleaned up."

Jack stood and hovered forward. The scent of his soap registered before he said, "That's a butterfly bandage on your forehead? You cleaned and closed the wound and put a butterfly bandage on it yourself?"

"No. My fairy godmother magically appeared and carried me to the house in a carriage made from a pumpkin, then the mice and birds doctored me up." She scoffed and tried to sound believable. "Of course, I did. I've been taking care of myself for years." She pressed her lips into a line. This was too much to deal with after the day she'd had.

A note of suspicion crept into Ellie's tone. "You got from the yard to the couch here in your cottage on that ankle, bleeding from your head?"

"It wasn't easy," Dani replied. That was a true statement.

"I'll bet. It had to hurt walking on this ankle," Luke said.

"Like the dickens," she admitted.

"And you got yourself ice? In your socks?" Jack must've picked up on Ellie's disbelief.

This was why she didn't want to call Ellie. Now she was getting the third degree from every side. She put a bit of defiance in her tone. "Socks seemed like a good idea."

"It was. But it must've hurt to get your socks and fill them with ice," Ellie said. "You should've called one of us. See. This is why it isn't a good idea for you to live alone."

No! They couldn't tell her what to do. "I did just fine and used what I had." She smoothed her sundress and found the cloth she'd used to stop the bleeding. It was soft in some areas and, in others, crusty from her dried blood. She balled it in her hand. "Can't y'all let it go and give me a minute to rest?"

"I can't get over how you made it back to the cottage and hobbled around and cleaned yourself up all alone," Ellie said.

She offered a slight shrug. "I was determined."

"And you did dishes," Ellie added.

"Those were from before."

"Hmm. Okay ..." Ellie tapered off with an I don't believe you tone. "And what's that bandana with blood all over it? You carry bandanas now?"

Ellie had her there.

"A cowgirl's got to have her bandana." Dani fingered the cloth Wyatt had given her. It was nothing like the delicate, embroidered antique handkerchiefs she found at thrift stores. Her aunt and Ellie made a point of surprising her with them at Christmas.

"Did someone help you?" Jack asked.

"Thea's fetching me some salve." She tried redirecting. They meant well, but dang, if they kept this up, they'd get the truth out of her, and she'd endanger Wyatt. "I'll be fine in no time."

"What color is your bandana?" Ellie asked softly.

Dani stilled, caught in the lie. "I ... I didn't check. I'm kinda shook up."

Luke secured the wrap and gave her foot a squeeze. "You're coming to our house tonight."

"I want to sleep in my own bed. Avery can sleep here."

"Avery can't," Ellie said. "She's spending the night at Emma's."

"Thea will stay with me," Dani said.

"That's actually a good idea," Ellie said. "We're heading to Arcadia to meet up with some of Luke's friends who came to town for the rodeo. We'll be gone from early until late."

The front door opened and shut. "Sorry I'm late," Thea called out. "Bud had a dizzy spell, and Garrick just got home. I brought the salve. Oh, dear. We'll need to unwrap her ankle." Thea unwrapped the bandage and held her hands over the injured part. Heat radiated from Thea's hands throughout her foot, and she was silent a moment before rubbing in the cream. If anyone else noticed the healing treatment, they didn't say.

Thea gave her foot a squeeze and rewrapped it. "There."

"Can you stay here with me tonight?" Dani asked.

"Oh. No, sweetie. Phyllis is picking me up shortly. We're off to Orlando for the quilt show tomorrow. I thought I mentioned we were going up early. Did you get those herbs packaged?"

"No. I tripped before I got to the herbs. I—"

"Hold up," Jack said. "Does that mean you can't help my dad tomorrow?"

"You never asked ...." Thea paused. "I can probably help the day after tomorrow." She laid a hand on Dani's leg. "You stay off your feet for forty-eight hours, and you should be okay in the garden with a seat. Make sure to reapply the cream."

"Humph." Jack stood. "Well, you can't stay here alone."

"We can skip Arcadia ..." Ellie offered.

"No," said Jack. "You go on. She'll stay with us. I can handle Dani and Bud."

"Hey. Y'all are talking about me like I'm a child or a pet or something. I get a vote," Dani said.

The room fell silent.

She frowned. What would Wyatt do if he returned, and she was gone? "I don't want to put anyone out. Take me to the bunkhouse. Brick can help me and bring me home in the morning."

"You're not sleeping in the bunkhouse with Brick and Striker." Jack snorted. "Ellie, you pack up Dani's things and get her dog organized. I'll get the golf cart and take her home with me." Then, almost as an afterthought, as though he heard how he sounded, Jack added, "Is that okay, Dani?"

"Sure ... I guess so. But where will I sleep?"

"You'll take my room," Jack insisted.

"No," Luke said. "We'll take you to our house and bring you to Jack's in the morning."

"We have a bedroom for you," Ellie rushed to add.

"She'll be fine in my room. I'll take the couch. But it's up to Dani," Jack said.

"I'll go with Jack. It's easier if I'm staying there tomorrow."

"You're ... taking Dani with you?" Luke said, his voice tight.

58n```

"Yes," Jack answered firmly. "I'll be right back." Jack clomped off, and the door shut.

"I'll stay here if you want me to," Ellie offered. "Luke can go without me."

"She'll be fine," Thea said. "You go with your husband, Ellie." Thea planted a kiss on Dani's head. "Don't let Bud give you any guff. Make sure he drinks that tea I left in the fridge. It wouldn't hurt if you got him to use the cream, too."

Thea left. A moment later, the room filled with the sounds of Ellie packing a bag and organizing dog food.

Luke took a seat beside her on the couch. "Are you gonna be okay? If you're not comfortable going with Jack ..."

"I'll be fine." She laughed.

"Just text if you need us." Luke squeezed her hand.

"Don't worry. Y'all go on and have fun." What was his problem with Jack? Luke's brother had been nothing but kind to her the few times she'd been alone with him. But she registered the warning in his tone.

*T*he hard couch beat sleeping in a jail cell, but not by much. Jack stretched to the left and right, unable to work the kink out of his neck. He'd been counting on Thea's help today, not that he was complaining about having Dani here, but now he was housebound.

Sausage patties sizzled in the frying pan while he finished cutting out biscuits and popped the second pan into the oven. He'd made coffee, set the table, and set out a bowl of the cut pineapple Dani loved. He grinned with satisfaction. It was worth finagling a grocery delivery last night. Breakfast would be perfect for her.

Garrick slipped into the kitchen, his shirt damp with perspiration. "I'm finished in the barn."

"Already? When did you get up?"

"Who says I went to bed?" Garrick huffed a laugh.

"I woulda slept in your room if I'd known you weren't using it."

"Nah. I caught a couple hours. Besides," Garrick angled his head toward Jack's room, "your pleasure, your pain."

"What's that supposed to mean?" Jack scowled. "Dani's here because she's hurt."

"Right." Garrick snagged a chunk of pineapple from the bowl. "Is she up?"

"I just checked. She's getting dressed."

"For real?" The corner of Garrick's lips edged up. "Did you have to ... help her?" He ate another few pineapple chunks.

"She can dress herself, dummy. And don't eat all the pineapple. It's for Dani."

"Decent of you, allowing her to stay here. In your room ...."

Jack scowled. "It's not like that."

Garrick scoffed.

Jack jabbed the spatula at his brother.

"Hey! That grease is hot." Garrick raised his hands in surrender and backed up. "Don't we have crutches in the attic?"

"Back in Montana."

"Can she use Dad's walker?"

"Probably. And walk right into the wall. Here." Jack handed over the spatula. "Watch the sausages. I'm checking on her."

Jack tapped on the bedroom door and then opened it a crack.

Dani sat on the edge of the bed, petting Lucky's head. "Can you help me to the bathroom? I'd like to wash up. And will you take Lucky out?"

"I'll take him in a couple minutes. I'm making breakfast."

"You cook for y'all?"

"Wait until you taste my biscuits. And there's pineapple. Let me carry you to the bathroom."

"I can probably walk."

"Not today, you don't. Hold on to me." He looped an arm beneath her and whisked her into the hall bathroom, positioning her near the vanity. Her soft hair brushed against his cheek. He backed up so fast that he bumped into the wall. What was he thinking carrying her?

"Jack?"

"Yeah?" Standing this close to her drained all coherent language from his brain.

"Are you going to stand there, or can you give me some privacy?"

What was wrong with him? "Yes. Will you be okay?"

"Sure. I can hold on to the counter. My ankle's much better."

He backed out of the room and shut the door. Should he wait?

Oh, hell! The biscuits.

He sprinted toward the kitchen and pulled them out of the oven. Garrick sat at the table, texting.

"Didn't you smell the biscuits?" Jack checked the bottoms. One pan had scorched, but the others looked okay, and the sausages had been moved to a cool burner.

"Something's burning," Bud yelled from his room.

"Ya think?" he mumbled, then turned to Garrick. "Can you stay a while?"

Garrick rubbed the back of his head. "Let me check." He scrolled through his phone, a grimace forming on his face. "Sorry, bro." Garrick snagged two biscuits and stuffed sausage patties between them. "The bottoms are brown. I think they're kinda burnt."

"They teach you that at detective school? That's what I just said."

"I'm not going to detective school. I'm checking into para-medic school."

Jack did a double take. "No kidding? You want to be a paramedic?"

"Yeah. Since I was a combat medic, it seems like a logical choice. The program starts later this summer."

Jack studied his brother for a beat. Garrick rarely talked about his time in the Army. The turmoil in the Middle East had followed Garrick home like a dark sky that never completely cleared. Evasive, slippery, an expert at changing the subject, he'd shown little interest in helping their dad. Veterinarian? Maybe. But people?

Jack never, in a million years, would've pegged his brother as interested in health care. Then it hit him. There went the help he'd been counting on. He and his brother owned the same number of ranch shares, but Garrick did far less work. And it looked like the situation would only get worse. "Where are you headed today?"

"I have a meeting."

He snorted. Garrick and his mysterious meetings.

"I already mucked one side of the barn and mowed the south field. It'll be ready to bale."

"Right. I didn't say you don't pull your weight." He slid his brother a side eye and refrained from stating the obvious. Garrick didn't pull his weight. But they'd been ranching for years without his brother.

"You got a problem?" Garrick's jaw ticked. He could match Jack's attitude any day. "I didn't even know about the move to Florida. I didn't have to come—"

"No problem, bro. Go. Do what you need to do. I'll handle this." Jack started down the hall but stopped when the front door opened, and Brick came in.

"Baler's broken, Jack. I got your text. Want me to work on the baler or walk the dog? It's gonna rain tomorrow. We need to get the hay handled this afternoon." Brick looked longingly at the biscuits.

Garrick passed over the pan.

Brick ate a biscuit in two bites and snagged another one.

"Go fix the baler," Jack said. "I'll take care of the dog. Tell Striker we'll meet here at lunchtime."

Brick left.

"I'll help Dad before I leave. Or should I help Dani?" A mischievous glint lit Garrick's eye.

"Help Dad." Jack glared.

Garrick's phone buzzed. "Oh. Sorry. I've gotta go." He left.

"Are you kidding me?" Jack shook his head. He helped Dani back to her room, took out the dog, and got his dad dressed and to the table.

"What's wrong?" Bud asked. "You look as bad as me."

"My neck hurts from the couch." He poured a steaming cup of coffee for his dad.

"The couch." Bud cackled. "You finally got the woman you want in your bed, but you're on the couch."

"You've got it all wrong." He set the coffee down with a thunk, sloshing a bit over the edge.

"Humph." Bud grunted skeptically.

Jack snorted, not in the mood to discuss women with his father. He might've had his share of women, but he wasn't a cheater like his dad and never had been.

"I need to fetch Dani." He slipped from the room, cracked open the bedroom door, and gaped. Early light pouring through the window made Dani glow like an angel. Aside from the bruise on her forehead, her face was nothing but beautiful, big eyes, smooth cheeks, perfect lips, and creamy skin. She'd pulled on a fresh top and still wore the yoga pants she'd slept in last night. Typically, she wore dresses, but he wasn't complaining about those skin-hugging pants.

"You ready to come out?"

"Took you long enough." Dani sounded like herself again. "I'm not sure I'll be able to give this hotel a good review."

"I guess we'll have to do better." He puffed a laugh. "Hold on to me, and I'll get you to the kitchen." He circled her with his arm to balance her, sweet torture, and helped her to the table, then finally got to sit. "There's biscuits, eggs, sausage, and pineapple."

They'd attended the same family meals, but in his effort to avoid her, he hadn't paid much attention to how food got on her plate. He pushed it all toward her place setting. "Do you need help? It's all at the edge of your plate where you can reach it."

"Will you butter a biscuit for me?" Dani asked.

Jack found one that wasn't burnt and buttered it. "Here you go."

"Is there jam?"

"I like strawberry jelly," Bud chimed in.

"Is there anything else?" Dani asked.

Jack pushed away from the table and dug around in the cupboard. "There's apple butter and this blackberry jam Avery made."

"Great. Will you open the apple butter for me?"

He uncapped the jar and paused. "Here. Or should I put it on your biscuit?"

"Yes. And serve me eggs?"

"Okay. Want sausage too?" He forced a polite tone despite his breakfast growing cold.

"Yes. Thanks. And can you dish up my pineapple?" Dani's polished fingertips traced the biscuit on her plate.

He met his dad's gaze.

Bud lifted a brow.

"Uh, sure." Jack scooped some chunks of pineapple onto her plate.

"And cut it?"

"Cut it? It's in chunks." He cut them anyway. "There. I cut them in half. Can you eat now?"

Dani looked like she was about to cough but burst out laughing. "I believe I can manage."

Bud broke into a grin. "She's workin' it."

"Listen, cupcake," Jack huffed, exasperated, then chuckled. "Mind if I eat my breakfast too?"

"Sorry." Dani wiped a tear from her face. "I had to mess

with you." She speared a chunk of pineapple and chewed. "It's so sweet. I may be giving this place a five-star review after all."

The three of them tucked into their food.

Lucky whined.

"I already fed him," Jack said between bites.

"This is when he usually gets his walk. We go all around the grounds using that path y'all made me. Do you mind taking him?" Dani asked.

"No problem. You gonna be okay, Dad?"

"I've got Dani here. We'll try not to get into trouble."

Jack stuffed half a biscuit in his mouth, grabbed the leash, and headed out with the dog. Ordinarily docile with Dani, Lucky leaped and pulled like a rodeo bronc out of the chute. Could he let the dog run off-leash? The cattle dogs ran free. But this dog was special, so he kept it tethered. "Whoa, boy. Settle down."

Trying to burn off his energy, he jogged Lucky in a loop around the barns and behind Luke's house, then approached the cottages. When he circled behind Dani's place, he abruptly stopped. Something was off.

The back door. Hadn't they locked it? The screen door hung slightly open, and the door to the house was ajar.

The trouble they'd had with one of the hands last year came to mind. He'd tried to block the sale of the ranch, causing all kinds of issues, and was now serving time.

Jack approached the cottage, scanning the area, listening hard.

Nothing.

Garrick's Jeep was gone, so it wasn't him.

He crept up to the house and opened the door, cringing as it squeaked. There went the element of surprise. Beyond the kitchen sat the master bedroom, and at the end of the living room, a short hall led to two smaller bedrooms. Most burglars would go for jewelry in the main bedroom. Unarmed, he grabbed a bottle of wine from the counter and made his way forward, cursing silently every time he stepped on a creaky floorboard. Lucky followed along, wagging his tail. A lot of good he was.

Whap!

The screen door shut.

Jack shot out the back door. "Stay here!" he yelled at the dog, slamming the door behind him as he sprinted into the backyard.

A flash of color rounded the bushes.

He ran toward the thicket and passed the stand of oaks. Huge flowering bougainvillea bloomed beside other shrubs ahead. He stopped and bent over, hands on his knees, scanning the area while he caught his breath. There was no sign of anyone. But someone *had* been in the house. It could explain the missing dinners and noises outside Dani's cottage the other evening.

Someone was on the property.

Were poachers in the area? Burglars?

Dani's house held little of value but nobody would know that before breaking in. He hustled back to her cottage and examined the door and windows. No sign of forced entry. In all the commotion getting Dani out of the house, had they forgotten to lock it?

After locking up, he hurried home with the dog.

Jack texted Brick and Striker: *Meeting bumped earlier. Be here ASAP.*

Someone was on their land.

They'd been in Dani's house.

He wouldn't rest until they were found.

After he pressed send, the clean bandage on Dani's cut came to mind. His brows drew down. Had she lied about doing that herself?

Jack cleaned the kitchen in record time, running on adrenaline. Should he tell Dani about the intruder? It might upset her. But she ought to remain with them until Avery or Thea returned and could stay with her. Unless the intruder was a guest of Dani's. But wouldn't she have said something? Why would they run?

Dani and Bud were having coffee in the living room, content for now.

Jack's phone pinged.

Brick: *on our way.*

Jack took a seat near Dani. "You weren't expecting any house guests, were you?"

"No."

"Did you give anyone the code to the gate?"

"No ... why? As long as you're here, can you help me wrap my foot? It's time to apply the cream and—"

"I'll do it a little later. Striker and I are riding out and— don't get upset." He searched for the best words to avoid scaring her. "There was someone in your house when I was walking Lucky. They fled before I got a good look at them. I need to check the cattle and horses and find out what's happening."

Creases formed on Dani's forehead. "They were in my house?"

"Don't you worry. I'll make sure you're safe. We'll find them. I'll have Brick stay here with you."

Bud lifted his chin. "You don't have to leave a damn babysitter with us. I can watch out for Dani."

In time, that may be true again. He hoped so. "Sure, you can. Humor me."

There was a knock, and Jack opened the door for Brick and Striker.

Jack had a plan. Considering the terrain they planned to cover, checking outbuildings and wooded areas, horses were the best choice. Brick stayed behind with his dad and Dani while he and Striker rode the fence line west toward town. They started at the far end of the property and found no sign of anyone in the thickets or the little park Luke had made for Ellie as a wedding gift. Over the next hour, they worked toward the house, checking the fences and cattle sheds and searching for signs of rustlers and other intruders.

"We'll check the west side first." Jack said as they rode along. "If we don't find anything, let's head east."

"What about McClure's?"

"Yeah. We'd best check that property too." McClure's farm was nothing more than a dilapidated barn, an abandoned house, and acres of decent grazing pasture they leased from a management company. Every so often, he'd ride over and check on the place, just to make sure it remained safe for their cattle. The doors were locked tight and windows were boarded. It was unlikely someone would be in there, but they'd check. "I'll send Brick over there if we don't find anything."

The wind picked up a colorful bit of debris. A candy wrapper? That made no sense. His gaze followed the direction the wrapper had come from. After dismounting and grabbing the trash, he led his horse closer. He wasn't sure what else he was looking for, but he'd know it when he saw it.

He moved through the pines into a protected clearing. The flattened grass might be from someone using the space to camp. He and Striker inspected the area, finding evidence of a small campfire. He cursed. The last thing they needed was a brush fire way out here.

Something shiny caught his eye. A can in the weeds? Pineapple. Like the ones in Dani's pantry. And it still held the scent of fruit. And there were more candy wrappers. "Some idiot ..." He growled as he fished the can and garbage from the brush and handed it to Striker.

Jack pulled off his hat and scratched his head while scanning the area for more evidence. Nothing. Dammit! They'd found the spot, but the intruder had moved. He leaned his arm on the saddle and stroked Whiskey's neck, calming himself. Anger charged through him, but a clear head was more useful. He sucked in a deep breath and released it on a slow seven count. Dr. Dave would be proud.

Striker squatted and ran his hand over a patch of roughed-up earth. "Looks like a tent stake made this hole. This is far from town for homeless folks."

"I've got no idea who it is." Candy bars? Canned fruit?

Striker pushed his lower lip into a thoughtful frown. "You might've scared them off."

"Let's hope." He mounted up and took in a wide view of the surrounding landscape. There was no sign of anyone, but he kept alert as they rode toward the barn. The hairs on his neck prickled as though they were being watched. He spotted a red-shouldered hawk eyeing him from the fence.

They returned to the barn. "What now?" Striker asked.

"I'll call Kurt." The local deputy might know if rustlers or homeless people were an issue in the area. "In the meantime, we'll keep looking. And convince Dani to stay until it's safe."

A trespasser was camping on their property, posing a risk to livestock and possibly the residents. That was not happening on his watch. Jack left Striker in the barn and stormed toward the house, rehearsing what to tell Dani. They needed to find whoever broke into her house. His stomach burned. What if she'd been home? What if she'd been hurt?

His natural inclination was to demand that she stay. But a

different tactic may be more successful. Remember water, Dr. Dave would say. Water cut the Grand Canyon out of rock. It's okay to flow, to take the softer approach.

Soft? What did that even look like?

He pushed through the front door and headed into the living room. Bud's head lay back, and his mouth hung open. He was about ready to check his dad's pulse when his old man snored like a train barreling down the track. Across the room, Brick had Dani's foot balanced on his lap, and he was ... rubbing it?

Jack narrowed his gaze at Brick. "What's going on?"

Brick leaped up, looking guilty, setting Dani's foot on the ottoman where he'd been sitting. "Hey, boss, I was—"

"Brick's fixing my foot. Rubbing on my anti-inflammatory cream," Dani broke in as if sensing the tension. "I told your dad he ought to use it too."

"Did you find anything?" Brick wiped his hands on his jeans.

"Yes." Jack clenched and unclenched his jaw. Dani wasn't his. And Brick was close to her age, helpful, and friendly. Too damn friendly. It wasn't spelled out for employees not to fraternize, but the situation irked him. Was Dani an employee? He'd think about that later. "Looks like someone was camping out in the back middle pasture. But they're gone." He shifted his gaze from Dani to Brick. "Keep an eye out when you're working. You may want to carry one of the hog rifles. We don't know if this guy's armed."

"Will do. I'll ... get back to work." Brick let himself out.

"Rifles? That seems a little drastic." Dani twisted the hem of her shirt in her hands.

"They're trespassing. It's serious. We don't need fire on our land. And they may be a poacher. You know what they used to do to cattle poachers?"

Her forehead wrinkled. "No. What?"

"Well, they didn't walk away from it." Jack sat on the ottoman and capped the jar of cream. "I'll rewrap your ankle." Her soft toes were polished, pink-tipped, and for a moment, he simply held her foot. He could kiss her right where her ankle curved to her lower leg. And then plant a kiss on her shin. His mouth dried.

"Jack ... is everything okay with my foot?"

Bud stirred, making a nasal snorting noise.

Jack snapped out of it and began wrapping Dani's ankle. "Yes. Looks like the swelling's gone down."

"That's the magic of the cream we made. I created the recipe myself. My first actual product. I'm making a big batch to sell and partnering with Wren. She'll bottle jars of honey with herbs, and I'll add honey to some of my creams. Win-win."

"Impressive." He finished wrapping, gave her foot a little squeeze, and gently shifted it to the stool. "I don't mean to scare you, but you ought to stay here another night, maybe longer."

"That's kind but—"

"At least wait until we have someone to stay with you. Keep your doors locked, and I'll see about getting you some kind of alarm."

"I'm not too worried."

He studied her. No, she wasn't. Dani didn't seem the least bit worried. Was she brave? Reckless? Or withholding something?

"But you'll stay tonight?" His breath caught in his chest as he waited for her answer.

Bud cleared his throat.

Jack glanced back at his dad, met his father's gaze, and held it a beat before turning back to Dani. His dad didn't get a vote. This had nothing to do with how much he wanted Dani to stay. He'd be a perfect gentleman. He was protecting her, was all.

*D*ani sat on Jack's couch in her yoga pants, wet hair piled on her head. You'd think someone in this house would own a blow dryer, but she'd settled for wrapping her hair in a towel and hoping for the best. She would've asked Jack to fetch hers, but after he'd searched for the intruder, who had to be Wyatt, she'd reconsidered. What if Wyatt had come back? It was too risky. Wyatt's safety came before her beauty.

Footfalls sounded in the hallway. Since Garrick hadn't come home this evening, it must be Jack. Besides, Garrick stepped lighter and moved differently.

Jack groaned and the couch moved as he sat at the opposite end. "Bud is in bed. Let me know when you're ready, and I'll help you to your room."

"If you want to lie down, I'll go now. Otherwise, I'll give my hair more time to dry." She pulled off the towel and brushed out the wet strands.

"I'll watch the game." He stretched and moaned again.

"What's wrong? I thought I heard you groan."

"My neck is tight, and my shoulders. Old stuff from years of working too hard. It didn't help that ... never mind." He turned on the TV and lowered the volume.

She reached into the tote at her feet and pulled out her jar of cream. "After I rub this on my foot, will you help me rewrap it?"

"Sure. Say when."

Dani massaged the anti-inflammatory cream into her ankle. It was already better, and the swelling had gone down considerably. "This cream is really helping. Why don't you come sit here, and I'll rub it into your shoulders."

"No. Thanks."

"Why no? You don't think it works?" She was taken aback by his rapid refusal.

"I believe you."

"So, what? You like being in pain? For real. This is why we make it and sell so much around here. Chet said it helped him."

"I said no."

"Chicken." She clucked a few times. "You're afraid of trying my cream. It's warm, but it doesn't burn. And this jar is the lavender version that helps you sleep."

"That's not it."

"Do you hate the smell?"

"No."

She clucked a few more times.

"Okay." He got up.

"Sit right here. On the floor between my legs." She shifted and patted the space on the cushion. "Take off your shirt and put your back here."

A moment later, he settled against the couch, his back between her legs, the sides of his arms warm against her calves. The lavender fragrance filled her nostrils as she scooped a good amount of cream into her hands and began massaging Jack's shoulders and neck. "You're as hard as concrete and full of knots." Dani dug into his flesh and kneaded his tight muscles. "That's better. Your muscles are relaxing." She stroked it over the tops of his shoulders and partway down his muscular arms. Very muscular arms. She swallowed hard. What had begun as a friendly offer to help ease his pain was turning into something else entirely. She wanted to lean in and kiss him. To bite his lovely deltoid muscle.

His breathing changed from slow and easy to ... oh .... did he feel something too? But her staying here wasn't about that. Ellie's warning to keep her paws off the ranch hands played through her head.

Jack was one of the ranch owners, not a hand. Did that make it better or worse?

This was why Jack had said no. Dani's hands on his shoulders made it difficult to breathe. For a moment, he'd relaxed, and then the reality of his arms touching her legs, her face so close, hit him. When she bent forward, her breath warmed his neck. His heart thudded, and his muscles tightened again, only different ones. The ones needed for maintaining control.

Jack's breathing became ragged, and his hands ached to touch her. To turn around and be in the exact place he'd dreamed about too many times. The idea wouldn't leave him alone. Dani needed to stop.

He scooted forward, ready to break the spell or take it to the next level, and right now, the two ideas were battling to the death in his brain. "That's enough. Thanks." The words came out rough, his throat thick with emotion, with need.

She capped the cream. "I think I'm ready for bed now, after all."

He stood and faced her, hands shoved in his pockets, and

studied the pink climbing into her cheeks. Dani seemed uncomfortable, vulnerable. It was a hot look on her. But Dani was here for reasons of safety, not for easier access. And he had self-control. Besides, there was the ranch and his fragile working relationship with Luke to consider. "Give me a minute," he said. If she touched him now, he might combust. He forced his brain to review his favorites in the NHL playoffs.

The front door opened. Garrick strolled in. He took one look at Jack standing there bare chested, then swung his gaze to Dani and hiked his brows before hustling into the kitchen.

Crap. This wasn't how it appeared, although he wished it was. Jack pulled on his T-shirt, wrapped Dani's ankle, and helped her down the hall—to his room.

It was going to be another long night on the couch. But that's where he belonged.

With reluctance, Dani stuffed her remaining things into the backpack tote. After two nights under Jack's roof, she needed to go home. But it tore her in two. Last night she'd enjoyed rubbing cream into Jack's tight shoulders and could make a habit out of it. It was really nice staying here. Even though Jack had supplied clean sheets, the rest of the bedding and room held his spicy, warm scent. There was something comforting and delicious about sleeping in his big bed. As much as she hated to, she pulled the sheets off the mattress, making it clear she was leaving.

Wyatt needed her. She had to warn him. He'd probably been at her cottage looking for her, and he might be in grave danger. The men were talking about carrying rifles when they worked. Brick was probably too sweet to shoot Wyatt. And Luke handled the books, social media, and marketing. He didn't work the cattle. But Striker or Jack ... she shuddered to think what would happen if they came upon Wyatt.

Footsteps creaked on the wooden floor outside the bedroom, and Jack's deep voice came from the doorway. "You can stay another night if you feel safer here."

"Oh, Lordy, no. Thanks. If I stay at your house any longer, I'll be as big as Peppercorn."

"He does like his feed." Jack chuckled.

A thousand butterflies fluttered in her belly. "He's the biggest and greediest eater of all the minis, bless his fat little heart. And you're an excellent cook. I like my feed, too." She could get used to Jack serving her meals.

Jack huffed.

"I'm almost packed up."

When he walked toward the kitchen, she laid back on the disheveled bed and fanned her arms the way she did when she floated in a swimming pool, moaning in pleasure at his lovely mattress. Going back to her own house was bittersweet.

Lucky whined.

"You know we're getting ready to leave, don't you?" She shrugged on her backpack tote and stood carefully. With her cane taking some of her weight, and holding Lucky's harness with her other hand, she inched down the hall.

Bud's steely tone filtered out of the kitchen. "I don't need some bossy old woman telling me what to do. Oh, Dani. Mornin'."

"Why Bud, you old devil. Are you calling me bossy? Should I be offended?" Dani limped into the kitchen.

"No. It's ... never mind." Bud slurped his drink.

"Want me to boss you around?" Dani asked. "Rumor is, I'm quite good at it."

Bud scoffed. "Luke warned me about you."

"Can't blame a girl for wanting to have a little fun, can you, Jack?"

"Hold on, Dani. You should've asked for help. Let me take this." Jack helped her out of the backpack.

"I'm better. I want to get home. Avery can hang out with me. Or Ellie. I'll be okay. I texted them." At this point, she'd say whatever she needed to in order to leave. She was desperate to get home and warn Wyatt. His life could depend on it.

*D*ani stood outside her back door and bit her upper lip, worried. Several times a day, for the past few days, she'd gone outdoors and listened. Where was Wyatt? She needed to warn him.

Avery had stayed over for two nights. They'd listened to described movies and eaten pizza. It should've been fun. Avery was more like a younger sister than a niece. But a cloud of worry hung over her. Was Wyatt okay? Did that bad man find him?

Shortly after Avery left for school on Tuesday, there was a knock on the door. Then the sound of a key.

Dani bubbled with excitement. Wyatt?

Lucky woofed.

She stood.

The door opened and shut before she took a step.

Familiar boots strode across the floor. "Hey, Dani."

"Oh, Jack."

"Were you expecting someone else? I had a key. Is it okay I used it? I didn't want to bother you."

"It's fine. I figured you'd text if you were coming over."

"I came to install a security system, and I got you a voice-activated thermostat. Brick and Luke are coming down in a few, and we'll get you set up."

Those gadgets were probably costly, and she was likely leaving. "Thanks. But you shouldn't have gone to the trouble. I'm not sure I'll even—"

A knock sounded on the door and Luke and Brick came in, talking about wires and circuit breakers. Power tools buzzed, and the men moved from room to room.

They took a break. "Help yourself to tea or soda in the fridge," she offered.

The four of them gathered in the living room, and talk turned from electronics to working cattle and which ones would be going to auction.

When the conversation paused, she asked, "Y'all seen any more of that person you were searching for?"

"Not a hair," Brick said. "When are you coming back to help with the horses?"

"Probably tomorrow." She wiggled her foot. Thanks to the magic of the creams and Thea's healing treatment, it didn't hurt at all.

"Kinda lonely doing it without you," Brick said.

"Brick," Jack said from the other room. "Bring me the standard screwdriver."

"You're all set." Luke put a remote control in her hand. "Press this button to activate the alarm when you're home. This one is a panic button. It alerts me and Jack, and this one brings the sheriff.

She rubbed her fingertips over the remote, memorizing their order. "I'm sure I won't need this. But thank you."

"Let's hope you don't." Jack returned and sat in the chair across from her.

The creak and metallic snap of a toolbox closing were

followed by Brick's steps. "I'm heading out." The door shut behind him.

Luke and Jack remained, Luke taking a seat to her right on the couch.

"I'll go over the thermostat with you," Jack said.

"I can do it," Luke insisted. "Don't you have to meet up with Striker?"

"After I talk to Dani." Jack's tone was steel.

"I can explain it. Tech's my thing." Luke's voice had an edge.

"I bought it for her," Jack said firmly.

Luke shifted, and the couch squeaked. "I've got the time now."

The atmosphere had become thick with tension. What was with these two? Dani broke in, "I sure appreciate y'all taking the time for me. As long as you're here, can one of you check the toilet? It keeps running."

Luke stood.

"Go on home, Luke. I've got this covered." Jack wasn't dropping it.

"Don't you need to check on Dad?" Luke asked.

"Thea's with him."

Luke released a hard breath. "Dani, text if you need help with anything." He let himself out.

Jack checked her bathrooms and returned. "Guts in both tanks need replacing. I'll get the parts in town. Can you stand, okay? I'll show you the device and then go over the commands in case you can't find the remote."

He helped her into the hall, and went over how to use the thermostat, standing closer than usual, sparks filling the air between them. Her heart beat a little faster. Did he feel it too? "Thank you ... for all of this."

He touched her arm and asked, "Do you need anything else before I go?"

Shivers ran up her skin. *How about a kiss?* "No. I'm ... fine.

She placed a tentative hand on his arm. There was no doubt he wanted to kiss her.

She leaned forward.

"I'll check in later and make sure it all works okay," he said softly.

"Okay. Thanks." Her hand slipped down, grazing the thin fabric covering his hard stomach.

Jack inhaled abruptly. "Do you need help back to the couch?" He directed her away from him.

"No. No, I'm fine." Confused as all get out, but fine. If you called crushing disappointment fine. She'd been sure they'd kiss.

"I'll handle the horses with Brick this week. You rest." Jack slipped out the front door.

She was alone.

The house echoed.

"Come on, boy." She harnessed Lucky and went out back to the steppingstone path covering the short distance from her cottage to the garden behind Thea's house. Taking care not to trip on the edge of a stone, she listened intently and called, "Wyatt?"

There was no reply.

———

On Dani's second day back in the garden, there was still no sign of Wyatt. He was probably gone. Moved on. And he hadn't even returned her key. Which might mean he was hurt. Or they'd taken him back to wherever they worked. An unholy mixture of dread and disappointment sat heavily on her chest.

She perched on the garden stool and carefully snipped bits from the fragrant rosemary. Each herb had a separate basket so as not to get them confused. She inched forward on her taped ankle and started working on the valerian.

The sweet perfume of jasmine wafted on the April breeze and sunshine warmed her cheeks. Lucky woofed softly.

No growl, but the woof put her on alert. "What is it, boy?"

Twigs snapped in the distance.

Lucky panted and moved around. "Woof."

"Who's there?"

Nothing.

"Wyatt?" she called out. "Is that you?"

"Shh! Don't yell my name." The branches crunched as he strode toward her.

She practically lifted off the stool in happiness. "It's just me and Lucky here. I thought you'd left ... or ...."

"I stopped by. You were gone. And there've been too many people around."

"I stayed with Jack and Bud. Then Avery stayed."

"I know."

"Oh."

"I watch what's going on. Who's coming around."

"You need to be careful." Her face tightened. "The men here are looking for you."

"Tell me about it. I had to move camp. Twice."

"Are you hungry?"

"Are you offering food?"

"There're bell peppers over there. Kale."

"You're joking, right?" He scoffed. "I'm eating like a freakin' vegan. Can I pet Lucky?"

"Go ahead."

"Can I have another can of pineapple?"

"I'll do you even better. Come inside. There's leftover pizza in the freezer." They walked toward the house together.

"You can hold my arm. Take some pressure off your foot." Wyatt bumped her with his elbow.

She grasped Wyatt's arm. Strong but not big like Jack's, Wyatt had the arm of a teenager. "I don't mean to be rude, but your clothes have an odor. I can't place it. But it's disagreeable."

"It's from where I worked before I started camping. Funny thing. There's no laundromat in the woods."

"Do all your clothes stink?"

"Probably. I'm used to it."

"I have a washing machine. Want me to wash them?"

"You'd do that?"

"Sure." She brightened, filled with purpose. "You helped me."

"I'll get you to the house, then I'll go get them."

"I'll have the pizza ready for you."

"Can I take one of the horses?"

"No. I can't give you permission. Plus, you'd best be careful you're not seen."

"Just kidding. But don't worry. Jack's still in the barn. How come you live alone? Everyone except that old lady lives with someone else. Why don't you move in with her since you're blind and—"

"I can manage on my own. I'm fine."

"Yeah. Me too. I'm fine camping in the woods."

His resigned tone gave her pause.

Wyatt wasn't fine. He was young and vulnerable and didn't even have a way to clean his clothes. "Do you want to sleep in my guest room? You'd have to hide your things during the day in case someone comes in."

"I said I'm fine." His arm tensed beneath her hand. "I'm good on my own. I'm camping ... But I might stay one night. Can I get a shower too?"

The laundry room sat between the kitchen and the big bedroom. Dani had set the cycle for a heavy-duty wash to rid the garments of that odd chemical odor. Now the aroma of reheated pizza and the fresh scent of laundry soap filled her home.

When the dryer buzzed, she pulled out a piece of laundry and held it to her face. Warm and soft, the clean cotton scent of the T-shirt was a vast improvement.

The beeping and crashing of the video game Wyatt was playing on her computer drifted over from the living room, and an unfamiliar warm feeling filled her. This might be what it's like to be a parent. "I've got a shirt and pants ready."

"Okay. Just a sec." The game drew to an end, and the sound of Wyatt's bare feet slapped the floor as he moved toward her.

The fragrance of her shampoo wafted over from Wyatt, and a pleased sense of doing good bloomed in her chest.

"Thanks." He snatched the clothes from her hand, and the ruffle of clothing and zip of his pants told her he was nearly dressed.

"Hey, Dani." Jack's voice sounded from the front door.

"Shit!" Wyatt slipped into the nearby bedroom, closing the door.

"I picked up the plumbing parts in town." Jack's voice drew nearer. "Okay if I fix the toilets? And I wanted to ask you about riding to Heron Park tomorrow."

Jack approached her in the laundry room, stopping so close she smelled his earthy scent. "What's going on?"

"Just doing a little laundry."

"Those look like men's clothes."

"Oh. I ..." Her stomach dropped. She needed to distract him.

Jack pushed past her. "These are men's clothes. What's ... do you ... have someone here?"

She walked past him into the kitchen. "No. I'm—"

He followed her. "There are two glasses on the counter. Who's here?"

"No one."

A cough came from her bedroom.

Jack brushed past her.

"Hold on," she said. "You don't get to just—"

Jack opened the door. "Dani. Who is this ... this kid?"

"I'm not a kid," Wyatt snarled.

"That's my friend. Wyatt."

"Your friend?" Jack sounded skeptical. "Have you been camping on the property?"

The hum of the washer and dryer filled the silence.

"Answer me," Jack said.

"So. What if I have?" Wyatt had that belligerent tone that was sure to get him into trouble.

Dani winced.

"It's private property to start with." Fury filled Jack's tone. "And that's only your first problem."

Dani placed a hand on Jack's arm. Tension vibrated from him. "Calm down, Jack."

"You were in the house the other morning, weren't you?" Jack stepped closer to Wyatt, pulling out of her grasp. "How'd you get in?"

"Dani gave me a key."

"What?" Jack sounded angry enough to spit barbed wire.

She squeezed her hands together. Oh, dang. Why'd Wyatt have to tell Jack?

Jack huffed loudly. "You let some random kid have a key and use your house?"

"He's not random. Wyatt helped me when I was hurt. I was bleeding, and he took care of me."

"Where'd you come from, anyway?" The steel in Jack's tone softened a degree.

"I'm passing through. Looking for work. I had a job a little east of here, and it ... ended."

"Over by the Whitehall's?"

"Yeah. Right."

"You've barely got hair on your face."

"I'm eighteen."

"Prove it."

"Why would I need to prove it to you, old man?"

"Because I'm friends with the local deputy, and you've been trespassing on our land," Jack bit out.

Wyatt had better not push his luck.

A stretch of silence filled the space. The laundry clicked and tumbled in the dryer.

Wyatt sighed deeply. He walked across the room and, a moment later, came close again. "Here."

"Your license says you're seventeen," Jack said.

"I'll be eighteen next month."

"You're a long way from Texas. What are you doing here, kid? Do your parents know where you are?"

"No." Wyatt scoffed. "My dad did this ..."

"So? You've got a scar. Was it an accident?"

"No. And there's this." Wyatt's hard tone matched Jack's. "I'm not going back there."

"Right ..." Jack sounded more cautious now. "What about the bruise? That looks recent."

"My eye? It's from the guy I worked for."

"You ought to report it."

"Uh uh. I'm under the radar. He's bad. His friends are meaner than rattlesnakes."

"That doesn't sound like the Whitehalls I know."

"It was someone else there."

"Right." Jack was silent a beat. "Okay."

"Okay, what?" Wyatt asked tentatively.

"Let's see how it goes replacing the flush valve and gaskets in the toilet tanks. If you pass the test, I may hire you on. You can stay in the bunkhouse."

"For real?"

"I'm not a charity, kid. You have to show aptitude."

They moved down the hall and Dani breathed a heavy sigh of relief. Wyatt might be okay. But if someone was still after him, Jack needed to know.

What was a man doing in Dani's cottage? Jack studied Wyatt. No. This was a boy. A kid who'd been helping Dani. Why had she hidden the fact Wyatt had been the one in her house? After all those times he'd ridden out searching for the intruder. She could've saved him time and trouble. A thread of tension moved through him. Dani wasn't telling him everything, and that bothered him almost as much as having his time wasted.

"You bandaged Dani's face?" he asked as Wyatt tightened the gasket beneath the toilet.

"Yeah. I'm pretty good with cuts."

When Wyatt reached to reattach the water, his shirt moved, revealing several scars on his upper arm. Jack's stomach twisted. There was no way he'd send that boy back to a home where he'd get hurt. And he'd be eighteen soon enough.

His own brother came to mind. Luke's arm had been in a cast when Bud brought him home to live with them. Later he'd come to find out his half-brother had been abused. He hadn't exactly rolled out the welcome mat. The atmosphere at home had changed when Luke arrived. At night, his parents' angry voices erupted behind closed doors. They'd never fought like that until Luke came. And there were several times he'd caught his mother crying. Through conversations he'd overheard her having with his aunt, he'd learned his dad had cheated. And it wasn't the only time. But evidence of it was now living under their roof.

For years, Jack hated Bud for it. And hated Luke too. His new half-brother tore their family apart by his very existence.

He and Luke were nearly the same age, but instead of being close like twins, a fire of resentment had raged in his heart.

He handed Wyatt a rag and rubbed the tension from his own forehead. Things had always been difficult between him and his half-brother. And Luke had probably been a lot like this kid, only much younger. An odd sensation tightened his chest. He shoved it away and focused on the youth working beside him.

They cleaned up, and Wyatt flushed the toilet. It worked perfectly. They headed back to the kitchen.

"Impressive, kid. You've got yourself a job if you want one."

"What's the pay?" Wyatt cocked his head.

"You're trying to negotiate?" He suppressed a grin. The kid had attitude. "You get minimum wage, room, and board. Talk to Striker about groceries. You do your own cooking."

"Days off?"

"Do you want this job or not?" Jack scoffed. "Typically, on a ranch, there're no days off. But here we give you one day off a week unless it's calving season. Then it's twenty-four-seven."

Watt nodded, but his face wrinkled up, not inspiring confidence.

"You were out at Whitehall's?"

"Yeah." Wyatt looked away.

"What were your duties?"

"The usual."

"Like?" Jack folded his arms and leaned on the wall. The boy was lying. Why? "Stuff like...? Milking cows?"

"Yeah, milking the cows."

"And goats?"

"Right. The goats."

"Listen, dummy. They aren't a dairy, and last time I checked, they don't have goats. What did you do?"

Wyatt paled. "Ranch stuff. You know...."

"And if I called them?"

"They didn't pay me. I ... er ... worked for someone staying there."

Jack snorted. "I don't know what your story is, and maybe I don't want to. But you'd best walk the straight and narrow here, or you'll meet the business end of my fist. Got it?"

Dani gasped.

Wyatt's eyes rounded. "Got it."

Something about Wyatt didn't sit right. Hiring the kid might be a mistake, but Jack had worked too many days mucking stalls. Wyatt's youthful energy would come in handy. Dani did have a sense about people. And she liked Wyatt.

"Trial period. Two weeks. I'll introduce you to Brick and Striker. They're the bosses who'll train you and assign your tasks."

"What are you?"

"The boss you don't want to mess with."

"Okay. Thank you, Sir."

"Not sir, Jack. Don't screw up. Now get in there and handle your own laundry. Dani's not your servant, and she's not your mom. You have to pull your own weight around here."

Wyatt started down the hall and turned. "I won't let you down." He hustled into the laundry room.

Jack rubbed his face. *Business end of his fist?* What was he saying to the kid? That was technically assault. Wyatt was a minor and had probably been abused. Man, he was a jerk. Dr. Dave would give him the stink-eye when he related this on their next call. He moved toward the living room to find Dani but paused and veered into the laundry room where Wyatt was folding his clothes. "Wyatt?"

Wyatt jumped. "I'm almost done."

"Take your time. I wanted to say...." He studied the floor for a moment. This was more difficult than expected. "I wouldn't really hit you. You know that, right?"

Wyatt's brows lifted. "Okay."

"See you in a while." Jack started walking away, then paused. "But Wyatt?"

"Yeah?"

He lowered his voice. "If anyone hurts Dani, I'd kill them."

"If anyone hurts Dani, I'll help you."

"Good." He chuckled. "And you're gonna have to learn to be a better liar, or you'll lose at poker every game. And Wyatt, never throw your trash on the ground where animals can eat it. Most of our livestock costs more than you'll earn in a month. Got it?"

"Got it, sir. I mean, Jack."

"When you finish here," Jack continued, "meet me at the bunkhouse. It's across the driveway."

"I know where it is."

Jack frowned. Yes. The kid was a wild card. He'd need to keep a close eye on him.

*B*rick and Wyatt had finished most of the stalls when Jack crossed through the barn carrying the box he wanted to go through.

"Hey, boss," Brick called over.

"Hey, boss," Wyatt copied Brick.

Jack addressed Brick. "How's he doing?"

"He might be worth keeping." Brick called Wyatt a quick study and a hard worker. Wyatt was up to speed on the heavy barn work, showed mechanical aptitude, and drove a tractor like he was born to it. He rode okay but roped and used a whip as if he was holding wet pasta.

Jack brought the box of odds and ends from the office to the house and set it on the kitchen table. Most of the stuff he'd stuck in there would probably end up in the trash, but the notebook looked interesting. He parked himself on a kitchen chair and cracked the book open to a page of flowery handwriting.

Louise, the wife of the previous ranch owner, had created something between a journal and a record of the plans for growing the miniature horse rescue. A dream that'd never come to fruition before she passed away. Sure, they'd collected miniature horses. But her vision had been more extensive than giving miniature horses a safe place to live out their lives. She'd stuffed the journal with folded, printed articles about the healing power of animals. Pieces about equine therapy. Chills ran down his arms as he got caught up reading stories of people with PTSD who found peace caring for the horses.

He closed the book. Louise had been the same age as his mother when she'd died, but they weren't much alike. His mom had grown weary of ranch life and would've tried to talk his father into living in a beach condo or something. And Bud might've gone along with it, but he'd have been miserable.

Louise, like him, had wanted to expand the ranching operation and diversify. She'd left her dream unfinished. It was good he'd taken those five additional rescue horses. But they weren't utilizing them to their potential. An idea scratched around in his mind but didn't fully form. Just a seed. But it felt important.

Thea entered the room behind him. "Oh, you're still here." She'd been in the living room with his father. "I'm heating up more tea."

"I can't believe you've sold him on drinking that."

"After the first two cups reduced his pain, it sold itself. Next, he needs to use that new cream Dani made. I'd like you to rub it on his hip and lower back tonight."

He winced. Wasn't he already doing enough for his old man? "He doesn't like the smell."

"A small price to pay."

Jack stood. "I'm driving to Heron Park for a tractor part."

"Dani said she's riding along with you." A slight crease formed in Thea's forehead.

"That's right. We're headed to a couple of stores. Do you need anything?"

"I need you to take good care of my girl." Her tone held a warning.

"Always." He couldn't keep the side of his mouth from

curving up. The old woman was another one of Dani's protectors.

"That's what I thought. You're a good man Jack. Stay that way."

Good? Him? That's a new one.

They left Lucky at home and rode into Heron Park. Jack parked and led Dani inside, stepping lightly. He was crushing his fresh start, being a better man.

Once inside the big home decorating store, they stood close together and might've been newlyweds setting up their house. A wide variety of necessities and goods for making life more comfortable, half of it useless, crowded the aisles. He'd been in stores like this before but had managed to avoid them for over a decade.

A knot formed in his gut and gripped his lungs. He and Abagail had shopped in a place like this when they'd first married and been expecting. But this would be nothing like that. Today, they'd get what Dani needed and get out. How long could it take? She was blind and wouldn't get distracted by every shiny object.

"What do you want? Pillows, towels ...."

"Let's get me something soft for the couch. But Jack, I need to shop the sale rack. My credit card is already groaning."

"Cupcake, this is all on me today."

"But why?" A smile teased her lips. "Why are you being so nice to me?"

He studied the woman on his arm, and his heart squeezed. For the love of Pete, she owned him. But he was too old, and she was too related to Luke. "Because I can afford it, and you ... you've been goin' without on my watch. I'm responsible for the folks on the ranch." It sounded reasonable.

"That's why? Because you take care of the people on the ranch? Like you took care of Wyatt?"

"Right. Like that." Nothing like that. He wanted to brush her hair off her face and kiss her on the lips right there among the other shoppers.

"Let's find me something soft for my couch. So I can curl up if it's chilly."

They headed over to the aisle holding a staggering variety of small blankets.

"What color—" He stopped himself. What kind of idiot asked a blind person what color they wanted?

Dani shoved her hands between the blankets stacked on the shelf. She felt for the next pile and ran her fingertips down those, perusing the selection with her sense of touch.

"There are a bunch over here." He took her hand and guided her to the row of hangers.

"Oh, my. Oh, Jack, try this. It's as soft as a kitten or a rabbit. And this ..."

"Do you have a color preference? Is that a weird thing to ask?"

"It's not weird. I associate colors with things I enjoy. I like a light blue for the sky. And pink, of course. And yellow is like lemons or butter. Who doesn't love butter? But mostly, I have a softness preference. Check out this one."

The throw was light pink, like a baby blanket. They'd bought a blanket that color for their nursery. His stomach tightened. "Nice," he ground out.

"No, really feel it. Close your eyes." It was her turn to take his hand.

Her touch sent shivers over his skin, a pleasant distraction from unwanted memories. He brought his focus to the blankets.

"Notice how smooth this one is, but cool to the touch, and this one here, it's thicker. It might be too hot." She moved his hand to a stack. "And this one, so silky. Now, without looking, which one would you want?"

"I don't know. They're all ...." He wanted to say they were all the same to him, but when he paid attention, there were variations.

"Don't go all tough cowboy on me. You know they're different."

"You're right. How about this one?"

"Excellent choice. That's one of my favorites. We'll get it for you."

He cracked his eyelids. "It's hot pink."

"Perfect."

"For you." Come to think of it, she did wear a lot of pink. "Why do you like pink?"

"It's feminine, silly. And the color of strawberry ice cream. Or roses. But pretty much any pastel works for me."

"This isn't pastel. Aliens can probably spot this blanket from space. It's probably too intense for them."

"Sometimes I like intense." Her hand rested over his for a beat longer than expected.

Did she mean something by that?

His mouth dried. "Let's get you a few different ones." He removed the throw from the hanger. "This hot pink one and a different one for your chair and another for your bed." The image of her laying on that plush blanket, her soft hair fanned out. And then ....

He rubbed his face. Yes, she was kryptonite, burning through his resolve. "Okay, let's move along. We don't have all day." He could kick himself. Earlier, he'd told her they literally had all day, but his IQ dropped about thirty points standing this close to her.

They moved from the throws to the dishware. Dani examined the spring inventory and picked out a rabbit-shaped platter. "Where's the cowboy stuff?" She ran her fingertips over the various dishes on the sale shelf.

"We won't find cowboy stuff in here." He winced. Palm trees and shell-themed décor dominated the shelves.

"No horse-shaped dishes or anything?"

"Nope. Let's go."

"Okay." Her tone dropped.

When they made their way toward the register, the cart piled high with fluffy towels, velvety pillows, uniquely shaped dishware, and throws, they passed an aisle with tiny statues and other items to display. A pair of horse sculptures caught his eye.

"What do you think of these?" He set one in her hands.

"I love it!" She explored the intricate details of the sculpture with her fingertips.

"It reminds me of a Remington."

"A gun?"

"No." Jack chuckled. "He was a famous cowboy artist. This resembles his work."

"I had no idea you knew about art."

"Besides PE, it was my favorite subject in school." He guided her hands to the other figurines. "There're several horses here."

"I want two. I'll think of them as a couple. On this podcast I was listening to about feng shui, they said if you want to find a mate, put some sort of couple in your relationship corner."

"What's a relationship corner?"

"Your home has sections, and they have names. In my house, my bedroom is in the relationship corner. I'll put them on my dresser."

"Because you want a relationship?" He winced, glad she couldn't see his expression.

"Well. Yes. I do. I'd like someone special. I had a bad breakup before I came down here. But I might be ready now."

Did she want to bring a man into her home?

"Don't you want someone?" Dani asked. "I know you were married once."

"Twice."

"What happened?"

"It ended." He didn't want either of his exes back, but it'd been a painful time, and there was no point dredging that up.

"Why? If you don't mind my asking."

"You like talking about your exes?" He scowled.

"It depends."

"Let's not ruin the day with old stuff we don't want to think about. But I have an idea. After we finish with the sculptures, let's get you a bookcase to display them."

"I love that idea." Dani squeezed his arm.

He brought his hand to her hair and let it slide down to her shoulder, then quickly pulled it away as the friendly impulse turned into something else.

For the next half hour, they explored sculptures. "What's this?" Dani asked.

"It's a replica of a compass. It says *true north* at the base."

"Show me."

He guided her fingertips, naming the letters as she touched them. It was personal and tender. Something in his chest rearranged, like tumblers in a lock clicking into place.

"I love it." She held the compass with both hands. "I want it to remind me to stay on course."

"And that means?" He held his breath. Why did it matter what it meant to her? Suddenly, her future plans were important to him.

Dani set the compass sculpture in the shopping cart. "The herbs." Her fingertips traced along the figurines on the shelf as she spoke. "Deciding what to do with them, where to ... oh. What's this?" Dani lifted the small statue.

"That would be a replica of 'Michelangelo's David.'"

"Oh. My, it's ... anatomically correct."

"You got that right."

Her face pinked.

He grinned. This was getting interesting. "This here's the 'Thinker.'" He placed a small version of Rodin's sculpture in her hands. "He's got his hands under his chin like he's deep in thought."

"He's naked too."

"That's a thing in art. Didn't you ever take art in school?"

"No. I was busy taking classes to help me survive. I didn't get art electives. But one time, I took chorus. I loved singing. I like the sculpture of David. I want to get it."

"Because?"

"He's the little guy. Standing up to a big giant. It's an empowering story."

They added the sculpture of David and a boxed shelving unit he'd need to assemble to the cart and wheeled toward the checkout.

David. The word brought to mind Dr. Dave. What would the doc say when Jack revealed he'd spent the day with Dani, taking care of her like she was his?

How would he react if she brought that cowboy from the diner back to her cottage?

His jaw tightened. That couldn't happen. But it likely would. He rubbed the back of his neck. This was getting complicated. He needed to either go back to keeping his distance or tell Dani he was interested.

Keeping his distance held no appeal.

"I'm hungry. Is there a place around here to eat?" Dani asked.

"I know the perfect spot."

This close to the coastline, it would be a waste not to eat near the water. Jack drove them to a seafood restaurant and requested a table on the deck near the sandy shore. They were having lunch, and this was starting to feel like a date.

It wasn't a date.

This might be the place where he'd taken a few women when he'd first moved to town. That was dinner, and he'd had specific intentions. This was about food. He had another errand to run, and people needed to eat. But his heart lifted as he led Dani to her seat.

He needed to settle down.

"Read me the menu." Dani leaned back and turned her face to the sunshine.

He read her the list of items, surprised at the intimacy of performing such a simple act.

"Ew. I hate it when they call fish *fingers*." Dani wrinkled her nose.

"You'd best not ask me about mountain oysters."

"What are they?"

"I told you not to ask. What's your stance on shrimp tacos?"

"I want the Greek salad wrap with shrimp. It'll be easier to eat."

"I'll get that too." He laid down the menu.

They ordered, and the server returned with their drinks.

He stared over white caps frosting the blue-green water where the bay met the gulf and frowned. What was he thinking, bringing her to this beautiful view she couldn't share?

Dani removed her sweater and stretched her arms long. "I love it out here."

"Why?" The view was the main thing this place had going for it.

"Seriously?"

"Yeah. What's the appeal?"

"It smells fresh, clean, salty." Dani hung her head back,

inhaling. "I love the sound of the waves hitting the shoreline. They make recordings of the seashore you can play. But I prefer rain if I'm playing nature sounds. And there's the warm sun and wind on my skin. There are gulls and songbirds, too. I hear a cardinal. Do you hear it?"

He closed his eyes and listened. A truck needing mufflers roared by. Several types of birds called from various directions, and the waves rolled in. It sounded different with his eyes closed. He inhaled the scents of the seaside, damp grass, and fried fish. His stomach growled.

"Yes. There it is." He surveyed the area and spotted a dot of red in a tree.

Dani played with the moisture on her glass. "You know those horse statues you bought me?"

"Yeah?"

"They make me kind of sad. Well, more wistful, I guess. I brush horses every day. But other than being led around on ponies at camp, I've never ridden."

"You've lived at the ranch, what ... over ten months now, and haven't been riding?"

"Luke promised to teach me last summer, but there was too much going on with the wedding and his new business. We never got around to it. To be honest, I'm kind of scared."

"I ..." He shouldn't offer.

"I can probably ask Brick or Striker."

"Brick has his hands full teaching Wyatt to ride and handle a cow whip."

"What! Why do you whip them? Doesn't it hurt?"

"We don't whip them. We crack the whip, and the sound gets them moving. Bottom line. Brick's busy right now."

"I'll ask Striker. He's been teaching Avery to work with the new mini horses."

No way was that know-it-all teaching Dani to ride. But that left him and, hell .... "I'll take you riding."

"You have time to teach me?" She grinned broadly. "How will I get up on them and back down? They're huge."

"Not a problem. I'll be there." What was wrong with him? Pressing the boundaries by taking her shopping, taking care of her like she was his ... what? His little sister? No. What he felt for her was hardly brotherly. He was treating her like a girlfriend. A serious one.

What happened to keeping his distance? "We can start tomorrow."

*D*ani was nervous and had hardly slept, but that wasn't going to stop her. Today was her first riding lesson. Something brand new, which was exciting. And, also, a little scary. Jack was teaching her, which was enough to make her heart flutter—in a good way. The jittery feeling was because she had to climb on a big, unpredictable animal that could buck her off.

She knew people who'd been thrown from a horse. Avery's horse reared last year and she'd hit the ground hard and hurt her hip. Just a bruise, but it had been painful. Luke had been thrown from a horse and suffered a broken leg that had required surgery. It had taken months to heal and had ended his career in the rodeo.

Jack had promised he'd find her a gentle horse.

She squeezed into her jeans, tucked in her shirt, and sucked in her belly to do the button. All those slices of apple pie were catching up with her.

With her hands on her hips, as her sister had shown her, Dani lifted her chest, inhaled deeply, and imagined calming energy filling her body. I *can* do this. I can get on an enormous horse. It'll be okay.

She poured a cup of herbal tea and inhaled so much lavender oil she'd probably sprout flowers. That wasn't enough. Courage. She needed courage and had the perfect blend of oils, including frankincense, geranium, and spruce. She rubbed the rollerball oil dispenser below her throat and inhaled from the vial.

Lucky whined.

"I know. You think I'm stinky. Let's go. You'll be on the ground. I'll be way up high. I have to do this alone."

Jack met her in the big barn and gave her a tour of the tack, naming the parts. Next, he moved on to the horse.

"I know what a horse feels like," she said. "I've brushed enough of them."

"It's good for you to touch Domino, get to know him. He's gentle, but he'll pick up on your fear."

"Who says I'm afraid?"

"Dani. Your fingers are like ice. C'mon. I'll help you up these little steps. Let's get your foot in this stirrup and lift your leg over the horse." He explained how she should mount.

She held the saddle horn and, with his help, wedged her foot in the stirrup, tried getting her leg over the horse, and knocked her knee into the saddle. "Ouch!" The horse was a mountain her leg wasn't crossing.

The horse moved. "Wait!" she called out, her pulse spiking.

"Whoa!" Jack grabbed her.

"I can't do it."

"Get back over, Domino. I've got you, Dani. Let's try again."

"This isn't a good idea." Jack must think she was a clumsy cow.

"You're not giving up that easy, are you?"

"I'm not giving up. I just changed my mind, is all." She tried backing down the little steps, misstepped, and tumbled off the side.

Jack caught her.

For a quick moment, the world was reduced to Jack's chest and arms. That and humiliation.

"I'm done here."

"I didn't peg you for a quitter." There was a challenge in his voice.

Her face tightened. "I am not a quitter."

"If you say so."

She could practically hear his smirk. She climbed back up the steps. "Okay. One more time."

Jack helped lift her, and Brick came over and guided her foot from the opposite side.

And then, she was on the horse. Mostly, it felt like a big leather saddle. She reached forward and stroked Domino's mane. He raised and lowered his head. "You're a good horse. Please don't bite me."

"He's not a biter." Jack patted Domino. "Hold the reins like this." He positioned the leather straps in her hands. "I'm gonna lead you around the ring. Domino here is gentle, so when you feel comfortable, I'll let go."

They circled the ring a couple of times. This was fun. Not a whole lot different from the pony rides she'd been on as a kid, but she was riding and enjoyed the rhythm of the horse beneath her.

"He knows to stay close to the fence," Striker's voice came from across the ring. "Why didn't you say Dani was riding today?"

"Hey, Striker." Dani sat taller in the saddle.

"I thought you were going over the books with Luke," Jack said tightly.

"I'm finished. I can help Dani," Striker offered.

"No. I've got her." There it was, that tone Jack took with

Luke. Now he was using it with Striker. "Why don't you take Wyatt out and show him how to check the water systems?" Jack said.

"We do that on Mondays." Striker came closer.

"Whoa." Jack slowed Domino. "And today would be good for Wyatt to learn."

Striker was right below her now. "No sense—"

"I'll do it," Brick offered.

"No. Striker can. You finish up in the barn." Jack sped them up again.

It struck her as she sat in the saddle—these men were arguing about her. *Her?* A smile curved her lips. "I'm ready for more whenever y'all are finished chitchatting." Dani stroked the horse's neck.

"Go ahead, Dani. You can ride Domino around the ring on your own while I get Whiskey," Jack said.

She rode Domino, exuberance charging inside her. She was riding. On her own. No cane. No dog. With the horse beneath her, she had sight. Tall. Mighty. Powerful. She could get used to this. True, the horse was only walking, but she'd take the win.

"Tell him 'whoa.'" Jack came alongside her on his own horse.

"Whoa," Dani said.

Domino stopped.

Triumph! She nearly burst with happiness.

"There're no cows in the cow pens. We'll ride from pen to pen and through the corrals. Domino will follow along. We'll go slow today. Give him a little squeeze with your heels and say 'walk'."

She squeezed, and the horse moved forward.

There she was, riding, telling this huge animal what to do. She wasn't exactly a rodeo queen, but the strength of the animal beneath her, the sun on her face, and the scent of the horse lifted her heart. How could she ever leave here and live somewhere else?

They rode for a while, and the horse turned and walked a little faster.

"You're doin' so good. Let's head into the pasture. You up for that?" asked Jack.

"Sure." Would she even know the difference? They rode out of the ring, and the scents of fresh grass and blossoms filled her nostrils. Yes, it was different from riding in the ring. And the freedom, the free feeling of being outdoors, not thinking about working Lucky or tripping over something, was liberating. This was wonderful. She sat taller and threw back her head.

"Hey," Jack's voice came from beside her. "Stop your horse."

Dani brought Domino to a standstill.

"Hold out your hand. To the right."

She held the reins in her left hand and reached out. Jack was there, on Whiskey, right beside her.

He grasped her hand. "You've got this, Dani. You really do."

They sat on their horses in the mild afternoon sun and listened to birdsong, holding hands, Jack rubbing his thumb over her fingers. Butterflies launched in her belly. Was it the excitement of the horse? Or the thrill of Jack holding her hand? Either way, this moment could go on forever.

Too soon, they rode back to where she'd started.

"Let me help you dismount." The leather squeaked as Jack climbed off his horse and tied Domino. Then he was at her side, gripping her while she brought her leg over the steed. Jack held her waist as she slid down the side and into his arms.

"You looked really good up there, Dani." His voice was husky.

Her heart sped up. Was he going to kiss her? She felt that electricity, like when she rubbed his shoulders the other day in her house. "Thanks. I loved it."

"Your hair came loose." He tucked it behind her ear, and his hand remained there.

After sitting on the horses, holding hands, wouldn't a kiss be the next step? What was she supposed to do? She leaned in and tipped up her face, ready.

Nothing.

Just thick silence and heat filling the space between them. She moved her hand, brushing her fingers against his.

He stepped away. "I need to untack the horses."

Her cheeks warmed, and she hurried to redirect, pretending she didn't notice. "I'll brush Domino."

"No. You go on."

"I really don't have—"

"I'll handle it." Jack's tone left no room for argument.

Her chest sank with frustration, and she wanted to argue. Why was he trying to get rid of her? "Can I ride again tomorrow?"

"You might be sore."

"Can I let you know how I feel?"

"Sure. But I may not be able to take you for a while." His tone sounded like a door shutting. What was his problem?

"O ... kay. I guess I'll ask Strik—"

"No. I'm Striker's boss. I'll ... check the schedule and get back to you." He led her to the fence where Lucky awaited. "I've got work to do."

His boots clomped in the distance, and the jangling and thunking told her he was busy with the horses.

Dani grasped Lucky's harness and directed him to Thea's garden. For a moment, she and Jack had been close. What went wrong?

This was why she shouldn't let herself have feelings for him. Not only was he sighted, but he obviously didn't think of her as a desirable woman.

Jack watched Dani head toward Thea's house, her back stiff.

He'd almost kissed her. Right there in front of God and all creation. In front of whoever might be watching. And Luke was around somewhere. He wasn't in the mood to go at it with his brother.

"Are you always that smooth with women?" Wyatt stood a few feet away, leaning on a pitchfork.

"Weren't you going with Striker to check the water stations?" Jack unsaddled Domino.

"He said they were checked yesterday."

Jack's face hardened. As usual, Striker had his own way of doing things and wasn't taking orders from him. But if Luke had been giving the orders ... he growled under his breath.

"He'll show me later this week," Wyatt smirked. "Dani liked her lesson."

"Yep." That kid was too perceptive for his own good.

"You giving her another one?"

"Why?" It might demolish his resistance if he had to help her on and off a horse again.

"Dani liked it. You liked it." Wyatt's eyes crinkled with amusement. "But you might've blown it. She's pretty upset."

"Don't you need to help Brick?"

"We got the stalls done."

"See that cow whip?"

"Yeah ..." Wyatt shifted his gaze to the coiled whips hanging from hooks.

"You aren't done until you can crack that whip. Get out there and practice."

"Striker and I are practicing later. He says once I master cracking, he'll teach me to work on targets."

Jack groaned inwardly. Not only did his foreman know Florida cattle ranching better than any of them, but Striker also had a shelf of ribbons from target whip competitions. But he was Striker's boss, and Wyatt would do well to remember that. He gave Wyatt the stink eye.

"Okay." Wyatt raised his hands in surrender. "I'm going."

After he finished with the horses, Jack stalked into the office and plunked down on the chair. What had he been thinking, taking Dani's hand in the field? Him, the man who hooked up. Good time Jack, holding a woman's hand on horseback like he was in some sappy movie. Hell, his friends wouldn't even recognize him.

How long had it been since he'd wanted a woman like this?

He'd gone on a tear after his second divorce and earned a reputation that'd worked in his favor when he wanted to pick up women. Why not? Everyone blamed him for his marriage ending anyway. Unlike his dad, he'd never been one to cheat. But with two failed marriages, he didn't have the skill set to be a good husband. And if he failed at a relationship with Dani, it'd mess up everything here on the ranch.

Yet, here he was. In deep.

This is what came from breaking his rule about steering clear. How was he supposed to go to Dani's cottage, assemble her shelves, and pretend he didn't want her after holding her hand in the field?

Dani wanted him to give her another riding lesson. He'd do it because he was a man of his word, and there was no way he'd let Brick or Striker help her. As a ranch resident, she was his responsibility.

But he needed a few days away from her first, to shore up his resistance.

"Jack?" Luke entered the office, his expression dark.

"What's up?"

Luke stood several feet away, swinging a hammer. "Where's my hammer?"

"In your hand?" Jack raised a brow.

"No, the red-handled one. This is the black one. I prefer the red one." Luke scanned Jack's tools on the pegboard above the desk.

"I haven't seen it." He was in no mood for his brother.

"You sure you didn't use it?"

"I didn't touch your hammer."

Luke swung the hammer in an arc, then tossed it from hand to hand. "I hate it when someone uses a tool that belongs to me without asking. And then they don't put it back."

"Can't you use the black one?"

"No. I prefer the other one. It was expensive. I bought it." Luke glared at him.

Jack met his brother's hard gaze. "I'm sure it'll turn up." He stood, refusing to be intimidated. He could get all over his own case, but Luke had best not get territorial with Dani. "You've got a hammer. Use it. You can always buy another."

"Sometimes we get a new tool, and it's our favorite. Then the newness wears off, and we cast it aside. Don't want it anymore. People are fickle like that. Some people take other people's tools. Not me."

"Your point?"

Luke's tone grew a harder edge. "Sometimes we find a keeper. I want to keep my good hammer. You might be the kind of person who tries new tools and gets tired of them. For no good reason. That's no way to live."

"I used to like collecting new tools. Maybe I've changed. Maybe I want to stick with the ones that work. Like you." He waved to the pegboard. "Now I've got my tools in order."

"So you say." Luke glanced up and back down. "Order can get messed up."

"Are we about done here?" He couldn't keep the irritation from his tone. "I have to get up to the house. Thea's leaving, and the agency is sending someone new." Before Luke answered, he spun on his heels and left his brother standing there. The chip on Luke's shoulder went back to their time in high school. Or earlier. If he hadn't moved on by now, that was his problem.

Marrying Ellie didn't put Luke in charge of Dani. And his brother wouldn't warn him off. Not anymore. Screw Luke. A twenty-five-percent greater share of the ranch didn't make Luke the dictator.

He got halfway across the drive when an unfamiliar car pulled through the gate. The new caregiver had arrived. He needed to get to the woman before Bud had a chance to scare her away.

$\mathcal{A}$ week passed before Jack finally made it to Dani's place with his toolbox in one hand and his power screwdriver in the other. Despite keeping himself busy during the days, she'd occupied his mind every night. He'd resisted the impulse to walk those few hundred yards and see her. It hadn't been easy.

Today he was on a mission. Get the shelving assembled and get out.

He rapped on the door with the hand holding the power tool. "Hey Dani, it's me."

Dani opened it. "Jack? Usually you let yourself in."

"My hands are full. I brought tools to assemble the shelves."

"C'mon in. Can I get you an iced tea?"

"Only if it's sweet like you," he tossed off, cringing immediately. That's not how he wanted to talk to Dani.

"Of course, it's sweet like me. Do you need a little sweetening up?" A flirty smile graced her face.

"Yes ... er, I'll take an iced tea." The box holding the shelving unit leaned on the far wall where he'd left it. He tore the thing open and got to work.

Dani set his tea on the end table. "I thought you were coming days ago."

"I got busy." Busy firming up his boundaries. Had a stern talk with himself and even had a session with Dr. Dave, who offered a reality check. If he wanted to be an effective ranch manager, he had to think strategically and consider the big picture. That meant getting along with Luke, who owned the largest share of their operation.

Damn his father for dividing their business that way. Even though money wasn't an issue, he'd need Luke's cooperation when he expanded the mini horse program and launched the horse breeding operation. His dad had said he'd even up the shares if he and his brothers proved they could work together effectively. That was plenty enough motivation to get his head on straight. He'd even started reading books on leadership and management while his father snored in front of the TV at night.

Dani, standing nearby, made focusing difficult. He may as well put her to work. "If you hold this piece, it'll go faster."

She held the end steady while he drove in the screws.

It was grim work, ignoring her while he assembled the unit. A screw was missing, and he had to hunt for another in his toolbox. Then one of the holes didn't line up correctly. All the while, Dani's floral scent wafted over, messing with his head.

He directed her for the next half hour, and they got the unit assembled. As the shelving came together, the cottage filled with the aroma of something delicious, making his mouth water. "What's that I smell?"

"Apple pie."

His mood brightened. "Seriously?"

"It's from the diner. I put it in the oven when you texted you were on your way. Are you ready for a slice?" She headed into the kitchen.

He hadn't planned on staying. This wasn't a social visit, but his stomach rumbled. "Almost." He tipped the piece and tightened the last screw. "That should do it. Now you have a place for your statues."

Dani stood by the oven with long mitts over her hands, carefully placing the pie on the stovetop. She removed the mitts, sliced the pie, and served it up. "Ouch." She stuck a finger in her mouth, removed it, and blew on it. "That's hot."

"Are you okay?"

"I'm fine. I just got a little hot filling on my finger."

He should've offered to help. "Where do you want to eat?" Jack scanned the area and scratched his head. She had no table. "I don't mind standing to eat, but where do you usually sit?"

"I sit on the couch and use that TV tray in the corner."

There was a single TV tray leaning on the wall. He gaped. That just seemed ... sad. Didn't Ellie and Luke know she needed a table? "We should've bought you a table—"

"I'm fine. Could you set up the TV tray, and we can share?" She inched toward the living room holding the two plates.

"Sure." In a flash, he set up the tray and moved to intercept her. "I'll carry the pie." He carried it to the living room, waited for her to sit, and slid beside her.

This was a mistake.

Between the aroma of the pie and the nearness of her, he trembled inside. Should he have brought the shelving back to the house to assemble? Or sent Brick over? He needed to eat fast and get out of there.

When he bit into a forkful of pie, he moaned.

"I'll take that as confirmation you like it."

"They know how to make a pie." He wolfed it down like someone had threatened to take it from him and was about to stand when Dani placed her hand on his thigh.

He froze. Swallowed hard. All of his attention was fixed on the spot where her hand burned through the fabric of his jeans.

"Jack?"

"Huh?" Warmth pooled in his belly, and everything inside him charged with energy.

"You know, the other day. After riding. When you ... you know ... touched my hair?"

"Yeah?" His breath caught in his throat.

"I thought you wanted to ... kiss me. And if you did ..." She brought her hand to his chest.

His heart thudded under her palm. He should get up.

"It would make me happy. If you kissed me."

Months of carefully cultivated resolve crumbled. "We can't have you unhappy, can we?" He brought his hand behind her neck and pulled her in, dropping his mouth over hers, tasting her sweet cinnamon-apple-flavored lips. He held her face in his hands, pressing into her for a take-no-prisoners kiss. Filled with need, he brought his mouth to her neck and nibbled her delicate earlobe.

"Dani." His words came out rough. Arousal pulsed through him, pushing him on.

She laid her head back, giving him easy access to her throat, and he complied, covering her skin with open-mouthed kisses.

Someone knocked on the door. It opened. "Dani? Are you in here?" Luke called.

Oh, hell no. Jack pulled himself away from Dani and scrambled to his feet, adjusting his shirt and pants.

Luke entered the room holding a plastic container. "Ellie sent over some chicken parm...."

Luke stared at Dani, her hair mussed, lips swollen from Jack's kisses, and her face flushed. Then he took in Jack, and his lip curled.

Jack leveled a bland look at his brother.

"Hey, Luke." Dani rearranged the strap of her dress and shoved her hair back behind her ears. "We were enjoying a piece of apple pie. Would you care for some?"

Luke swung his gaze from Dani to the empty plates and back to Jack. "No thanks."

Jack had always been the one to start their fights and could easily overpower Luke, but the venom in his brother's eyes gave him pause. Besides, he was finished with hot-headed behavior and needed to get along. The two of them hadn't come to blows in a long time. Still, his arms tensed. If Luke wanted a fight, he was ready. "I just assembled that shelving. Want to help me move it?"

"Where does it go?" Luke's tone, exceedingly calm and polite, contrasted with his hard face.

"In my bedroom." Dani gathered the two plates and stepped toward the kitchen.

Luke shifted his gaze from the bedroom door to the shelves to Jack. "I'm sure you don't want to drag it into her bedroom by yourself."

They lifted the bookcase and carried it into Dani's room, positioning it against the wall.

"What are you doing here?" Luke asked.

Jack gestured to the piece of furniture. "Building her shelves."

"Just shelves."

Jack exhaled hard. "Someone needs to take care of her."

"I see the care you're taking."

"No, bonehead. I bought her stuff for the house, the shelves. She doesn't even have a place to sit to eat for meals."

"We're getting her a table."

"Yeah, she's been here alone for over a month. There's no table."

"I've been gone."

"And I'm here to handle it."

"You don't need to handle my wife's sister. I've got it. She's my kin now."

"Really? It looks like you left, and she's fending for herself."

"Dani doesn't need …. She's not one of your—"

"I know that. I was helping her." He hadn't initiated the kiss with Dani. That wasn't what he'd come over for, but he'd enjoyed it. He dragged in a breath and counted to five before responding. He could remain calm.

The muscle in Luke's jaw ticked. "And now you're done helping."

"Just because she's Ellie's sister doesn't make her yours."

"She's not yours either."

They stood, nostrils flaring, muscles taught.

Dani appeared in the bedroom doorway. "Jack, can you help me organize the little statues? They're in that box on the floor."

Luke's gaze shifted to the figurines with open curiosity and then returned to Jack.

"Sure." He set the box on the bed with a look that dared Luke to say something. Whatever he was doing, one thing was for sure—Luke wouldn't run him off.

Dani scooped a tablespoon of dried valerian from a bowl and dumped it in a small jar. The loud ticking of Thea's kitchen clock made her speed up. "Whoops. I spilled some." That's what happened when she was distracted and trying to hurry.

The problem was, she couldn't get Jack out of her head. The day they'd held hands on the horse and when he'd come by to assemble the shelving unit. She'd served him apple pie and laid her hand on his wall of a chest. Beneath her fingers she'd felt his muscles, defined and hard. Now she understood the phrase sculpted abs. He'd reminded her of that statue of David. Then they'd kissed. Oh, mama mia, how they'd kissed. That memory played over and over in her head like a song that wouldn't stop. It was nice. Very nice. And hadn't happened again. She'd thought they might talk about it. But it was as though it'd never happened.

Jack, being sighted, older, and the ranch manager, heck, one of the owners, was never going to be her boyfriend. She'd be wise not to make too much out of the kiss. Most men she'd known would take a kiss if offered. They were friends. Because what else would they be? He might be part owner of the ranch, but he wasn't her boss—was he? She got free room and board and a small allowance, which probably counted as a paycheck. But Brick usually told her what to do and helped her if needed. Striker, being the ranch foreman, was Brick's boss.

Luke was her brother-in-law, and Jack was his half-brother. She didn't know genealogy or how that stuff worked, but Jack wasn't exactly her relative. So, they were friends. Friends. She wouldn't push it again. Honestly, she had no idea what had come over her. Despite all the flirting, she rarely made a move on a man. It was too awkward since she couldn't tell where his lips were without touching him.

Those moments kissing Jack filled her with longing. If Jack wasn't an option, she'd find someone else. She ran her fingertips over the bits of herb on the table around the jar.

"Don't try to use what you spilled. The herbs are all mixed together. Lord only knows what kind of tea that would make. I'll take care of the mess." Thea was usually patient, but today her tone had a slight edge.

"Thanks."

The older woman had insisted on reviewing the properties of the plants before they began assembling the blends, and this afternoon session was taking way longer than Dani had predicted. "That makes twenty jars. Is it enough?" She slid her thumb under the thin nitrile and began to remove her gloves.

"We need forty, dear. We still have lavender and chamomile. What's your hurry? I declare. It seems like you're not here today."

Forty? Dang. She needed time to change clothes, but she sat back down and scooped another spoonful into a small jar. For the past couple of hours, she and Thea had been making products to sell at the produce stand next door and the coffeehouse in town. Most were promoted as remedies, although their claims were vague since they weren't government approved. Names such as Catch a Nap and Sharp as a Tack graced the labels.

"How about I stay for fifteen more minutes? I'm riding into town with Jack. He's dropping me at Mac's while he runs errands."

"You're enjoying your time with him." Thea's simple statement seemed to carry a lot of meaning.

"I am. Jack's been helping me. He bought me some things for my cottage."

"That's very generous."

"He's my friend."

"Is he? Humph."

For some reason, she wanted to explain or validate that statement. "He's a lot nicer than I thought. We live on the same piece of property, but for months I hardly ran into him. I could've been miles away. Now he's giving me riding lessons. I love being up high, letting the horse watch the path. It feels so free. This morning I rode out to check the cattle with him and Brick."

"You worked cattle?" Thea asked, alarmed.

"Oh. No. I rode along, and they checked on a few of the new calves."

"And now you don't have time to work in the garden?"

Dani cringed inwardly. "I know. My riding has cut into our gardening time." Packing herbs and preparing remedies was interesting, but working in the soil didn't bring her joy the way it did Thea. "Can I do it when I return? I'm picking up dinner and meeting someone." She didn't have anyone particular in mind, but there were always people to talk to at Mac's. And Tanner might stop in.

"Let's meet in the garden first thing in the morning before you work with the minis. I promised Jack I'd come over at four. The caregiver's leaving, and I'm staying through dinner."

"I can pick up food for you." Dani paused. Thea didn't drive, and Dani didn't ask. As far as she knew, Thea didn't have a visual impairment, but when the topic turned to driving, Thea always changed the subject.

"I suppose you could bring me soup. Get a quart and drop it by. I'll heat my rosemary bread. Bud loves it."

"I'm impressed that the new woman Jack hired has stuck it out so long."

"So far, she's holding her own." Thea chuckled. "Bud tried firing her yesterday, but she came right out and told him Jack's her boss. Did you know she was an elementary school lunch lady before she became a nurse?"

"They have nerves of steel. We were bad in the lunchroom. It was the only time we could cut up."

"At the school for the blind?"

"I attended a regular school first. Then I switched to the residential school."

"How was that?" Thea's chair scraped the floor, and the jars on the table clinked. She'd started cleaning up.

Dani placed jars in a box while Thea swept. "Most kids at regular school ignored me. Some were mean. When I got to the residential school, my mom had recently died. One of my teachers took me under her wing. She had a daughter my age, Jessica, who she sometimes brought to work. That's how we met. So going there had a silver lining."

"I'm glad you were able to make those connections."

"Thanks. I miss Jessica ...." She stopped, held the edge of the box, and said tentatively, "Jessica split up with her boyfriend and needs a roommate again. Her cousin is there through the summer, and I figured I might go up there when her cousin moves out."

"You're leaving?" Thea asked sharply.

"Maybe." She cringed inwardly. Jess needed a definite answer soon. "I'm thinking about it, anyway. I was hoping to continue this on my own. You can send me herbs, and I'll blend them and sell tea and creams in Jessica's friend's shop. I already emailed my old boss. He'd take me back."

Silence grew in the space between them, a tense uncomfortable silence thick with disappointment.

Thea had been welcoming and kind, but working with the herbs wasn't enough to outweigh the general isolation and trapped feeling from living this far from town. Back in Jacksonville, she'd be hanging out with Jess and swimming regularly. Aside from walking Lucky and riding, she got little exercise here, and her clothes were getting too tight.

"If that's what you want to do. I thought you were happy here with Avery and your sister. And the horses. I thought you'd stay on."

"I love it here. I do. Those little horses, and riding the big horses is amazing ...." Was she supposed to live out here like a spinster and step into the old woman's shoes? She'd hardly found a pair of her own. "But there's no public transportation here. No way to leave the ranch. It costs too much to get a ride into town. You and Phyllis are always going off shopping and other places. I guess it'd help if I had a Phyllis in my life."

"You want more—variety? To go to town?"

"I'm not sure what I want, but I don't think I'll find it way out here. I don't know how to *create my best life,* as they say on this podcast I listen to. But Jessica invited me back, and that's a start."

"Hmmm. You might start by imagining what you want."

"Right. Well. When you don't have much money or ... anything. You know what they say, beggars can't be—"

"Wait. Don't even think that way. Did you ever have Jell-O made in a mold?"

That was a random thing to ask. "Yes. My mom had these little heart-shaped molds, and she'd add pineapple. When the Jell-O set, she'd plop it onto a plate. I loved it. Why?"

"Knowing what you want is like pouring liquid Jell-O into a mold. If you have something in mind, if you have the Jell-O mold, you're more likely to get the result you want. You get the shape of the container you mix it in unless you make a specific choice, like when we make teas or creams for a specific ailment. You didn't ask. But my advice is, before you make a big change, get clear on what you want."

"Well, right about now, I want a Greek salad. And I know how to make that happen." Dani stood.

"Can I ask you for a favor?" Thea walked her to the door. "Would you be interested in taking over for me at Wren's? I have this big quilt project—and with Bud and then the garden ...."

"You want me to work there by myself? Like, go in your place? And meet with customers alone?"

"I think you're ready for that. If you have a question, you can call. I've got too much on my plate."

"Wow." Until now, she'd only assisted. Could she handle it alone? "Have you talked to Wren?"

"She said she'll train you, and she'll be on site."

What did on-site mean? The hundred-acre farm sounded big. Yet, the chance to get off the ranch and meet new people made her buzz with excitement. The money would be challenging. And if Thea counted on her to work there, it might become more difficult to move away. But it was an opportunity to be independent and do something different.

"You mentioned wanting to get off the ranch. It's not far, but Brick or Striker could give you a ride, and you'd need to bring product. Would you be able to manage the money?"

"I think I can." She had an app on her phone that could read paper bills, and in her experience, people didn't try to cheat. "I should go now. Oh. Can I bring a couple jars of that pain reliever cream? In case Chet's there?"

"You're already thinking like an entrepreneur. And that cream you made, I told Jack to massage it into Bud's hip. You have a gift, Dani. Every new formula you've come up with has hit the mark."

The compliment made her smile. Thea trusted her. Or was this request designed to make her stay? Dani accepted a bag with the jars of cream and headed home to change.

———

Jack started down the path and spotted Dani in front of Thea's house. "Ready?" He'd promised to give her a ride to the diner. The idea of leaving Dani there to flirt with local men made his stomach twist, but it was her social life, and he had no room to make demands.

"I'm heading home to change and feed Lucky."

"You look fine, cupcake." She looked a whole lot more than fine, but his mind wasn't supposed to be going there.

"But I bought a new dress for wearing into town. You know, in case I meet someone."

He groaned inwardly. Those were details he didn't want to hear. When she reached for his elbow to walk sighted guide, he pulled her a little closer than necessary and led her home.

"Why do you call me cupcake?" she asked, grinning as if she loved it.

"Because you're so sweet."

"I'm not."

He huffed. "Which makes it even better. And sometimes you are."

They headed into her cottage, and he fed her dog while she

slipped into a different outfit. When she stepped out in a snug red dress, he about dropped to his knees. "Where'd you get that?" he choked out. It seemed a little much for the diner, but Dani was always overdressed.

"I made it in my spare time."

He scoffed.

"I ordered it online, silly."

"How'd you know it would fit?"

"I send them back if they don't. It's not rocket science."

"Jeans are fine for the diner."

"Jeans are too warm. Besides, I like dresses. And I like looking pretty. What's your opinion? How do I look?"

"You look fine."

Her smile slipped.

"You looked fine before. Let's go." He hustled her out of the house, feeling like a tool for not giving her the compliment she wanted.

"Just fine? In this dress? My friend, Jessica, checked it out online and thought it would be pretty."

"Okay. You look nice." He shut her door and stomped around to the driver's side.

She was back on topic as soon as he climbed in. "Dang it. I'm going for better than nice."

"Okay. You're beautiful. Smoking hot. And probably too good for the likes of whoever's hanging out at Mac's diner."

A bright smile lit her face. "That's more like it. It didn't hurt to say that, now did it?"

That's where she was wrong. He ached with desire. And the idea of leaving Dani at Mac's, where she might meet some other man, made the nuclear power plant inside him spark.

He drove them west and changed the subject. "I asked Wyatt to come along. I wanted to take him to Hudson's with me. But he's funny about riding into town and had some excuse again."

"Wyatt didn't tell you where he came from before camping here?" Her tone held a note of caution.

"No. Not much. He mentioned that guy who beat him." He glanced over. "What do you know?"

"I'm not sure what he did. But he made his boss angry."

Jack shrugged. Hell, angry was his middle name. "What does that mean, made him angry?" The bruise on Wyatt's face flashed across his mind. He should've asked for more details.

"The man's after him, like planning to hurt him bad. I sense what they were doing was, well, I don't know .... But Wyatt's clothes smelled really weird before I washed them."

"Weird? Like how?"

"Like ammonia or plastic, some kind of chemical, like they were handling the pest control stuff or fertilizing or something. It was nasty."

"Huh." He ran through a mental inventory of the products they used on the ranch.

"Anyway, he thinks the man is still looking for him."

"I'll have a talk with Wyatt."

"No. Wait. Don't tell him you got it from me."

"How am I supposed to deal with it if I don't—"

"Please. I like Wyatt. I don't want to get him in trouble."

"I'm trying to help. Sounds like he's already in some kind of trouble. I wish you'd told me more before I hired him. We don't need any more issues after dealing with Mitch and all the mess he caused last year."

He pulled up to the diner. "Will you order dinners for us?" He intended it to sound noncommittal, but if she was buying them meals, she wouldn't be eating with Tanner.

"Yes. I already texted Wyatt to come over later. And I'm getting soup for your dad and Thea. She's heating him her rosemary bread."

He brightened. "Which means I have the night off. Mind if I eat at your place? I was hoping ..." He stopped himself. What was he hoping for? For a repeat of the other night? That was not happening. It couldn't happen. Not if he wanted to keep the peace on the ranch.

A beat-up white van cut him off, pulling into the parking lot at Mac's. It slipped into the last space in front, parking beside the motorcycle he'd seen at Turner's.

He felt uncomfortable leaving Dani there, and part of him wanted to blow off his errands and stay. "The spots out front are taken. Give me a second. I'll park on the side and walk you around."

"That's okay. I have my cane. Just let me off by the entrance steps."

"Are you sure?"

"I've been getting around on my own for years. I can find my way inside."

"That's not what I meant."

"Don't worry. Thanks. Text me when you're heading back." Dani climbed out and shut the door.

Something in his chest squeezed as he drove away. An unfamiliar feeling. Would she find a place to sit? Would she be okay? And worse, would Tanner be there to notice her in that dress?

———

Jack parked beside a familiar Jeep in front of Hudson's Farm and Ranch supply. Why was his younger brother here?

Garrick held down a stool in the checkout area with Flash and Tate.

He raised a brow and zeroed in on Garrick. "I hope I'm not interrupting your meeting."

When Garrick said he had a meeting, Jack assumed he meant one of the groups at the VA Center in Heron Park.

"What can I do you for, buddy?" Tate asked, closing his laptop.

"Need a part for the tractor. And set up a delivery...." Jack swung his gaze from one man to another. Why did he have the distinct sense he'd interrupted something?

Tate showed him the options for the parts, while Garrick followed Flash into the back of the store. They talked about equipment, weather, and hay. "So, Garrick spends time here?" It still blew his mind to learn Garrick had more than a passing acquaintance with Tate and Flash. Those veterans were stand-up guys who'd helped them out a time or two, but that was before Garrick showed up.

"Solid guy, your brother," Tate said absently.

"He come here often?"

"Now and then." Tate's brow creased. "Why?"

"No reason." He and his brother rarely spent time together since Garrick had come home from overseas. Garrick did the minimum required at the ranch, leaving more grunt work for him, then came down here to shoot the breeze? It grated on Jack. He was all for giving Garrick space but not shirking the ranch and hanging out with Tate and Flash. Fourteen years changed most people, and his brother had lived through combat. At least Garrick returned home with all his body parts. But it still irked.

The next stop should be the pharmacy and the grocery store. But Jack texted Dani he was running late and steered the car toward Heron Park. Pounding the hell out of the bag at the boxing gym was just what Dr. Dave would've ordered. He needed time to think.

*I*n the world according to Dani, it didn't count as eating a slice of pie if you left part of the crust. She took another bite and let the scrumptious apple filling melt on her tongue. Only the edge of the crust remained.

Before it got busy, she'd enjoyed chatting with Amber, the woman working the counter. Now, patrons surrounded her, and some of the conversations were getting interesting. She pushed the plate away and strained to hear the men arguing in one of the booths. Try as she may, she couldn't quite make out what they were saying.

"You hated it, huh?" Amber had a smile in her voice.

"That pie was excellent. Can I buy a slice to take home? No, wait. Add an entire apple pie to my cake order." Given the effect it had on Jack a of couple weeks ago, she needed more. *You're supposed to be friends.* Yes. And he wanted her to pick up dinner and eat at her house. *Friends do that.* But so might someone who's interested.

Interested in what? As if an older, twice-divorced ranch owner with a history as a player wanted her in some serious way. She chewed her upper lip, then stopped herself. Just

because he took her riding didn't mean he wanted a relationship.

But she'd still bring home an apple pie.

Two of her favorite diner friends, Chet and Roy, got up from
where they'd been sitting beside her.

"You got that cream for me?" Chet asked.

"I almost forgot. Here are two jars." She handed over the
sack.

"I was hoping for three. I told my brother about it. I'll have
Maryjane come by and pick some up."

"Send her to Wren's Produce. I'll be working there on
Fridays."

Chet placed two twenty-dollar bills in her hand. This visit
to the diner was already a success, and she still had a while to
hang out since Jack was riding all the way to Heron Park before
returning.

"Hey Dani," Chet called from the end by the cash register.
"Are you coming to visit the kittens? This Sunday's good."

She bubbled with happiness. "I'd love to if I can find a ride."

While Chet paid, a man sat in the vacant place to her left.
Her nose wrinkled, and she breathed through her mouth. Oh,
my stars. He stunk.

"Weren't you sitting in the booth?" the counter server asked.

"They left. I moved," the stinky man said. The sharp edge to
his tone dared Amber to argue.

Dani's senses went on alert. His voice. He was one of the
men who'd been arguing.

"Well, good to know," Amber said, unperturbed. "We can
use the booth for a four-top."

"And I'll take a piece of what she's eating. And throw in a
couple brownies to go."

Dani leaned a little closer despite his pungent odor. "You
won't be sorry. They make wonderful brownies."

"They do, huh?" A little pep entered his otherwise monotone voice.

Usually friendly, tonight she was Miss Nosey Pants. All of her warning bells sounded in his presence. Pine Crossing was a friendly small town, but not as sweet as she'd first thought. After the goings-on last summer when one of their ranch hands had been stirring up trouble, it became clear there were some oddballs in the area.

"I didn't catch your name." She kept her tone light.

He scoffed. "I didn't give it."

"There are a lot of regulars in here. I don't recall us ever meeting. I'm Dani." She must be crazy to press it, but there was something about his odor. He might be one of the men Wyatt had worked for.

"I don't get into town much."

A plate thunked on the counter, and he began eating, shoveling it in. Chewing loud like hungry livestock.

"Do you have a name?" The hairs on her neck prickled. What was she doing playing Nancy Drew? But she had to know if Wyatt might still be in danger. She waited. Sometimes people filled the silence if she remained quiet.

He continued eating.

"What do you do for a living?" She asked with feigned nonchalance. "A lot of the men I meet here work on the local ranches or farms."

"Why do you wanna to know? You wanna go out? I'll show you a good time." He snorted softly. "I have a van."

Good lord! Absolutely not. "Thank you kindly for your offer, but no."

Beneath the counter, he placed a large hand on hers, his bony fingers cinching tightly around her wrist. "You sure?"

A chill ran through her. "I need to get back to the ranch. I'm bringing dinner. My ride will be here shortly."

"We can meet here tomorrow. I know a good place to swim. Or I'll pick you up. Tell me where you live."

That was never happening. "Uh, no, thank you." She tugged her hand away from his tight grip and rubbed her wrist.

"Leave her alone." An unfamiliar deep voice boomed from her right. "Weren't you leaving?"

"No," snarled the man to her left.

She sensed a large presence move behind her. "I think you were." His tone left no room for argument.

The air practically vibrated with tension.

She looped her tote over her shoulder, ready to move if a fight broke out.

"I don't need this crap." The stinky man vacated his stool.

"Did he hurt you?" the man behind her asked.

"I'm okay." Her wrist burned, and she needed to wash off his filthy touch.

"Good."

"You are?"

"They call me Bear."

"As in a teddy bear?"

He laughed heartily. "More like a grizzly."

"Well, thank you, Bear. Something about that guy gave me the creeps."

"Yeah. Sleazebags like him will do that. Don't you go off with him, you hear?"

There was no chance of it. She shuddered to think that he'd wanted her address. Fortunately, he didn't come to town much.

Jack had taken the edge off of his anger at the gym. It was bad enough leaving Dani at the diner wearing that hot dress. Now, every time he thought about Garrick hanging out with the guys at the feed store, a twist of something painful formed in his chest. Being five years older, he'd barely had time to get to know his brother as an adult before Garrick had enlisted and left the ranch in Montana. Now, Garrick chose to hang out with strangers in town? Sure, Flash and Tate were good guys. But he was family.

After texting Dani, he finished his errands, drove to the diner, and parked beside a filthy guy climbing into the grimy, beat-up white van. He'd hung out with some tough men back home, but this guy made his skin crawl. While he hadn't gotten to know many of the locals, the people passing through were more troubling. Plenty of day-worker farmhands and cowboys were in the area at any given time. Hell, he'd hired some himself. Most seemed harmless, but others were sketchy drifters.

According to his friend Kurt, the local deputy, central Florida was fertile ground for a number of illegal goings-on—human trafficking, drug smuggling, meth labs, animal poachers, and people trading in illegal exotic animals. It hurt his brain to think of Dani getting mixed up with any of that stuff. Until Wyatt showed up, he'd believed the ranch was insulated and safe. But maybe not. He oughta be more careful about who he hired on. Tonight, he'd get the full story from Wyatt.

Jack climbed the steps to Mac's Diner and powered through the door. Dani sat half-way down the counter, talking to that big biker he'd run into at Turner's. A bad feeling came over him. She had no idea who she was flirting up.

He'd promised his therapist to keep a lid on his temper, but if the biker was bothering Dani .... In a few quick steps, he was at her side. "Is he—"

"Hey, Jack." Dani beamed a smile in his direction. "This here's Bear, as in Grizzly. Not a teddy. He was just talking to me."

Bear furrowed his brow. "Aren't you the guy who bought me and my friend a drink at Turner's?"

"Yeah ..."

"This your woman?"

He glanced at Dani. Was she? No. "Yes." He'd kissed her a couple weeks ago, but he wasn't about to have her harassed by bikers or anyone else. "Yeah. She's mine."

Dani's mouth formed an "O."

He'd have some explaining to do.

"Take care of her, man. She needs to watch out for scum bags." Bear offered him a conspiratorial look before lumbering back to his seat, boots thudding and chains clanging as he slid into a booth.

"What happened? Are you okay, Dani?" he asked.

"I'm fine. I'll explain on the way home." She stood, ready to go.

He collected her carry-out order and paid, in a hurry to get her out of there. "Was someone bothering you?" He helped her into the truck and steered them toward the ranch.

"Not really. There was this one man. He was persistent, and, well, I didn't care for the way he squeezed my hand. It felt like he ... I don't know."

"He touched you?" Jack whipped his head to face Dani and checked out her wrist. In the dim light, it appeared okay. He'd been gone too long. "Was he still there when I came in?"

"No. He'd just left. Something was off. Maybe he'd had too much to drink at Pete's, but he didn't smell like alcohol. And there was an odd odor. Anyway, it wasn't that big of a deal."

Fury raged inside him. "Next time someone gets too close or feels off, you text me. I'll be right back. Got it?"

She scoffed softly.

There he was, being overly bossy. He laid his hand on hers. "I'm saying I care about you and don't want you getting hurt."

"What can happen in a public place? I'm safe at the diner."

"Probably."

"Your 'woman' has her many admirers to offer protection." Dani's tone was snarky, but her lips curved up.

"Right. I was just ..." Words failed him. In hindsight, it was a boneheaded thing to say.

Violet claimed the sky as they turned into the Tall Pines driveway. "I saw three dinners. You got one for Wyatt, too?"

"Yes. I want him to come over for dinner. It's—"

"Good. We'll invite him over. It's about time I got some answers. I'll deliver the soup and be right back."

While Dani took her dog out, Jack carried over the soup for his dad and Thea. Before he stepped out the door, his gaze fell on the old drop-leaf table pushed against the wall. For a while, Ellie had used it as a desk. Now it was gathering dust. He carried it to Dani's cottage, then texted Wyatt to come over.

Wyatt bit into a drumstick and moaned. "Mac's food is the best, but I was hoping for meatloaf."

They were seated at the drop-leaf table Jack had set up at the end of Dani's living room.

"Meatloaf is Mondays," Dani said.

"You've had their meatloaf?" Jack had a strong suspicion about where his meatloaf dinner had disappeared to the first night he'd brought Dani home.

Wyatt glanced away sheepishly and dug into his mashed potatoes. "I heard it's good."

"I gave Wyatt part of my leftover meatloaf. It was in the freezer," Dani continued, unaware of the missing carry-out dinner. "Tuesdays is fried chicken or Tacos, you know, Taco Tuesday."

"I'm glad you got fried chicken. I've had enough tacos to last a lifetime. That's about all we ate at ... where I was working and, uh, staying. Sometimes it was taco shells and spray cheese." Wyatt wrinkled his nose.

"Yeah. I've been meaning to ask. Exactly who was your boss at your other job?" Jack leveled a stare at Wyatt. Striker's friend was the manager at Whitehall's, and they'd never heard of Wyatt.

"A bunch of people ordered me around."

"Who did you report to?" He narrowed his eyes. The kid wasn't getting out if it this time.

Wyatt shrugged. "Mostly a guy they called OD."

"OD? What kind of name is that?"

"A nickname, I guess." Wyatt kept his gaze on his meal.

"And you never heard him called anything else?" Jack put down his fork and leaned forward. Wyatt was holding something back.

"Just OD." Wyatt shoveled in a big forkful of mashed potatoes.

Jack huffed. "I want the truth. Now. I took you in. We're feeding you. I need to know I can trust you. It starts with the truth."

Wyatt was silent for a long moment before exhaling hard. "His name was Oscar. Nobody called him that. He gave me that name when I first met him at the gas station."

"What were you doing at the gas station?"

"Buying water. I'd just got into town."

Jack chewed thoughtfully. The station in Pine Crossing was a local drop-off and pick-up for the bus line. "And this Oscar hired you?"

"Uh-huh." Wyatt crammed a biscuit in his mouth. "He's the one looking for me."

Dani piped up. "I wonder if he was the man who sat beside me at the diner. He left right before you got there, Jack."

"What?" Jack sat up taller and laid down his fork. That

sketchy-looking guy who'd been climbing into the beater van and leaving the diner had to have been the one sitting by Dani.

"Well, first, he was in a booth arguing with someone. Then he changed seats and sat by me." Dani got a pinched expression. "And he had that same odor as your clothes did, Wyatt. It was foul. But your clothes smell good now, don't they?"

"Why didn't you say something sooner?" Jack studied Dani, the hairs on his arms raising.

"I'd planned to." Dani picked apart her corn muffin. "The entire episode with the stinky man was so upsetting. I tried putting it out of my mind."

"He never told me his last name," Wyatt continued. "They all called him OD."

"What was your plan for after buying water?" Jack stared down Wyatt until the kid looked away.

"I was figuring it out." Wyatt exhaled sharply. "I might've been sitting on the curb at the side of the gas station. OD saw me and offered me a job."

Now they were getting somewhere. "And you went to work for him." Jack stared at Wyatt with fresh interest. The boy had probably had more than a few adventures since leaving home.

"It's not like I had a lot of options. He offered me a place to stay and meals."

"You worked at the Whitehall place?" Jack waited for the lie. After having Wyatt on the payroll for several weeks, it was clear he hadn't been working cattle or caring for animals. Hell, there probably wasn't a single one of Wyatt's tasks at Tall Pines that Brick hadn't taught him. "You did ranch chores ...."

"Right." Wyatt scowled. "What is this? The third degree?"

Jack glanced at Dani, who'd grown uncharacteristically quiet. The conversation seemed to be upsetting her, but he had to know.

"You work here now. You need to be up front about who you

are and why you were camping on our property." Jack snorted. "What'd he hire you to do?"

"Like I said. Ranch stuff." Wyatt stared at his food, his expression guarded.

"How about the truth?" Fury propelled Jack to his feet. Then, just as quickly, he sat. Looming over the kid was intimidation. He'd try a different tactic. "You know Striker is friends with their manager."

Wyatt stopped with his forkful of mashed potatoes halfway to his mouth and glanced toward the door.

"And the manager there hasn't heard of you. So, how about you start over?"

The kid paled. "I worked for some men. They live in RVs, set up a camp, and move every few months. I saw a sign for Whitehall's ranch near the campsite. I don't know who owns the property. I ran errands."

"Errands?" he asked.

"I had to—deliver packages."

"Packages?" Jack's chest tightened. "What was in those packages? Where did you take them? How'd you—"

"I used one of their trucks. At first, I didn't know what was in the packages. They told me not to worry about it. They were ... manufacturing." Wyatt scoffed. "They had all kinds of equipment. When I figured it out, I left."

"You just left?" His brows pulled together. "What was it? Drugs?"

Wyatt nodded. "Yeah."

"Were they growing weed? It wasn't fentanyl, was it?" Oh hell. This was worse than he'd imagined.

"It was meth. They used a lot of chemicals. Some they bought and some ... I think they stole them from a farm." Wyatt huffed and shook his head, making a sour face. "I didn't want to be involved. I don't want to go to jail. They were just a place to stay and food. I got up early to escape, but OD caught me hiking into town. He tried to bring me back. Said I couldn't leave." Wyatt touched his temple. The bruise had almost disappeared. "I got away. That's why I was hiding. They're looking for me." Desolation was etched into his features. "They think I took money. Said they'd—"

"Did you?"

"No. Well. A little."

Jack scoffed loudly. "Shit."

Wyatt continued. "I took some food when I left. But this other guy, Raymond, was stealing from them. And he paid me not to tell. Threatened to say it was me. They'd never believe me over him. And they weren't paying me. They said I had to work off my rent. I figured they owed me." Wyatt set down his fork and pushed away from the table, looking ready to bolt.

Jack gentled his tone. "Okay. I believe you." Did he believe Wyatt? Hard work and willingness to learn were turning him into a man. He wanted to believe the kid.

Wyatt rubbed his face and, for a moment, looked like a sad, lost boy. "They're crazy."

For crap's sake. His suspicions were correct. Wyatt was trouble. What was he supposed to do? They'd had enough issues on the ranch last year. He had half a mind to send Wyatt away.

"Hey, Wyatt." Dani stood. "I got a cake for dessert. I remembered."

"What?" Jack asked, exasperated with the whole conversation. He shifted his gaze to Dani and back to the kid.

"And you get this." Dani fetched one of the throws he'd bought her at the home store. It still had the price tag. She extended it to Wyatt.

"It's my eighteenth birthday." Wyatt offered a weak smile.

"Jack paid for the cake and the throw. They're from both of us," Dani said.

Jack nearly gaped. Birthday present? From both of them? As in a couple?

He held Wyatt's gaze for a long moment. "Well, let's have cake. Happy birthday, kid. Now you're old enough to go to adult jail.

"Thanks?" Wyatt shook his head and looked from Dani to Jack. "I'll catch hell if the other guys see this." He rounded his eyes.

It was the bright pink blanket. You could probably see it from space. Jack held back a laugh and exchanged a wry smile with Wyatt.

Dani cut the cake, and they dug in. The mood had lightened and conversation segued into the merits of different kinds of cakes and pies for celebrations. He favored apple pie and apple cake. Wyatt thought the chocolate cake Dani bought was perfect. Jack cleaned his plate and had a second slice. He wasn't complaining. It was almost as though they were a family, sharing a meal. Having a celebration. Awareness hit him like a two-by-four. He could get used to this.

Wyatt had finally left, and Jack helped Dani clear the table. What should he say about claiming her as his, right there in the diner? How long would it take for news to reach the others at the ranch? He needed to come up with a story. He'd said it to protect her. That should fly. Although it wasn't the entire truth. When he'd seen her talking to that biker, he'd been filled with a hard jolt of *she's mine*. Eating dinner with Dani and Wyatt had only made it worse.

Even though he'd confronted Wyatt and gotten an earful of bad news, the meal ended well, and he'd enjoyed himself more than expected.

His phone buzzed with a text.

Thea: *I'm leaving.*

Crap.

Jack: *On my way.*

"I have to go," he told Dani.

She stilled. "I thought you might stay." Those words were heavy with meaning, the invitation tempting.

That was the problem.

He'd like nothing better than to stay. And he owed her an explanation for what he'd said at Mac's. "Thea's leaving. I should go."

"I wanted to tell you I can't ride on Friday or Saturday. I'm working at Wren's farm stand. Ellie's driving me over Friday morning."

"Okay. I'll stop by if I can."

"I'd like that."

He hustled out of her house before he gave in to his impulses again. If anything else happened between them, it'd be with intention. And he needed to get clear on what those intentions were. Dani messed with his brain, making him want things he hadn't wanted in a long time. Something between them had shifted. He needed to figure out what to do with the situation.

More than a little relieved at postponing an uncomfortable talk, he hiked back to the house and found Garrick pulling up. How's that for timing? He glanced back at Dani's cottage, fighting the urge to return, but it was just as well he'd left.

He and his brother climbed the steps together.

"He's been like that for a half hour." Thea gestured to their dad snoring in the recliner while some nature documentary played on the TV. That had to be Thea's pick. She nodded to him and Garrick and let herself out.

Jack went straight for his beer in the fridge, popped the top, and took a long pull.

Garrick moseyed into the kitchen behind him. "Rough day?"

He glared at his brother, still irked about finding him

hanging out at Hudson's, and leaving most of the chores and issues at the ranch on his shoulders. "You could say that."

"What's up?"

"It's Wyatt. He's ..." Why explain? His brother had enough trouble with insomnia and nightmares.

Garrick leaned on the doorframe with his arms folded. "Something wrong?"

His younger brother wanted to talk? That was a new one. Jack gave Garrick the short version of his conversation with Wyatt.

"Damn." Garrick scratched his chin. "Guess it's good he's here now."

"I just hope that jerk doesn't come looking for him. I think I spotted the guy in town at Mac's tonight."

"I was just there." Garrick's gaze sharpened. "What does he look like?"

"He'd have been gone by then." This is what he'd wanted to avoid. His brother was already reclusive and jumpy. "Nothing for you to worry about. I've got it under control."

"You're a bad liar." Garrick pulled open the fridge and got his own beer.

"You gonna be here a while?"

"Sure. You going back to Dani's?"

That caught him unaware. "No. I wanted to turn in early. If you could handle Dad." His brows drew together. "Why'd you ask?" Aside from the riding lessons, he'd returned to keeping his distance. Well ... until tonight. And he'd made a point of being more circumspect, even asking Brick to ride along with them several times.

Garrick's tone held a challenge. "You're out riding with her all the time."

"No. Only a few times a week." When was Garrick even around to see him?

"Uh-huh." Garrick's eyes narrowed. "Luke was pretty bent out of shape about something the other day."

"Luke's got a bug up his butt half the time."

"This seemed different." Garrick huffed.

Wait a second. Was Garrick taking Luke's side?

That was the thing about his younger brother. Garrick didn't remember a time when Luke hadn't been with them. Couldn't recall when their dad and mom got along and when he was the only older brother. It didn't help that he and Luke were practically the same age and Garrick had only been two.

Those were the best years of Jack's childhood, before the age of seven, when he'd been his dad's favorite. Before Luke had come to live with them. Growing up, Garrick treated him and Luke the same, like their older sister did. Which irked.

"You've made some friends in town." Jack changed the subject. He may as well call out Garrick for hanging out with Tate and Flash in town, when he implied he was up at the Veterans' Center.

"What's with the attitude?" Garrick squinted at him. "Anyway, don't deflect. Luke might have a point. Dani's ten years younger than you. And blind. And his sister-in-law."

"Tell me something I don't know."

"And Amber said something when I grabbed dinner at Mac's."

Crap. He'd expected word to get around but figured he'd have a few days. "Whatever you heard, it didn't mean anything."

"I'm just saying. Luke might not be off base."

"You didn't take issue when Dani stayed over those two nights."

"That's before I thought you might be serious." Garrick pulled a face. "Things could really go to hell around here. Why not go to Heron Park ...."

"Nothing's going on." The denial rang false. He didn't know

what he wanted, but he wanted something. He wanted something to happen with Dani. The days he rode with her were the highlight of his week.

"So that's your official position?"

He didn't need his younger brother's interrogation. "Right."

"And if word gets back to the ranch .... Because Pete was at the diner when I was there. And people on the ranch might be interested."

"You can tell people it didn't mean anything. I was protecting her. And for your information, I haven't looked for women in Heron Park in months. If you were around more, you might know that."

"Why not?"

Yes. That was the question. "I've changed."

Something in Garrick's expression shifted. "Make sure."

Now his younger brother was giving him advice?

They were quiet for a moment, and Jack finished his beer. "You care how things go down around here?" He studied his brother. "I was thinking you might want to sell me your shares of the business."

Garrick's gaze became shrewd. "Give you controlling interest? I think I'll keep them."

His chest fell, and he scoffed softly. "Handle Dad, okay?" He tossed the empty Bud Lite bottle in the recycle bin and tromped down the hall, needing to be alone. As manager of the ranch, it was up to him to set an example. To keep harmony on the ranch and be a cool-headed leader.

But there'd be no harmony, no peace of mind because Garrick didn't want to sell and keeping his distance from Dani wouldn't cut it.

The spring morning carried the sweet scent of damp grass. Dani and Lucky climbed into Ellie's new hybrid sedan and rode to the neighboring organic farm with a box full of teas and creams.

"You're sure you want to work at the stand all day?" Ellie asked.

"Yes. I'll cover the hours Thea worked. I'm leaving all the horse care to y'all on my work days. I want to focus on our products, and this seems like a low-key way to start. It's temporary. Probably." If she left, they'd have to cover the mini horses without her. They may as well figure it out now.

"And you're fine on your own? Because I can move my schedule around and come back."

"No thanks." Her teeth set on edge. Ellie still underestimated her. How would she manage independently in Jacksonville if she couldn't do it here? "You know I'd love to have you around, but I'll be fine. I've got my money reader app." Money wasn't really the issue. Other concerns had been playing through her mind. Would she be able to answer people's questions and manage everything in the stand by herself? Locals probably wouldn't steal or try to pull anything, but what about tourists who might stop in? This was different from dealing with customers with Thea there—someone sighted to assess people on the spot.

Within minutes, they pulled into the roadside parking lot of Wren's Organics. The farm stand carried various seasonal vegetables, fruits, and jars of raw honey and was the primary outlet for their teas and remedies. Wren ran the farm, harvested her own honey, and had to actually deal with swarms of bees, which sounded dangerous. She also gathered pastured organic eggs, which were probably less hazardous, unless you ran into an angry chicken. Usually, Wren was pretty busy when she was there with Thea, and they didn't have a lot of contact.

"Are you sure you'll be okay?" Ellie walked her to the stand.

Being her first day, she didn't want to worry about her guide dog and had Wyatt looking in on Lucky. "I can call Thea. But I've learned a lot from coming with her."

When it was slow, she and Thea sometimes talked about the produce or the herbs. Often, they'd while away the afternoon gossiping about locals. Thea was old enough to be her grandmother, but on those slow afternoons, she imagined Thea as a mother. She was only seven when her mother died and could hardly remember her mom's voice anymore. Aunt Pat, who was older than old, had helped raise her but didn't have a nurturing personality like Thea.

"Hey, y'all," Wren greeted them. "You ready to work?" She looped her arm through Dani's elbow. The scent of honey wafted around her like an aura.

Dani put a bit of sass in her voice. "As long as it doesn't ruin my manicure."

Ellie's phone buzzed. Then buzzed again. "I'm sorry, I need to take this." Ellie stepped aside and spoke in a low tone. "Sorry," she said when she returned.

"Is everything okay?" Wren asked.

"That was about Avery's birthday present," Ellie explained. "You're invited to the party, Wren. Put it on your calendar. The last Saturday of next month. I special ordered Avery custom boots, a whip, and chaps."

"She's really embraced ranch life," Wren said.

"More than I would've predicted." Ellie chuckled.

"She wants a big cookout," Dani added.

"I'll definitely be there. Avery's mentioned it. She's pretty excited to be turning eighteen. Want me to bring that citrus cake?"

"Sounds great. We'll probably have chocolate cake too. But the more, the merrier," Ellie said.

A car pulled up. "Looks like we have our first customer." Wren let go of her arm. "I'll take care of them, and you can take the next one."

Ellie's phone buzzed again. "Oh, sorry. It's a client. I have to take this."

"We're good, Ellie. Go on. Wren can show me what to do," Dani said.

"Really?" The relief in Ellie's voice was evident. "I can stick around ...."

"Don't worry," Wren said. "We've got this."

Ellie's car crunched out of the parking lot, and Dani pulled her shoulders back, determined, independent.

The first group of customers simply wanted produce. Wren assisted them, and Dani listened in while she unloaded a box of cabbages and organized the heads in the bin.

"Do you work here? Can I pay for this?" a man asked. "Miss?"

Was he talking to her?

"Oh, Wren," Dani called out.

"Hold on a minute. I'm busy with these folks." Wren answered from the far end of the stand.

"Can you help? I'm late to work," the customer said.

Even though she had the money-reader, she'd hoped Wren might handle the sales. "Of course. Right over here." Dani pushed past her nerves and rang up the man's purchases, mentally calculating as she filled his bag. She'd learned to count out change in school, but she rarely handled money. Credit cards and online payments were easier.

"All I have is ones," he said.

"That's fine." Big relief. There'd be no need for her money reader to manage ones.

She slid the money into the cash drawer and handed back coins. There. That wasn't so bad.

Wren worked alongside her for the next hour as morning commuters stopped by the stand. By mid-morning, the steady stream of customers thinned to nothing.

"Well, that covers the morning rush. You cover the midday slump and restock the tomatoes. I'll finish in the honey house. I have a large delivery, and tomorrow we have a group from the girls' center coming for the day. There's a ton to do. Are you good?"

Seriously? Wren was leaving her alone on the first day? "I uh ..."

"You did fine this morning. If you need anything, text, and I'll be back here in five minutes." Wren's footsteps receded in the distance, crunching over the shell pathway, then the dried grass.

Dani was arranging the tomatoes when a car pulled up. "Hi, Dani." Maryjane entered the produce stand. "Chet sent me down for more of your pain relief cream. And I need some of Wren's tomatoes. What's this? Honey with rosemary?"

"Yes. Wren and I are experimenting with different blends. That one is amazing on biscuits."

They talked about the kittens. Then Maryjane paid for her order and left Dani with a little too much time on her hands. Naturally, her thoughts turned to Jack. The other evening, having the birthday dinner with him and Wyatt gave her a taste of something like a family. The kind where she was the lady of the house. She'd liked it, wanted more, and had hoped Jack might stay after dinner.

The warm day stretched on, and she sat on the stool and listened, hearing into the distance. How far away could she detect sounds? Birdsong, insects, and the occasional vehicle on the road. The humming of farm equipment or power tools filled the quiet.

Tires crunched on the shell parking lot.

Finally, another customer. She stood and smoothed her skirt.

The vehicle's engine kept running.

She waited.

And waited.

Were they lost?

Just turning around?

The engine cut off, and she prepared to greet the customer. But no doors opened and shut. They didn't come over. They hadn't left. What were they doing? A chill crept over her arms. She patted the cell phone in her pocket. Of course, she was being silly. People sometimes pulled off the road and finished a phone conversation or texted. But feeling vulnerable had her heart pounding.

A few minutes later, the vehicle started again and pulled away.

She wiped her sweaty hands on her dress. That was weird.

After she settled down, she decided to refill the other bins that were low. She lifted the crate of radishes. It was heavier than she'd expected, and the contents rolled to one end. The corner of the wooden box caught on the edge of the table. She yanked, and a piece of the bottom came loose. Radishes tumbled into nearby bins and covered the ground around her feet. Her chest fell. Dang!

She knelt and attempted to gather the radishes before either Wren or a customer came along. This mess would not make a good impression.

"It went well?" Ellie asked as they rode home.

"Sure. All good. Except for a rain of radishes when the box broke. It took me a while to find them."

"At least it made the afternoon more interesting."

"Yes. It was thrilling when people remarked about the radishes being in with the fingerling potatoes. Should make for some interesting side dishes," Dani said.

"I can't drive you tomorrow morning. And Striker is having the veterinarian out, so Jack will have to bring you to work."

Her heart leaped. "I'll try to manage."

"I'll bet you will," Ellie said dryly.

"What?"

"Luke said ... never mind."

"What did Luke say?"

"Nothing ... just ... just be careful, okay? Jack is a lot older and more experienced than you. And he's been divorced twice."

"I'm aware of his history." Her fingernails dug into her palms, hating that condescending tone. Ellie had no right to boss her around.

"Which is why—"

"We're friends, is all. Anyway, even if I did like him, I might be leaving at the end of the summer. Jessica invited me back up there. She needs a roommate."

"You'd leave?"

"Don't sound so surprised. You know how important transportation is for me. And there's not much of a future for me at the ranch. How will I meet a man here? I love y'all, but I don't want to play the part of the spinster aunt."

"Oh. I wasn't thinking. It's just that you'd said you wanted to stay on the ranch and study with Thea."

"Which I've been doing for going on a year. I don't plan to do it for the rest of my life."

Ellie sighed loudly. "That's why I wanted to get us a place in town somewhere."

"And it's okay. You married Luke and stayed. I'm not angry at you. But I may need a change. You get that, right?"

"I do. I guess that means I don't need to worry about you and Jack."

"Nothing to worry about at all." Ellie might be disappointed, but at least now she wouldn't interfere. And there was an apple pie in her freezer waiting for the right moment.

Since early Saturdays were typically slow, Jack dropped her off, and Dani worked the produce stand by herself. She organized the inventory and rang up a few orders. Eventually, the sound of a vehicle came up the road and pulled into the parking lot.

Heavy footfalls came her way. "Well, hey there." A deep voice greeted her. "You're working here solo?"

Why did he want to know if she was alone? It took her a moment, but she placed him. "Bear?"

"You remember."

"Yes." She relaxed. He was the one who'd stood up for her at Mac's. "I'm not alone. If you need Wren ...."

"Thought I'd stop by for some of that magnesium cream you were talking about at the diner. For my back."

They discussed the properties of the different creams, and the conversation turned to the local area. It turned out he was renting a trailer out east and working as a mechanic in Pine Crossing.

"As long as I'm here, I may as well see what else you have."

The sound of basket handles snapping into place was followed by Bear rummaging through bins.

Another customer arrived. "Is this the place where I can get custom teas?"

"Yes, if you tell me about the issue, I can make a recommendation." She paused, stilled her mind the way Thea had taught, and listened deeply to the woman. To listen to the words and to what wasn't being said.

"I'd like one for stress ...." The woman told her about the issues with her youngest son and his new wife.

The woman settled on Sunny Day tea for vitality, Let it All Go for stress relief, and Fresh Face anti-aging cream with citrus.

Bear came to the check-out area while the other customer selected produce. This was starting to feel like a bonafide midday rush.

While Dani rang up the items, another vehicle crunched into the parking lot. Her heart leaped at the familiar sound of the engine. It was lunchtime, and Jack was back.

Jack strode across the Wren's Organics parking lot, carrying a bag filled with lunch from the diner. His chest lifted with pride while he waited near the entrance, watching Dani discuss her remedies. One of her customers was that big biker. This made the third time in a few weeks that he'd run into that same biker, but there was no motorcycle in the parking lot.

Jack was hard and strong from a lifetime of ranching and time spent at the boxing gym, but this guy was huge. The man had a bit of a beer gut but a lot of muscle and was taller than Jack's six feet. Not someone to be messed with.

The biker squinted as he approached. "We meet again."

"Where's your Harley?" Jack asked.

"In about fifty pieces. I'm rebuilding it."

"You're a mechanic?"

"Motorcycles are my first choice, but I can fix damn near anything. Worked as a mechanic in the Army. I'm Bear."

"Jack." He studied the man with fresh eyes.

"Just got a job in town at the service station," Bear said.

"Good to know. That other mechanic ...?"

"Was fired." Bear gave him a meaningful look. "If you want honest work, stop by."

Jack glanced at Dani, who was finishing up with another customer.

"Your woman's something," Bear remarked. "She's handling this alone?"

Was she? An uncomfortable feeling blanketed Jack. "I'm sure there's someone else around."

"Is this your place?" Bear asked.

"No. We have the adjacent ranch."

Bear frowned. "Right. It's just ... nah."

"What?" Jack glanced over sharply.

"Bein' she can't see ..." Bear looked like he wanted to say more.

"The farm owner's here." Jack scanned the area. Wren's pickup truck sat parked near the house, but there was no sign of her.

He caught Bear looking around too.

Should he trust Bear? Could Bear be one of the men looking for Wyatt?

"Right. Well, gotta go." Bear climbed into the Ford pickup and headed east as another vehicle pulled in.

Tanner from Parson's Ranch parked and swaggered over, not giving him a second look.

Dani finished ringing up a customer, and Jack was about to announce himself, so she'd know he was there, but Tanner moved past him first. "Hey, Dani. How's it going? No Thea today?"

"Tanner?" Dani's face brightened. "Hey there. I'm holding the place down on my own. I thought you'd come by earlier."

"Me too. I got busy," Tanner replied.

Jack froze, hardly able to fully follow their conversation. Had they decided to meet up here? His heart beat in his throat, and a rock-hard lump—a new and crappy sensation—formed in his chest while he watched Tanner and Dani.

"Come on back here. Wren set your order aside." Dani gestured under the bins. "Don't worry about paying. It goes on the account."

"That's what she said." Tanner reached under the bin.

"It's heavy," Dani warned.

"Nah. Easy."

"Like I always said, you're cowboy strong," Dani quipped.

Jack could hardly believe his ears. Were they flirting? No. That's just the way Dani talked to people. But it never bothered him like this before.

"Will you be at Mac's tomorrow? Roy and I are coming in for breakfast. I'll buy yours if you show up. I owe you a meal. Remember?" Tanner stared at Dani, blatant admiration on his face.

He couldn't take another second of their friendly banter. "Hey, Dani." He approached and stood so close he was practically touching her.

"Hi, Jack." She smiled broadly. "Tanner? You've met Jack, haven't you? From Tall Pines?"

"Not officially." The easy expression on Tanner's face morphed into irritation. "Jack."

"Tanner." Jack dipped his chin. "You've got time midday to buy produce?" He leveled a hard look at the ranch hand. The tension between them practically crackled.

Tanner's brows pulled together. He glanced from Dani and back to Jack.

Jack nodded. "I brought our lunch." He put a hand on Dani's back and kept his gaze locked on Tanner.

"I'd best be getting back." Tanner lifted the crate and headed out to the truck.

"See ya." Jack moved his hand over her back and closed the short space between them. He'd made up his mind. He was staking his claim before men like Tanner took advantage of Dani's easy accessibility at the produce stand.

"What's with your tone?" Dani sounded angry.

"It concerns me you are working here on your own." He unpacked their lunch.

"It has nothing to do with Tanner?"

He clenched his teeth. "More like concerned about your safety."

"Tanner is a friend."

Right. She wasn't buying his explanation. After months of court-ordered therapy, he was better at identifying and discussing his feelings. Still, they weren't having that conversation now. And even if he was being possessive, his concerns were valid. "I picked up lunch at Mac's." He set their sandwiches on a clear section of the counter near the cash register, and they tucked into their food.

A car drove by. Then a truck full of cowboys towing a horse trailer. "Where's Wren?" Jack asked. "Isn't she supposed to be here?"

"She's in the honey house getting an order ready. And setting up for a group coming out to tour the farm. Groups come out fairly regularly."

"Wren's off working somewhere, and you're on your own?" He couldn't let it go. Dani might not think working all alone was a problem, but it chaffed. The two-lane state highway wasn't busy, but the stand was too close to a road used by tourists, day workers, all kinds of people driving by.

"Yes. That's the plan. I'm good. I have the money reader app."

"It's not about that." He studied the honey house in the distance. With the doors and windows shut, Wren wouldn't know what was happening at the stand. He needed to do something. Dani couldn't work here on her own. It wasn't safe. When he got home, he'd talk to Striker. The foreman had known Wren a long time and might be able to convince her to level up the security. Striker's opinion might be helpful for a change.

He finished his sandwich and balled up the deli paper. It was time to move forward with his plan. "Are you free tonight? Garrick can handle my dad. We could go into Heron Park for a burger."

"Are you asking me out to eat or on a date?"

"I brought you lunch. Now I want to feed you dinner." He winced at how abrupt that sounded, but none of their conversations had gone as he'd intended. After spotting her talking to Tanner, he had no chill.

"So, it's a date?"

"Yes. That's what I said."

"I'll have to check my calendar."

"That doesn't sound like a yes."

"Just messing with you. Going out sounds wonderful. I should be home by five-fifteen. And I wonder if we can check out the kittens at Chet's ranch this Sunday."

He winced inwardly.

"And piglets. They have baby pigs."

This just got better and better. But it meant spending time with Dani. "It's a deal. And I think this lunch should count as a first date."

"Why?"

"Because I meant what I said in the diner the other night. I want to go out with you, Dani. And since we're officially dating,

I can do this." He cupped her soft cheeks in his hands and covered her lips with his.

When he pulled away, she looked shocked.

"Was that okay?" he asked.

"Absolutely. And I didn't even need to feed you apple pie." She touched her lips.

"Oh, don't worry. There's apple pie, too." He pulled the containers from the bag and slid one over to her with a fork. "Did you know apple is my favorite flavor of kiss?"

Dani took a big bite and chewed. "It is delicious."

He leaned in. "Even better when it's on you." He kissed her again, tasting the sweet apple on her lips, his insides lighting up. They were doing this. And if he was careful, he could keep it under wraps until he figured out whatever *this* was. All he knew was that he wanted her and couldn't keep his distance anymore if he tried.

*D*ani easily swung her leg over the saddle and slid down the side of the horse into Jack's large hands. They'd been riding a few times a week for the past month, and she was proud to be getting the hang of it. Sometimes Brick rode with them, which was fine, but she preferred days when it was just the two of them.

"You looked good up there today, cowgirl." Jack planted a kiss close to her ear. That meant they were alone. He wanted to wait to tell people they were dating. It had seemed reasonable at first, but what was he waiting for, after weeks of lunches, dinners, and riding time together?

She dragged her fingertips over his scratchy jaw. "I never thought I'd say this, but I feel good in the saddle. As though I'm one with the horse. We have a connection."

"Glad you like it, cupcake because I meant what I said. You're a natural. Like you were born to it, and that's saying a lot because I've been riding since before I could walk. I get what you're saying."

The compliment made her feel lighter. "Thanks. I've had a good teacher."

"The very best."

She gave him a playful swat.

"Give me a minute to untack the horses and come over for lunch if you have time. Bud's caregiver is taking him into town, and we'll have the house to ourselves."

"Are we still going to the Timmons' farm today? Chet says the pigs are growing fast. It's too late to bottle-feed them. I don't want to miss seeing the kittens."

He got quiet.

"You said—"

"The surveyor is coming, and I'm meeting with the builder."

She deflated. "Darn."

"I guess we can slip away for a couple hours."

"Good. I'll go shower and change." With Bud gone, lunch may lead to something more.

"If you plan to hold piglets, you may as well leave your riding clothes on. You think you stink now? Wait until you spend time at a pig farm."

"Worse than cattle?"

"Cattle?" he huffed. "I don't even smell them."

She scrunched her nose. "Horses are one thing. If I could bottle their scent, I'd add it to a cream. But cattle. Nobody would buy that."

He chuckled. "I'll make us sandwiches to eat in the car."

"Okay, thanks." Well, that sealed it. They weren't fooling around at Jack's while Bud was gone. When would they take it to the next level? There'd been intense, amazing kissing, but they hadn't made love. Why was Jack taking it so slowly? He always pulled away before it went that far. Weeks had passed. They'd better get on it if she was having a torrid affair this summer. Jessica was expecting her in two months.

They finished with the horses, cleaned up, and drove south and east to the Timmons' farm. Dani lowered her window and enjoyed the scents on the warm June air. She took a big bite of roast beef, tomato, and banana pepper sandwich and let the wind cool her face while she chewed. "I love the sandwich."

"You and Thea have quite a pepper section going in that garden."

"I know. Some of them are so hot I need to use gloves when I handle them."

He scoffed. "Why grow those?"

"We're expanding. We've been meeting with Wren and developing a plan for different honey infusions and teas, adding peppers and various honeys to our creams."

"You're getting to be quite the wellness-entrepreneur."

"All fueled by the lunches you bring me."

They pulled into Timmons' Farm and were greeted by Maryjane, who led them to where they kept the piglets. Fat little bodies swarmed her calves as she fed them pellets.

"These are adorable." Dani ran her hands over the greedy piglet nosing her leg. "He reminds me of my dog trying to get more food. Lucky is really a pig."

They washed up and headed inside, where Maryjane had the mama cat and kittens. "Go on," Maryjane said. "You can pet them."

Dani sat on the floor while Jack guided her hand to the fuzzy babies.

"You're keeping the cats indoors?" asked Jack.

"Yes. We have barn cats too, but Misty is my special kitty. She lives indoors."

"Indoor cats?" Jack made a disapproving sound.

"Meanie. I'd want to keep them inside, too. Ouch. Those itty-bitty claws are scratchy." Dani lifted a furry baby and held it to her cheek. "This one is so sweet. He purrs."

"That kitten can be yours. We'll be letting them go before long," Maryjane said.

"Oh. I'd love to. I want this little sweetie." She kissed his warm, soft belly. "But I'm not sure." Jessica wasn't a fan of cats, and if she was moving into Jessica's home, a cat was out of the question. But how she'd love to have one. And Lucky's puppy raiser had owned cats. He was good with them.

At that moment, she wanted to stay at Tall Pines more than anything. To stay in her cottage, get a cat, and spend her days with Jack and the horses, working the herbs and produce stand. To be with Jack. But what if she stayed, and she wasn't with Jack? How serious were they? If she stayed and they broke up, and he married some other woman ... the idea made her shudder.

Memories of Mark breaking it off and marrying Sandi played through her mind. That was gut-wrenching. She'd gone from a horrible breakup straight into a relationship with Parker, who'd tricked her with promises while he was dating sighted girls on the sly.

Heartbreak was awful. She held the soft kitten against her chest. There was no reason to think it couldn't happen again. A man like Jack wasn't a forever bet.

All morning it rained. Mist carried on the damp air, and Dani's skin felt wet and sticky. Nobody stopped by the produce stand. When the lightning was close, Lucky panted. She should've left him at home. She soothed her dog, texted with Jessica, and listened to her podcasts. When the rain ended, the day became muggy, hot, and dragged on like someone had stopped time. By the time five o'clock rolled around, she was fighting a headache and ready for a cool shower and dinner in a nice, air-conditioned restaurant with Jack.

Dani finished covering the crates while Wren pulled down the awnings.

Wren snapped a padlock. "All locked up."

"I don't get why you lock it if the underneath is open? Can't animals or people get inside that way?"

"What you can't see is the chain link fence. And I lock the gate at night. There's chicken wire around the bottom of the stand. The dogs and the donkey are pretty effective at keeping out predators. This is as good as it gets." Wren huffed. "For a while, food was disappearing on a regular basis. If someone really wants to get inside, it's easy. That's why I put in the dog door last month. The pups have excellent hearing, and when something's out here, they let themselves out and bark like hell. But that's only happened a few times." Wren had taken one of their puppies last year and now had the Border collie and two mixed breed rescues on her farm. They were sweet dogs but were kept away from the produce stand.

"Someone broke in?" Dani asked. Had it been Wyatt?

"Yes. It happened a couple of times this spring. They cut the chicken wire. But we don't keep money here, and people in the area are mostly honest. Someday I'd like a block building and a proper shop. There's room, and I can get the permit. But I haven't worked out the financing, meaning I haven't set up a printing press to print my own money because that's the only way it'll happen." They walked into the parking area. "Do you need a ride home?"

"Avery's coming."

"Good. Will you be okay waiting here? I have work to do in the horse barn."

"Sure, I'll be fine. Hey, did I tell you? Jack's been teaching me to ride."

"That's wonderful. Did he ever get those horses from Ocala?"

"What horses?"

"If you don't know, then he must not have. I saw him at the grocery store, and he was all excited about a stallion and a foal that'd become available. Outstanding bloodline. We talked about breeding it with my mare."

A car pulled up. "That's Avery now," Wren said. "See you tomorrow."

Dani put Lucky in the back of Avery's car and slid into the front seat. They pulled out of the lot. "Wait. Did you turn right?"

"Yeah, we're picking up Emma, then getting a pizza at Pete's before going home. I ordered you one too. Small, pineapple and ham, just how you like it," Avery said.

Dang. She wanted to get ready for her dinner plans with Jack. "That was thoughtful. But I wish you would've asked."

"Why? Do you have a hot date or something?" Avery chucked.

"I might."

"Really?" Avery didn't need to sound so shocked. "Who?"

Would it be so bad if Avery knew? "I'm supposed to go out with Jack later. I need to get cleaned up."

"Jack? As in Luke's brother?"

"That's the one."

"So, the riding lessons are really—"

"No," Dani said. "I'm learning to ride. And we're dating."

"He's so ... I mean, he's hot in an older man kind of way, but ...."

"Jack's not that much older than me. I'm almost fourteen years older than you."

"I know. You seem younger to me. Anyway, ten years. That's still a lot. Plus, I don't know ... doesn't he have a sketchy past? He was in jail. And he's divorced—twice. I thought he was ... well, Luke said they can't even go back to that one agency because he slept with the owner's daughter and—"

"Hang on. How old was she?"

"It's not that. She was in her thirties or something. And Ellie said the bump on Luke's nose is because Jack broke it. They've had a lot of fights."

"Recently?"

"No. Back when they were growing up. I mean—don't get me wrong, I love Jack. He's taken me riding a bunch of times, and he knows a lot about horses. He even took in those new minis. So, he's a good guy, I guess."

"I'm well aware of the extra minis." She watered, fed, and brushed them, usually alone.

Avery paid no attention to what she said. "My aunt is dating my uncle. How weird is that?"

"Is it weird? I hadn't really thought of it that way."

"It's totally weird."

"How about you let me discuss it with Ellie?"

"She doesn't know?" Avery's tone rang with alarm.

"I haven't told her, and I don't think Luke knows. I'd prefer to be the one to—"

"Got it. We're at Emma's. I'll be right back." Avery's car door shut and cut her off.

Dani waited in the car, with Lucky panting in the back seat. She fisted her hands, angry. Avery sounded so judgmental. Most of what she'd said wasn't new information. Jack may have been a hell-raiser, but lots of people went through a phase like that. The details about his divorces were a mystery.

But Avery's comments got under her skin like a splinter. Was it weird that she and Jack were starting a relationship? He'd asked her to scale back her flirting and be exclusive. That meant him, too, didn't it? She'd been foolish enough to believe Parker's lies. Jack was often busy in the evenings, and she'd assumed it meant ranch business or his father. Was he seeing someone else on the side? Was that why he was taking it so slowly with her? He'd better not be pulling a Parker.

How awkward would it be at the ranch if things didn't go

well with her and Jack? No wonder she hesitated to discuss Jack with Ellie. Getting serious with him might be a bad idea.

Her heart sank. Too late. She was already in over her head. But a little space wouldn't hurt. She needed to think.

She texted Jack: *I'm exhausted. I'm heading to bed early when I get home.*

Jack: *need anything?*

Dani: *no*

Jack: *I'll give you a ride in the morning.*

Should she let him? She might have more clarity in the morning.

Dani: *okay*

Jack gave Dani a lift to Wren's farm. She'd put him off last night, and she'd been blathering nonstop since she'd climbed into his truck this morning. It blew his mind that he was the one who wanted to have a conversation. "Dani—"

"There should be more people around today. Another youth group is coming out, and they'll play with the goats and gather eggs. They'll even help Wren harvest honey," she prattled on, interrupting him. "Oh, can you get that box?"

He carried the box she'd brought along. Despite working on verbalizing his feelings with Dr. Dave, it was still uncomfortable. When she fell silent, he couldn't think of how to bring it up. But something felt off in her text and the way she was acting this morning. "What's in all these jars?"

"Those would be different tinctures. Wren's buying them."

"They look like brewed tea."

Dani chuckled. "We plan to start selling premade designer blends, but you don't want to drink that tea. Those are highly concentrated. One is pretty bitter, the other will make you sleepy, and the other is hot enough to burn the hair off your chest. Wren's experimenting with sweet hot honey sauce. If it works out, she may start growing hot peppers."

He set the package down and tried to find the right words. "When we talked on the phone last night—"

"Jack! You're here. Perfect timing." Wren carried in a crate of lettuce. "I need someone stronger than I am to budge a piece of equipment in the honey house. The kids will be here soon."

He bit back a grimace and accompanied Wren to the building she called the honey house. It was in far better shape than the farm stand. The outside was a plain cinder-block structure, but inside, it gleamed with polished concrete flooring, clean wide counters, commercial sinks, and stainless-steel equipment.

"What happened with those horses? I thought you were interested." Wren showed him where the extractor was jammed. "It's a pretty simple piece of machinery, but it's stuck."

"I couldn't get up to Ocala in time." It still grated. He tinkered with the crank and maneuvered the other moving pieces. "You might need to order a part."

"Can you get it working just for today?"

"I'll try." By the time he had the extractor operational, teens were filtering toward the building.

"Hi, Wren." A teenage girl sauntered in like she owned the place.

"Hey, Maya." Wren glanced over from rinsing buckets. "You're early. Good."

"Yeah. My dad dropped me off. He's taking Lita to Hudson's store. Well, he had to go, and she tagged along." Maya shrugged. "She wants to buy boots, and they're having a sale. She wanted to get there early."

"Maya. This is Jack. Maya comes out from Starfish Key once a month to help. And this is the perfect day. I'm already short-handed because Andrew called out sick." Wren carried the buckets over to the extractors.

"Where should I start?" Maya washed her hands at the smaller sink.

"Thanks for everything, Jack. Unless you want to stay and help?"

"That's my cue to leave." Jack strolled outside and then paused. One of Wren's farm hands stood in the fenced-in area with a couple of teens and the goats. Youths gathered at the fence, laughing and cutting up while the man instructed how to feed the baby animals.

"Look! Horses." One of the teens pointed to Wren's palomino out in the field. A real beauty.

"I know, but we can't ride them," said the other girl.

"I wish we could at least pet them." The first girl sighed dramatically.

They gazed at the pasture where the paint had wandered over to check out the commotion. "I know," the second girl said. "And feed them carrots. Is that what they eat?"

The mare raised her muzzle to the wind as though showing off her flowing mane.

What he'd read in Louise's journal filtered through his mind. She'd wanted to bring out groups like Wren was, only using the mini horses. Those little horses had more potential than a life of eating and being loved on by family—a potential that was being wasted. Now that they had Wyatt and calving season had ended, he was uniquely positioned to do something about it. Only a hazy idea had formed, but the urge was there. Of course, Striker and Luke would probably shoot it down, but he was the manager. That had to count for something.

Jack did an about-face. If he wanted to start an operation like Wren's, there was no better time to find out how it was done. He could hang out, help, and be perfectly positioned if Dani needed something. He texted Striker that he'd be away for the morning and texted Dani he was sticking around.

Jack hadn't returned from helping Wren, but customers were arriving. Dani rang up someone buying Forty Winks tea, her new mint cream, and a flat of strawberries. Her phone pinged, but she was too busy to take it.

"Mmm, this lavender cream is heavenly. Do you happen to have any other floral-scented products?" a woman asked.

"Only this citrus. But I take custom orders." As they talked, she mentally blended oils that might suit the customer.

"I'n the meantime, I'll take the lavender cream and this mint cream. Can you send the custom blend with Wren when she delivers to Starfish Key? I work at the Sugar Star Bakery, and I don't drive."

"Sure. That'll be forty dollars." Dani extended her hand. Typically, people placed the money on her palm.

"Let me help." A masculine voice said before placing two folded bills in her hand.

Dani touched the money, and a chill ran up her arm. The bills were folded exactly as they needed to be folded for people who were blind.

"She's got a big yellow service dog behind the counter," the man said softly. "I'm Noah," he spoke a little louder. "If you work here, you might know Maya. I just dropped her off. I'm her dad."

"Sure. I've met Maya. And I've heard all about the bakery. Are you the visually impaired woman who works there?"

"It's my cousin's bakery. Noah is her husband. I'm Lita," the woman explained. "And I'm flat-out blind. Can't see a darn thing."

"What do you do at the bakery?" Dani asked.

"Help with the salads. And I play the flute at the inn. For the guests. Do you know who makes these creams?"

"I make them. And blend the teas. Me and Thea. When I'm not taking care of the horses."

"Wow. Impressive," Lita said. "You have horses?"

"Why yes." Dani puffed up a little. "We have fifteen miniature horses and several larger ones. It's a ranch, and they ride horses to work the cattle."

"Must be nice. Wren brought goats and a pony to an event we sponsored. I don't know much about horses, but I couldn't get enough of that cute little guy," Lita said.

"Miniature horses are different. You should visit. I'll show you how to brush them."

"Seriously?" Lita said. They exchanged contact information and Lita left.

Buzzing with happy energy, Dani finished ringing up another customer and replayed her conversation with Lita, planning when to have her out to visit the ranch. It'd been a long time since she'd had a real-life visit with a blind friend.

And then she smelled it.

That odd odor she'd detected on the man at the diner.

Her senses went on alert.

More customers had arrived, and there were several overlapping voices.

She listened hard.

Was OD here? Was he looking for Wyatt? Had he stopped in because she was here? In her distraction, she knocked over a basket of blueberries. They rolled all over the counter. She patted around, gathering them up.

"Oh, no. I liked that pint. They were the prettiest," the woman said.

"I'm sorry," Dani replied, loading berries back into the container.

"I'll get another." The customer sounded put out. "Some of them rolled to the ground. Oh. Oh! I didn't know you were .... Don't worry about it, dear."

"What's wrong with her? She's blind?" A man asked. "Don't they have someone who can see working here?"

"Shh! George," the woman said.

"Miss? Is it cheaper to buy an entire flat of berries?" Another man had stepped closer.

She answered questions and rang people up as fast as she could, only using the money reader once. It slowed her down. When the crowd thinned, she couldn't detect the odor anymore. Had she been imagining it?

Jack's head pounded with every step he took toward Dani's cottage. He'd take horses over kids any day. The girls at the farm had messed around, giggled, and shrieked. Especially when Wren pulled a frame of honeycomb from one of the supers, and the bees buzzed in the smoke. It'd been a whole thing. More than he'd bargained for.

He chuckled. Girls.

Then his chest pinched. Girls.

He might've had a daughter who looked like one of those kids. But his child had died the day she was born. It did no good to reflect on how unlucky he'd been in his first marriage and thinking about it was only adding to his sour mood. Shopping wouldn't help. He'd have blown off this whole trip into town if they didn't need to buy Avery's gift. But he made good on his word, as he'd promised Dani.

"Hey, Jack," Dani greeted him, wearing that yellow dress he loved. She offered him her lips. "Thanks for taking me."

She'd showered. Her floral scent, soft hair, and kiss sent tingles of pleasure through him. The day was about to get much better.

They drove into town to eat barbecue and to buy horse statues for Avery's birthday.

Either it was her company, or the Tylenol was kicking in, but by the time they pulled up to Smokey's Rib Crib, his mood had improved considerably. And Dani seemed back to normal.

They were shown to an outdoor seat on a concrete pad under a thatched roof. Large fans turned overhead. At the far end of the structure, musicians tuned their instruments.

"They have live music?" Dani perked up. "Exactly what I need. Oh, my stars, what a day I've had. There was such a crowd, and I spilled the berries and ... well, a lot of stuff. And hey, there was this blind woman who came in." She proceeded to tell him about Lita. "I want her to come out and visit the minis."

"That's doable. It's the kind of thing Louise had in mind when she started the rescue." He told her about the journal he'd found.

"You read her journal?" Dani seemed taken aback. "Isn't that a personal thing?"

"It wasn't a diary. There were records about the ranch in there."

"But all that writing about her dreams and such."

"Yeah." He hadn't given it a thought when he'd found it. "I figure she wouldn't have left it on the shelf if she wanted to keep it a secret."

"She probably didn't expect someone to come along and read it. She could've died before she could put it in a more discreet location."

"Fair enough." He laid down his menu and studied her. "Did one of Wren's bees follow you home? Because it seems like something's bugging you."

Before Dani could answer, the server came, and they ordered.

"I have a thing about privacy," Dani continued. "It's hard to get when you're blind and rely on audio texts and emails. I've had some embarrassing moments."

He took her hand. "Promise you'll tell me if I'm invading your privacy. Should I stop letting myself in your house?"

The corners of her mouth curved up. "You can walk on in if I'm expecting you."

"You look like you want to say more."

"That's all ... for now."

He cringed. That kind of statement had never boded well when he'd been married.

"Except," Dani continued. "Today, I smelled that same odor I noticed on Wyatt and that man in the diner."

"What! When?"

"At Wren's. This morning."

"Why didn't you tell me sooner? You should've texted."

"I was busy. When the customers left, I didn't notice it anymore. Whoever it was had left."

"You should've called right away." His stomach clenched. While he was scraping wax off honeycombs, some low life was up there where he could hurt Dani?

"I told you I was busy."

The server returned with their meals, but his stomach burned. Angry, he shoved his food away.

Dani bit into an ear of corn and sighed. "Oh lordy, I've gone to heaven."

Jack was in heaven watching her eat that corn. The aroma of the food got to him, and his rumbling stomach took over.

They ate, shopped for Avery's gift, and headed home.

He walked Dani to her door. Often, on a night like tonight, they'd spend some time on her couch, talking, listening to music, and kissing like they were back in school. Never before had he taken things so slowly with someone. It was driving him crazy. "Want me to come in for a while?" He tilted up her chin and kissed her on the lips.

"I need to rest. Thanks for dinner. It's been a long day." She stepped inside and began shutting him out.

"Wait." He pressed his hand on the door and stopped her. "What's going on? I thought we had a nice evening. Let me in for a minute. Just to talk." Damn, he sounded like a girl, but something was wrong. He couldn't face another night of being brushed off.

Dani hesitated, then stepped aside, allowing him to enter.

Instead of her usual spot on the couch, Dani sat on her swivel rocker and began moving back and forth.

He sat on the couch.

Dani balled her fists, not a good sign. "Jack...."

Oh, no. His forehead tightened. What was that tone for? He couldn't think of one thing he'd done to make her upset.

"I don't know what we're doing," she continued. "You ... you're older, and you've been married twice."

"You're holding that against me? Now? We've been seeing each other for a while." That couldn't be it.

He waited.

Was she serious? "People get divorced."

When she extended her hand, Lucky came over and she scratched the lab's head. "Right, and you're Luke's brother and you're the kind of man who goes out with a lot of women...."

"Who's been talking to you?" His jaw tightened. "I don't know where you're getting your facts. That's the old me."

"But—"

"You don't—trust me?" Indignation made the words catch on the way out. Hadn't he repaired things in her house and taken her shopping? Taught her to ride. Brought her lunches. "Luke, being my half-brother, doesn't have to come between us." He scooted closer and took her hand. "What do you want to know? Ask. I'll answer honestly."

"Okay. Why were you in jail?"

He snorted. She would ask that first. "Short answer, I punched a man. It was at this little dive bar back home. I'd stop in for a beer now and then. He went down, hit his head, broke a piece of furniture. Got cut up. He pressed charges, and the bar owner sued for damages."

"That's the short version? What's the longer version?"

"Too long to get into now. The jerk was hurting a woman. I had anger issues. It wasn't the first time I'd gotten into a fight there. The court ordered me to serve time, attend anger management classes, and get counseling. Our family attorney negotiated a deal to get me out of jail sooner." He rested his elbows on his thighs. "It turns out counseling helped me get a new perspective. I actually made some positive changes."

"So, you're different."

"Yes. I'm different."

"Why did you get divorced?"

"Which time?" A knot formed in his gut, and he glanced at the door. He didn't have to do this.

Her chin took a determined set. "Start with the first."

"Abagail wanted out. We divorced."

"Why? Were you chea—"

"No! I married my high school sweetheart. We might not have gotten married if she hadn't been pregnant. But I did the right thing." He dragged in a breath. It still tore him up. "Our baby had health issues. She only lived for one day. I was young, but I might've tried again." He scoffed. "She probably had better sense than me. But hell. We were already married. After we divorced, there was Molly. I was married to her by the end of the year."

"You ran out and got married again?"

The image of when he met Molly and her daughter Mindy at the gas station was seared into his brain. "She was a couple of years older than me and had a kid. Cute little girl. I probably wasn't ready. I understand the attraction now, in hindsight. But it didn't go well. Within a year, she left and returned to her ex, the baby's father. She moved in with him before we were even divorced. Kind of left a bitter taste in my mouth."

"Huh. So, you ..."

He exhaled hard, stood, and crossed the room. "When I think back, I'm not proud of the man I was. I was grieving and didn't know how to deal with my feelings. I was already so pissed off before any of that happened."

"But why? Why so angry?"

"I must've come out of my mom kicking and screaming. But it rose to a whole new level when Luke came to live with us. He had a different mother. It meant my dad cheated. Which I understood sooner than a kid ought to." He checked her expression. Her brows had drawn together, and she seemed to be listening intently. "I'm pretty sure it wasn't the first, but this time, the evidence was living under our roof."

Dani inhaled sharply.

"Don't get me wrong. I know Luke was just a kid. But my mom took it hard. And it caused a rift between me and my dad that's never mended."

Jack moved to the window and stared at the moonlight filtering through the trees. Unpleasant memories crowded his brain. He'd been his dad's favorite until that day Bud left and came back with a child only a few months younger than him. His new *brother*. A kid who looked like a miniature version of Bud. The rage, the jealousy, was beyond anything he'd ever felt before. "Our house wasn't the happiest place. But I had Garrick, and my sister, and cousins. I had the horses. They never let me down. And yeah, I could've been nicer to Luke."

He'd been a real shit to Luke. Always trying to put him in his place. He'd even gone as far as stealing the first girl Luke had gone steady with, just to prove he could. Not his finest hour. He continued, "But it is what it is. I can't erase the past." He faced Dani. Did she hate him now? She couldn't see his pain. Did she hear his sincerity?

"Have you forgiven him? I mean, your dad."

Her question hit him like a punch to the gut. That's exactly what he and his therapist had discussed at his most recent appointment. Jack sat back on the couch. "I don't know. It isn't easy handling my dad. And he'd rather have Luke up there any day of the week." Frustrated, he rubbed the bridge of his nose, then leaned toward her. "Listen. You're special. And not just because you're blind. But if you aren't interested, I won't waste your time. If you feel anything, I'm damn sure on board. And I don't say that lightly. Because you're right. I haven't been in a monogamous relationship in a long time."

"But what if we—"

"We can't let the what ifs rule us. You've got to live life. Know this. I will walk out that door and leave you alone, if that's what you want. We can be friends. Distant kin. Whatever. I'll still take you riding."

He waited.

Dani stood.

For a second, he thought she'd order him to leave. Why not? His relationships always ended poorly. But she took a seat beside him on the couch.

"Okay. I'm choosing to believe you. But I have to ask. Why do we have to be a secret? Is it, is it because ...."

He laced his fingers through hers. "We won't be a secret anymore. We're officially—something." The words were a fuse that could blow up the fragile working relationship between him and Luke and explode the relative peace they had at the ranch. It was a risk worth taking.

"Okay. And if I find I can't trust you, I'll come after you, and you'll be sorry." The corner of her mouth lifted.

"You can trust me." He cupped her cheek with his hand and covered her mouth with his, needing her, his tongue pressing into her mouth, tasting her, nipping her neck. He ran his hands over her curves, gasping at how she made him feel, arousal energizing him. Within moments, they were lying on her couch, and his breath was ragged.

He pulled back. She already thought he was some kind of dog. He wasn't about to prove it. Hadn't he told her he just wanted to talk? A lie. But he'd honor his promise.

"Is ... is everything okay?" Dani asked, touching her lips, uncertainty written on her face.

"It's more than okay. But I still want to take this slow." Summoning the strength of Hercules, he left her on the couch and let himself out.

He needed to help his dad get ready for bed. That ought to douse the fire inside of him.

Tomorrow, he'd take Dani on a proper date where they'd dress up and go somewhere different. It might be a long shot, but he wanted to give whatever this thing was a chance.

13

*I*t'd been a tough day in the hot sun dealing with an injured calf, and he was ready to blow off some steam. Jack collected Dani at her cottage, and they drove west. Simply having her in the truck beside him improved his mood considerably.

His growling stomach reminded him he'd skipped lunch. "You want to swing by the taqueria before heading to Turner's?" he asked. "They have excellent steak fajitas."

"Can we get something to eat at Turner's? Lita wanted us to meet them closer to six. Not that I minded having the extra time to get ready. But I thought you were picking me up around five."

"Right. Me too. Garrick was late getting home, so I had to help Bud after his caregiver left." One or the other of his brothers always dropped the ball, leaving his father to him.

"Turner's has good wings," Dani said. "Do you mind if we go straight there? I don't want to keep Lita waiting."

Turner's Tap wasn't what he'd had in mind when he asked Dani where she wanted to go, but at least the drive gave them time alone. The bar outside Cedar Bay offered live music and a good atmosphere. But their evening alone had somehow morphed into meeting up with her new friend, and Lita wanted to hear the country band.

He glanced at Dani, sitting beside him in his truck, a goddess in a pale blue dress that made his breath catch. He'd get on board with the idea if this made her happy.

Too soon, they arrived at Turner's. Apparently, they weren't the only people interested in this new band. Cars, trucks, and at least a dozen motorcycles jammed the parking lot. If he was alone, he would've kept driving. They pulled into the grassy overflow parking area, and he helped her out of the truck.

Dani reached for his elbow to walk sighted guide.

"Do you need to hold my arm? Can I put my hand around your waist instead? And we walk in together?"

Her forehead wrinkled. "I guess so."

"I'll be careful to guide you."

"I'm still opening my cane."

"Do you have to?"

"Why? Are you embarrassed by it?" She sounded defensive.

"No." He scowled. "It's nothing like that." But wasn't it? Didn't he prefer the woman with him draw appreciative glances instead of curious stares? And what kind of superficial tool of a man did that make him? "Go ahead. Unfold your cane."

Moot point. She'd already snapped out her collapsible cane and held it in her free hand. At least she hadn't wanted to bring her dog. In a crowd this size, it'd be an issue.

Loud music hit him before they stepped inside. The place throbbed with revelers and reeked of beer, sweaty bodies, and fried food. "Keep your cane close. It's crowded." Jack scanned the room, peering between bikers, cowboys, tourists, and drunks, searching for a blind woman Dani couldn't describe. He stifled the urge to groan and kept looking.

A tall man wearing a western shirt limped their way. "Are you Dani and Jack?"

Before he could answer, Dani spoke, "You must be Colt. I can tell by that sweet Texas twang."

Colt chuckled as he leaned closer. "You guessed correctly. You must be Dani. Lita's sitting across the room with me and my wife. I'll lead the way."

They followed Colt to a four-top and pulled up an extra chair. "Lita, they're here," Colt said above the music.

"Well, hey there, Jack." A pretty woman about his age grinned broadly but didn't look directly at them. "It's good to meet you. Dani, this is my friend Emily and her husband, Colt. They just got married on Valentine's Day. Isn't that romantic?"

Introductions continued, and the women got to talking. There was no hearing them over the music. Hell. This was nothing like what he'd had in mind when he asked Dani out. The two servers, one who he'd hooked up with when he'd first moved down, and the other barely old enough to drink, pushed through the crowd, skirting the rowdy bikers near the bar.

"They're short tonight." Colt lifted his chin toward the crowd formed around the U-shaped bar. "Go up yourself if you're feeling thirsty."

Jack got Dani's order, then wove through the throng to get himself a draft and Dani one of those frozen strawberry daiquiris. It took forever.

The band took a break and bits of nearby conversations filtered over while he ordered.

The bartender had just set down the drinks when a large bald biker in a leather vest leaned on the bar beside him. Chains hung from the man's grimy pants, patches covered his worn black vest, and skull tattoos covered his beefy arms. "Buy me another drink?" The biker laughed like it was a joke.

Jack snapped back his head. Was this guy serious? "Bear?"

"Just messing with ya. Yeah. Like it?" Bear ran a meaty hand over his shiny pink scalp.

Jack hiked his brows. "Looks sunburnt."

"No shit. Shoulda worn a head wrap. Buddy of mine has cancer. Solidarity bro. How's your woman? That creep leaving her alone?"

"Creep?"

"Dude at the diner. Real low life."

"I haven't seen him." The beat-up white van flashed through his mind. He'd know if he saw that scumbag again. Jack glanced at the man calling the driver of the white van a low life. If that was OD, then he was spot on, but he didn't have time to shoot the breeze. "See ya. I've got a drink to deliver."

"Hey, hold on." Bear dug something out of his pocket. "Here's my card."

Bear had a business card? Jack clamped his jaw to keep from gaping and tried to make out the writing in the dim light.

"You need any work done, you call. I'm at the shop every day now, and I ride by your ranch. I make house calls."

"You work on tractors?"

"Farm equipment, trucks, motorcycles ..."

"Will do." He shoved the card in his pocket and headed back to the table.

Jack stopped in his tracks.

Tanner had claimed his spot, leaning toward Dani—and she was laughing.

Fury charged through his veins.

Colt shrugged and cast a side-eye at Dani.

It was just like Dani to invite someone to take a seat if they stopped by to talk. That didn't make it okay for Tanner to take her up on it.

He fought the urge to toss Tanner off the chair. Problem was, he had a drink in each hand. Also, that might be assault, and he'd sworn off fighting. The old Jack was kicking and screaming to get out, but the difference between feeling an impulse and acting on it was huge. Thank you, Dr. Dave.

Tanner glanced up, and Jack nailed him with a look that left no doubt he was trespassing. Sure, he could've pulled up another chair, but why? The ranch hand didn't have sense enough not to encroach on his woman.

"Well. See ya, Dani." Tanner nodded to Jack and headed into the crowd.

"Here you go, cupcake." He slid the daiquiri across the table. But there was already a drink in front of Dani. "How'd you get a drink already?"

"Oh, Tanner knows one of the servers," Dani said. "Sorry, Jack. I wasn't sure what you were drinking."

He rubbed his forehead. This evening kept getting better and better.

Colt stopped the younger server as she walked by. "I think you need to bring this man another draft. He'll be needing it." Colt chuckled and added a variety of greasy appetizers to his order.

Lita placed a hand on Dani's arm. "Let me tell you about the new desserts my cousin is trying for her spring menu. We had a big tasting party ...."

The music started back up and more people crowded into the bar. Dani, Lita, and Emily had their heads together, talking and laughing. Jack couldn't hear a word. And he couldn't meet Dani's gaze because she couldn't see a thing. He may as well not even be there. He ground his molars. It irked. But Dani appeared happy. That counted for something.

He resigned himself to an evening of listening to music and talking to Colt. Tomorrow they'd do something, just the two of them. Something romantic.

————

After the loud bar, a quiet ride home together was the perfect ending to a wonderful evening. The daiquiri buzz had worn off an hour ago. Now, Dani was high on friendship, good music, and being out with Jack. And she thrummed with the anticipation of what might come next. It was late. Would he want to come inside? Should she invite him in? Sure, she loved flirting and banter, but it didn't mean anything. Even though she'd gone on a number of dates after she and Parker broke up, it'd been over a year since she'd been intimate.

She wasn't ready for the night to end. "That was so nice."

"Glad you liked it."

Was there an edge to his tone? "Is something wrong?"

"No. All good."

Oh, dang. Something was bothering him. "I thought you liked Turner's." Tanner had bought her a drink. The music was great. Lita and Emily were fun to talk to, but it'd been too loud to hear Jack from where she'd sat.

"Can't beat their beer, but—" he scoffed softly, then took her hand. "It's good you got to meet up with your friends."

Tension bled from her shoulders. Jack wasn't upset. He was ... was he jealous? Neglected? He was acting like a petulant boyfriend. She had to tamp back the happiness that sparked lest she grin inappropriately. Yes, they'd go in and cuddle on the couch. Or more.

She brought his hand to her lips and nipped his knuckle. "You're right." She nipped another knuckle. "I missed talking to you." She bit a third knuckle, then took her time kissing it. He inhaled sharply. Her ministrations were having the desired effect. "I appreciate you being a good sport. It meant a lot to me to meet up with Lita IRL."

"Come again?"

"IRL. In real life."

"Right. I guess I don't spend as much time virtual as you." He rubbed his thumb over her hand.

"Lita wants to come out to the ranch. She has another blind friend, a woman in Valencia Cove. Can they both come?"

"You don't need my permission to have friends in your home."

Her home. She liked the sound of that. But was it? She didn't pay rent, her name wasn't even on the lease, and her personal property was less than a load in a pickup truck. Still, Jack calling it her home put a warm feeling inside her.

"Thanks. But if they want to spend time with the horses, I'll need help from you, Brick, even Wyatt ...."

"Right. That can be arranged. I've been thinking about doing more with the mini horses. They're not being used to their potential, and I've been talking to a rancher in Ocala. I'm expanding the equine side of the business. Going to do some breeding." He described the ideas from the other day when he'd stuck around and helped Wren with the youth group.

"Wow. I'm surprised. With Luke and Striker always talking about bulls and calves and market prices. I don't keep up with all of it. I know there are the mini horses, but I thought Tall Pines was primarily a cattle ranch."

Jack pulled his hand away. "Now you sound like them."

Dang, dang, dang. She'd touched a nerve. What was wrong with her tonight? "Don't get upset. I don't know anything about it. I don't have an opinion." Besides, if she was leaving in August, her opinion was irrelevant. "I was going by what they said."

"Striker's an employee. He doesn't get a vote."

Now Jack really sounded put out.

"And Luke is more a silent partner," he continued.

"Okay. It's just that Ellie said that Luke—"

"Luke is preoccupied with his business up north. What I say goes." They paused for the gate, bumped into the driveway, and stopped the truck. Jack didn't turn it off. "We're here. I'll walk you to your door."

His door slammed, and a moment later, he was helping her out.

"I've got to go check on my dad." Jack walked her to the doorway and pressed a kiss to her forehead. "I can get away tomorrow morning. Want to go to the park?"

"Which park?" As in bugs? Heat? Sweating? The beautiful vistas and animals that wowed sighted people didn't excite her.

"The state park. Don't worry about the horses," he said, mistaking her hesitation for concern about her chores. "I'll get Wyatt to take care of them. Go on inside and lock the door. I'll text before I come by at nine." He brushed his lips over hers before stepping away.

That was it? One brief kiss? No cuddling? No couch time?

And now she was spending the day at a park? Thrilling. Riding was one thing. Hiking on a hot trail riddled with bugs was just this side of torture. Lucky nosed her hand and reminded her he needed to go out. She bent down to scratch his ruff, and he gave her a sloppy lick. "You love me, don't you, boy?"

She'd go to the park with Jack despite the heat, snakes, alligators, and bugs. Because he'd keep her safe, and it would make him happy. And, for some reason, the evening had upset him. She'd had fun. He hadn't. So, they'd go to the park.

Afterward, she'd tempt him with a sweet dessert. Not the pie in the freezer. She'd use the crock pot and when they came home, the house will have filled with an enticing aroma. She'd make something delicious. Something apple. And he'd want to stay.

*J*ack fist pumped the air. The message he found in his inbox made up for the disappointing time he'd had at the bar. He emailed the other men for an early meeting before heading to the park with Dani.

The breeder in Ocala had a horse. A stallion with an impeccable bloodline. The buckskin beauty had sired three champion foals. Two had gone to a polo club, and one was shipped to Kentucky for a life in racing. This was the horse he wanted.

Striker, Brick, and Wyatt met with Jack at the old pine table in the office at the end of the bunkhouse. Luke's flight wasn't getting in until later, so he couldn't be at the meeting. Jack smiled. What a shame. "I got an email about another horse coming up for sale." He wasn't in the mood to bring in his dad or defend his decision. After talking to Dani, he was determined. This was his dream, and he was making it happen. Period.

"You're serious?" Striker cocked his head.

"I'll bring a trailer when I go. We'll clear the stall at the end of the barn."

"If you're breeding, we're gonna need more room." Striker

scratched his neck and glanced at the chair where Luke typically sat.

Really? Striker was looking for Luke's approval even when his half-brother wasn't there?

Jack snorted. "Get a contractor out to start working on a new barn."

Wyatt's head moved left and right as though watching a volley.

Striker's grip tightened on his coffee cup. "We're expanding, for real?"

Jack turned up his palms as if making his case. "If anyone ought to be on board, I'd think you would." The foreman had been training Avery and Emma in horsemanship and acclimating the new minis. "You've been doing a hell of a job with the girls."

The corner of Striker's mouth edged up. That was more like it. Jack allowed himself a moment of satisfaction.

Brick nodded slightly, having the good sense to agree with whatever Jack said. The man understood where the power was. While Striker's contract wouldn't be up for another year, Brick was in a more vulnerable position.

"So, you want me to handle getting bids for a new barn?" Striker's brows scrunched together.

"As soon as I finalize the plans. I've got a few more ideas to add." Jack's phone buzzed. Ah, crap. Great timing. "I need to deal with my dad."

He left Striker to complete the task assignments and returned to the house.

"What took you so long?" Bud scowled. "Garrick needs to leave."

Garrick bugged his eyes. "Bye, Dad." On the way out, he clapped Jack on his shoulder and muttered, "Have fun ...."

He sprinted after his brother. "Hold up. I have plans today. You can't wait for Hetta to get here?"

"Text me if she doesn't show."

Jack tromped back inside, his attitude a storm. Of all days for the caregiver to be late.

He placed his dad's clothes on the bed, checked the time, and bit back the temptation to tell his dad to hurry. He was supposed to pick up Dani.

"Are you making those good biscuits for breakfast?" Bud asked.

"No. I don't have time."

Bud's face fell.

"I may have time to get a pan in the oven." If his dad got his butt in gear.

"Now you're talking." Bud grinned. He actually grinned.

While Bud took forever to snap his shirt, Jack glanced out the window, willing Hetta to arrive.

"Where's Thea?" Bud asked. "She can help."

"You—like Thea now?" Jack gaped.

"She's not so bad. Better than that old battle axe you hired. The woman's a damn drill sergeant."

He chuckled. "Emphasis on I hired. And you can't fire."

Bud glared at him, then laughed out loud. Was his dad laughing? Who was this man? He hadn't heard dad laugh since before the stroke.

Jack got the biscuits in the oven and was setting the timer when Hetta let herself in, apologizing as she made her way into the kitchen.

He pulled her aside. This was a perfect opportunity to make a special request. For double pay, she'd spend the night this week, and he could get up to Ocala—with Dani.

Up early, Dani put together a bean salad and whisked up a simple dressing. She assembled the cobbler ingredients, turned the crock pot on low, and smiled as she imagined how the house would be filled with the scrumptious aroma of cooked apples when they got back from the park. This was baking with intention. Her aunt used to say the way to a man's heart was through his stomach, but in her experience, it often started with the scent of something yummy. And Jack had already proved he could be seduced by a slice of sweet apple pie.

She splashed water on her face and pulled her hair up. It was already hot, which she was used to, but she preferred a dress, and Jack had told her to wear jeans. Who wore jeans in the summer, in Florida, when they weren't riding? Not her.

Jack met her at the door and whistled softly. "You ought to wear jeans more often, cupcake. You look good enough to eat." He nuzzled the side of her neck.

Maybe the jeans weren't so bad, after all.

The ride was easy, and they spent the hour talking about the mini horses, and the new creams she'd formulated. Before long, they paid at the park entrance. Jack told her about the landscape as they drove along the curving road. Slash pines and palmettos bordered open prairie. Alligators lounged on the banks of the river. Oaks and cabbage palms dominated the forest.

He slowed the truck. "We're at the outpost. There are canoes, bikes, and a pontoon boat. There's a food truck and picnic tables in the shade."

They climbed out of the truck, and she stretched. "I am kind of hungry."

"Can you wait? They have tandem bikes for rent. I reserved one. We can ride before lunch."

She gasped. "I don't think so. Been there, done that, landed on the ground." She tried to sound light, but it came out terse.

"Were you hurt?"

"Yes." She wrung her hands. This was his surprise? She couldn't pretend to like it. "I wish you'd told me or asked ahead of time." Her throat tightened, and she backed into the truck, feeling cornered.

"Seriously?" His tone was heavy with disappointment. "How long has it been?"

"It doesn't matter. I don't want to go."

"Was it ... within the last couple of years?"

She folded her arms across her stomach as the memories invaded her head. "No. It was when I was first at the school for the blind."

"You ever heard that expression get back on the horse?" Jack grasped her arms. "I've got you. I won't let you fall. How bad were you hurt?"

"I sprained my wrist. But ... that wasn't the worst part."

Jack kissed the top of her head. "What happened?" He was there, in front of her, strong and gentle, inviting her to open up.

She'd never told Ellie. It was so pitiful, so embarrassing. And she'd promised herself never to feel that kind of hurt again. "It was when I was at the residential school on a field trip. A volunteer took me on the tandem bicycle. We fell." She paused and gathered her breath. "I was hurt. My wrist hurt so bad ... and they wanted to call my parents, but ...." Her voice caught in her throat. "There was nobody to call. Nobody to come." She blinked at the water pooling in the corners of her eyes. "My aunt was out of town, and Ellie was ... I don't know where. But my mom had died the previous year, and ... I really wanted her. I missed her. And I missed my dad. And there was nobody else they could call." She shook, holding in the urge to sob. People may be watching. Besides, what good did it do?

Jack enfolded her in his arms and whispered, "How old were you?"

She palmed the moisture from her face. "I'd just turned eight."

He held her and stroked her hair. "We don't have to ride the bike. But I'll bet you I'm bigger and stronger than whoever was steering you that day. I'll do everything in my power to keep you safe. You have my word. Haven't I done a good job teaching you to ride the horses? But it's up to you. Why don't we eat first, and if you feel like riding the bike, we can try."

They ordered breakfast burritos from the concession stand and ate them at a picnic table in the shade.

"Listen, Jack." Dani tilted her head. "Do you hear the cranes?"

"No."

"There. That chortling ..."

"I hear it."

"And that ... a mockingbird. I love how many sounds it can make."

He put his arm around her, and she leaned against him. Together, they listened to the birds, the morning insects, and the grunts of gators in the distance.

"I'm ready for the bike ride now," she said.

"Are you sure?"

She tried to sound brave. "Yes."

Riding the tandem bike took effort. Jack had already caught Dani with her feet on the bicycle bar, letting him do all the work. "Are you even peddling?"

"Who me?" Dani laughed.

Despite their late start, this was a great idea. Clouds had moved in, blocking the midday sun, and they'd ridden farther than he'd expected. It'd been years since he'd been on a bicycle, and he congratulated himself on the idea as he steered them into a trailhead parking area and turned them around.

The sky to the east gave him pause. When had it become so dark? Rumbling sounded from the thick bank of steel-gray clouds. A cool downdraft brought a refreshing breeze that'd be enjoyable if the sky wasn't so menacing.

"It smells like rain," Dani said from behind him on the bike.

"Yeah." He kept his tone even, not wanting to alarm her. "We're heading back. We need to hustle."

Thunder growled overhead.

He pedaled harder.

They weren't going to make it.

When he'd moved down last year, he'd been surprised by the regular thunderstorms that came through in the summer. He could kick himself for not remembering to check the weather radar.

Lightning flashed like the lights were going on and off.

Not good.

He poured on the effort, his thighs burning.

Fat drops hit his arms. He glanced back to see Dani's face wrinkled in concern.

According to a small sign at the edge of the road, there were cabins ahead. He steered them to the potholed dirt drive. "Hold on, we're getting off the main road. There may be shelter ahead." The risk of falling became too great, so the two of them dismounted and moved forward on foot alongside the bike.

Cars sat in front of the first rustic cabin. That would only be an option if the storm was severe.

The rain intensified as they moved around the curve. Thankfully, the next cabin appeared unoccupied and had a screened-in porch. He dropped the bike in the grass and led Dani to the concrete steps.

The old wooden screened door stuck.

Rain pelted them, the slight overhang offering minimal protection. He was ready to punch through the screen, but after another good yank, the door swung open. They made it onto the porch. He peered through a window and found the cabin unoccupied.

"You know how to give a girl a thrill." Dani brushed water from her arms. "I'm soaked."

She was. And her shirt clung to her. Despite the circumstances, he enjoyed the view.

"Are you okay?" The last thing he wanted was to give her another bad memory. He hugged her from behind, resting his chin on her head. A perfect fit.

"Now I am. You're here. And I love the sound of the rain." She tipped her face up.

He brought his lips to her cheek.

"Listen," she whispered. "Hear how the rain sounds so loud on the roof and how it's pouring like a waterfall to the left? And how it makes that tapping sound. There must be metal somewhere. A gutter?"

"Yes. There's a gutter, but the rain is overflowing." He closed his eyes and listened. The rain made unique sounds in each direction, depending on where it was falling. "I hear the differences."

"It's nature's symphony. And the thunder, that's the drums." Dani leaned back into him and released a long breath, relaxing in his arms.

After a while they sat side-by-side on the porch bench. Dani told him stories about hurricanes rolling into the east coast of Georgia and in St. Augustine, where she grew up. He shared memories of blizzards and ice storms in Montana.

When the thunderstorm had moved through, they trudged across soggy grass and walked the bike back to the asphalt road. Steam rose from the pavement. Wet and hot, they rode around puddles and back to the bike barn.

The park ranger met them at the bicycle rack. "You get caught in that?"

"We found shelter." Jack explained. The ranger didn't need to know they'd used the porch.

The ranger gave him a questioning look. "Good."

Jack led Dani to the concession building. "Want something dry to wear? They sell shirts." He described the offerings.

Dani wanted the pink T-shirt with a sequined flamingo on the front. He found a black one sporting a gator. Not something he'd typically choose but he was wet and grungy, and it captured the spirit of the day.

"I had a wonderful time," Dani said once they were settled in his truck. "Even though we got wet, it was nice to get away."

"Is that so?" He studied her. "I'm heading to Ocala in a couple days. Do you want to come along? I can rent a cottage, and we'll make it an overnight trip, do something touristy."

Her face lit up. "I'd love it."

"We'll go as soon as I work out the logistics." His pulse jumped. This was finally happening. He didn't believe in love at first sight, but something inside him had come to life when he'd met Dani. She'd rocked his world since the first moment he'd set eyes on her. There'd be hell to pay if it didn't work out, but he couldn't resist the idea of a nice stretch of alone time with her. "How about the day after Avery's party?"

"Perfect. And I want to let Ellie know about the trip, and about us. Avery already knows."

"She does?" His grip on the steering wheel tightened. He wanted to control the narrative. For months, he'd kept up the appearance of friendship, of being brotherly to Dani. Of denying what was really happening. Never, since high school, had he taken things so slowly. Between Dr. Dave and Luke, and the need to keep things running smoothly at the ranch, it had seemed prudent. Now, it would be beyond his control. "Okay. We're public. No secrets."

He walked her to her cottage, intending to leave and go home to check on his dad.

"I made something, especially for you," Dani whispered and gave his arm a tug. "It's apple cobbler in the crock pot."

The moment she opened the door, the aroma of cinnamon and apples hit him.

"Hold up. You cook?" He followed her inside.

"I can. And I have dinners from the diner. Would you like me to heat the meatloaf, or do you want to eat dessert first?" she asked. "I kind of like the dessert first plan."

Bud could wait. "It all sounds good. I'm starving."

"Me too. And there's vanilla ice cream. You dish it up while I change clothes."

He topped two bowls of cobbler with large scoops of ice cream and set them on the table.

Dani reappeared in a curve-hugging dress. Pink and low-cut. "Do you want to eat on the couch again? Like we did the other night?" She fanned her fingers on her chest.

His knees just about buckled. "Danielle Tremont. Are you trying to seduce me?"

"Is it working?"

"Like a charm." He growled and backed her to the couch, covering her with kisses.

"Jack," she laughed gleefully and threw her head back, giving him more access.

He complied, nipping and tickling with his lips.

Playfulness turned into arousal, and they kissed long and deep. He adjusted her on the couch and traced the neckline of her dress with his mouth. "Want me to get the cobbler?" he ground out, too worked up to care about food.

Her laugh was low and throaty. "No. I told you we'd have dessert first."

He slid an arm under her bare legs and carried her into her bedroom. "I love dessert."

The ice cream melted.

*I*t was Avery's eighteenth birthday party and people would be arriving soon. While Ellie, Avery, and Emma finished decorating, Dani's job was making hamburger patties, shucking the corn, and spearing fruit onto sticks.

Dani popped another pineapple chunk into her mouth. "This is so sweet."

"Seriously," Ellie said. "Those will be grape kababs if you keep eating the pineapple."

"Who's guilty of eating the strawberries?" Dani asked.

Avery and Emma organized the chips and other snacks. Emma had spent the night and was helping them prepare for the birthday cookout. A year younger than Avery, Emma was typically quiet. The two teens had become nearly inseparable, and it was nice having her around, even if she didn't say much.

"How did your date go the other night?" Emma asked.

"It didn't happen that night. I was tired." She wouldn't admit that Avery's words had gotten to her. "But we had a date the next night and went to the park yesterday. I rode on a tandem bike."

"What?" Ellie came over. "You're dating? And you hate bicy-

cles. What's going on? How come I didn't know this? Is it
Tanner?"

"No." She stuffed another cube of pineapple in her mouth.

"Well. Who was it?"

Avery chuckled.

"You know, don't you?" Ellie said. "Why does Avery always
know before me?" Her sister sounded hurt. They needed to
discuss it anyway. Perhaps right before the party was good
timing. After all, Ellie would be busy and less likely to lecture
her.

Dani steeled herself for Ellie's reaction. "Jack."

"Jack, Luke's brother?"

"Yes."

"Oh, Dani," Ellie started in, "I don't think that's a good idea.
I'm glad he's been teaching you to ride. But you might want to
think twice—"

"It's not up for discussion." Dani jammed a cube of
pineapple on the stick, and it split and fell off.

"But he's family. And, you know. He's older than me, and he
was in... he's just so much more ... you know, it could be a problem. There are holidays and ... What if ..."

"It's already happening."

"Which explains the love bite on your neck." Avery
snickered.

Dani touched her neck. She hadn't known. "Where?"

"Here." Avery touched the side of her neck where Jack's
amorous attention had given her shivers the previous evening.
But now her cheeks heated. How embarrassing.

"Want me to cover it with concealer?" asked Ellie.

"I'll get it." Avery left.

"Seriously. You and Jack?" Ellie took a seat beside her.

"Yes and—"

Avery swished back into the room. "Want me to put it on
you?"

"Sure. Thanks." Dani angled her head, moving her chin out of the way.

"The grill's ready." Luke's voice came from the doorway. "Man, these strawberries look good. What's going on here?"

Dani squirmed. How long had he been standing there?

"I'm putting concealer on Dani. There you go." Avery stepped away.

"Is that a ...?" Luke asked.

"Yes," Ellie said softly.

"You finally went out with the guy at Mac's?" Luke asked warily.

"No ..." She wasn't sure if this was a good time to say anything. But she was a grown woman. "You may as well know. I'm going out with Jack."

"Going out where?" He said it so slowly she had to wonder if he had a hearing issue.

"Jack and I have been ... he's been helping me. We've eaten together. Yesterday we went to the park and rode the tandem bike ... We're ... going out."

"As in ... dating?" Luke's voice broke, as though the words were painful.

Avery and Emma were whispering, but she couldn't tell what they were saying. Dani sat a bit taller. "We're in a relationship."

Luke exhaled sharply.

She stuffed another piece of pineapple into her mouth. "Ellie, come take these fruit kabobs away before I explode."

Luke's footsteps quickly moved into the other room, and the sound of Avery and Emma heading outside and greeting friends on the porch filtered back into the house. She and her sister were finally alone.

"I wanted to talk to you," Dani said. "It's not a secret or anything. It's just that everyone's been so busy."

"Don't worry about Luke. I'll talk to him later. But honey, I wish you'd reconsider. This is complicated, and after Parker and Mark ...."

She bristled. "Jack is different. He's more mature." Wasn't he? "I'm going with him to Ocala tomorrow."

"Seriously? Why are you going there? Is he still thinking about—"

"Yes. We're checking on a stallion." Oh, she liked the way that made her feel. She knew something her sister didn't for a change. "And we're renting a cabin on a river."

"Luke got in pretty late last night. I don't think he knows about the horse or your trip," Ellie said.

"Jack is always up there looking after their father. It's about time he had a day off."

"It's not that. It's just .... This is crappy timing. With Avery's birthday today and Luke and Striker heading to Whitehall's Ranch to check on their bull. But it's none of my business."

"That's right. It's none of your business. Why don't you bring me the corn, and I'll start peeling."

"Here you go. I'll be right back." Ellie set the basket of corn at her feet with a clunk and left the kitchen.

Jack strolled toward Ellie and Luke's house, singing the song he'd been listening to back at the house. Garrick had offered to bring Bud to the birthday party. It was a free feeling to be responsible for only himself. The animals were handled, and he'd have a pleasant afternoon with Dani before slipping off to Ocala for a romantic overnight tomorrow. He had dad duty tonight, but Garrick had sworn to be there tomorrow evening.

Before he'd walked halfway there, his phone buzzed with a text.

Garrick: *running late.*

Jack jammed a hand through his hair. That's it? No other

explanation? He looked ahead at Luke and Ellie's house and back at his place. Thea was waiting with Bud until Garrick arrived. It wouldn't be safe for her to try and bring his dad to the party alone. And it wouldn't be right to ask her to wait. She wanted to go to the party more than Bud. *Dammit!*

He stormed back to his house and found Bud standing in the living room with his cane, Thea at his side.

"What are you doing back here?" Bud scowled.

"I came to get you. Garrick's running late."

"Figures." Bud waved a gnarled hand. "You go on. I'll walk with Thea."

"Dad." He groaned inwardly. "I'll get the car." Jack grabbed his keys from the table by the door.

"I'm walking." Bud took a few slow steps. At that rate, the party would be over by the time he got there.

"It's easier if I drive." He took a step toward the door.

"I said I'm walking." Bud's features screwed up in anger.

Thea laid a hand on Bud's arm. "Jack's trying to help."

A half smile curved the edge of Bud's mouth as he stared down at Thea's hand.

Jack blinked hard. Was he seeing correctly? His father ... and Thea?

"Besides," Thea said. "If you let Jack take you, you'll have more energy to enjoy the party and try Luke's new dart board." Thea moved her hand to Bud's shoulder and directed her gaze to Jack. "I wouldn't mind a ride in the golf cart. Jack, can we take the cart instead of the truck? Is that okay, Bud?"

"That sounds good," Bud replied. "Don't just stand there and keep the woman waiting. Get the cart. Thea doesn't need to walk that far."

"I'll bring it out front," Jack said, almost too stunned to reply.

The rusty old golf cart had transferred ownership with the property. By the time he drove it from the barn to the house,

Bud and Thea were down the ramp. Soon the three of them were tooling down to Luke's house with him as the chauffeur and Thea riding in the back seat with his dad.

Jack eased his dad from the cart and helped him inside, getting him situated in the game room while Thea excused herself. Wyatt and Brick were already throwing darts.

"Took you long enough." Wyatt pulled his dart from the bullseye. "You up for a game?"

Jack marveled. This tough kid was only a month older than Avery, yet Wyatt seemed to have a decade on her. "In a while. Where's Dani?"

"I think she's outside with Avery." Wyatt gave him a knowing grin.

Smart ass.

"Is Striker here?"

"The guy delivering the molasses was running late," Brick said, aiming his dart.

Jack strolled out the back sliding glass door. The screened porch ran the length of the house and opened to a deck. Avery, Emma, and half a dozen of their other friends were hanging out on furniture at one end, while Thea and Wren were talking at the other.

"Hi, Jack," Avery called over with a smirk.

"Hey there, Avery. Happy big eighteen." He nodded to the group of teenagers, who responded with giggles and side-long glances. And if he wasn't mistaken, one was checking him out. He stood a little taller. There was a time when, if that babe was of legal age, he'd be interested. He'd left that man behind once he hit his mid-thirties and did the math, not wanting to pick up women the same age his daughter would've been.

Ellie stood on the deck beside Luke, holding a platter as he slapped burgers on the grill. No Dani.

"Hey, Ellie, Luke." He dipped his chin.

The way Luke's eyes narrowed gave him pause.

Ellie left Luke at the grill. "Jack, I need your help. Come inside and get the other platter of meat."

Jack followed Ellie and found Dani in the kitchen washing her hands. Choosing discretion, he stood beside her and whispered, "Hey, beautiful."

Dani's lips curved into a small smile. "Hi, Jack. Hey, did you know there was a—"

"Can you take out the rest of the meat? It's on the table," Ellie called from the other end of the farmhouse-style kitchen. She was already slicing bakery buns with a bread knife.

Jack glanced around the kitchen. It was so big you could move a bed in there, and Luke didn't even cook other than grilling. He lifted the platter and wrinkled his nose. The beef at one end of the platter contrasted with some kind of carrot and grain-style patties. "You're calling these burgers?"

"Those are the new vegan burgers Avery likes. They're actually pretty good."

When Ellie turned toward the fridge, he laid a hand on Dani's back and pressed a quick kiss to her head. "I'll take this outside, then you come in the other room where I'm throwing darts."

"No. How about you help me peel the corn and slice tomatoes? You know it would be a catastrophe if I ruined my manicure." She fanned her fingers in the air before drying her hands.

"Tell you what, I'll run this meat out and be back to help in a second." He nuzzled her neck.

"Did I hear you right?" Ellie stopped and stared at him. "You're helping Dani with the food?"

He whipped his gaze to hers. What was that sharp tone? "I don't mind helping in the kitchen."

Ellie paused with her knife in the air. "Are you serious?"

"I enjoy cooking." He studied her. It wasn't like Ellie to be contrary.

"You honestly like preparing food?" Ellie huffed. "I figured when Thea wasn't bringing you food, you men lived on carry-out from the diner and frozen meals, you know—easy." She shifted her gaze from him to Dani and back, her brows pulling together.

He raised his chin defiantly and looked from Ellie to Dani. "You might be surprised. I don't mind a challenge."

"Really? I had you pegged for sweet and fast." Ellie pointed the knife his way.

"I think you know me better than that."

Ellie stared at her sister again. "You're willing to tackle more complicated dishes?"

"I can follow a recipe. I've been known to learn something new," Jack said, his jaw tensing.

She turned her back to him and vigorously sawed the remaining rolls in half.

He didn't know why it was so important, but he wanted Ellie on his side. "When I was younger, I helped my mom in the kitchen when I finished ranch chores. Which is unusual for a man where I'm from. But she needed the support, and my sister wasn't always there. I didn't mind lending a hand."

"Okay." Ellie met his gaze. "Help."

"Why do I get the feeling you're not talking about cooking anymore? And if you're serious about helping with the corn, it's time." Dani pulled an ear from the basket and peeled away the husk.

Keeping his eyes on Ellie, Jack pressed a kiss to the top of Dani's head. He would not be warned off. "I'll be right back, cupcake."

The parade of teens heading inside parted as he carried the platter out to the grill.

Avery held the door for him. "Luke is in a mood. Fair warning."

He carried out the meat and set it on the grill tray.

Luke's jaw ticked, wound tighter than a rubber band ready to snap.

"Need anything else?"

"Nope." Luke smashed down a burger, and flames leaped up.

It occurred to him, Luke might be aware he and Dani were a thing. And his half-brother was angry. Very angry. Jack was torn between a juvenile urge to challenge Luke and clear the air with a fight or working it out with words. This wasn't the right time for either.

"You need to step away. Now," Luke ground out, keeping his gaze fixed on the grill. He pressed on another burger. The flames roared.

"Kinda charred, don't you think?" If he stepped back, Luke would think he had the upper hand. But this was a whole new level of pissed off, and Dani was waiting inside.

What would Dr. Dave advise?

He went inside.

Wyatt stepped out of the game room. "We're starting a new game. You in?"

"Next one," he said, moving toward the kitchen.

The front door opened, and Striker entered, rubbing his neck, frowning. "Damndest thing. Bill just arrived to fill the molasses licks."

Jack asked. "Wasn't he scheduled to come?"

"Yeah. Except this old beater van followed Bill in like he was part of the crew. But Bill goes to the field, and the other guy gets out and walks around the barns. I ask what he wants, and he looks around, all shifty-eyed. Asked if we were hiring. I said no. Then he wants to know if we've hired anyone lately."

A shard of alarm caught Jack in the chest. "What color was the van?"

"White. Rusty, dirty."

"Is he still here?"

Striker scowled. "I told him he needed to get the hell off our property. Guy looked like he was a few sandwiches short of a picnic."

"He's gone?"

"Yeah. I made sure he left and saw that the gate was locked behind him. Bill will come get me when he's done."

"Good."

"Thing is, when he was getting in his van, I noticed he was packing heat. I've got no issue with firearms." He snorted. "But why would someone come looking for work armed? I might've given him a less friendly send-off if I'd seen it sooner."

"What'd he look like?" Jack asked.

"Skinny. Stringy hair." Striker lifted a shoulder. "Could be homeless."

Behind Striker, Wyatt had gone still. "Did he have a scar on his chin?"

Striker frowned and rubbed his own chin. "He had some beard, but there could've been a scar. Why?"

The color drained from Wyatt's face.

Jack put a hand on Wyatt's shoulder. "He's gone now."

Striker looked quizzically from him to Wyatt.

Jack told him the short version of Wyatt's situation and the threat posed by the man in the white van.

"Why are they searching for you?" Striker's gaze drilled down on Wyatt. "You're sleeping under my roof. I need to know what kind of trouble you're in."

Wyatt stared at the floor for a beat.

"Tell him," Jack said.

"He thinks I stole money," Wyatt said.

Striker's nostrils flared. "Did you?"

"It was someone else." Wyatt looked down.

"Must've been a good amount if he's hunting you."

"I don't know how much. Probably a lot. The guy who took it paid me to keep quiet. I wanted to leave anyway. But it was the kind of job you don't quit. They were ... well, I didn't know at first. I was only.... They hired me to run errands."

"Just spit it out, kid," Striker said.

"They were into a lot of things. I didn't know what they were doing at first." Wyatt winced. "But it was mostly cooking meth."

"You were a drug mule?" Striker gaped and nailed Jack with a hard look. "And neither of you saw fit to tell me?"

"They'd been talking about packing up and leaving. They don't usually stay in place for more than a few months. I figured they'd moved on by now," Wyatt said.

"Are you armed?" Striker asked.

"No." Jack pulled back. "Are you?"

Striker glanced at the bunkhouse. "Not yet."

Jack dry-scrubbed his forehead. "With the fence, gate, and security cameras we installed all over the place. And the dogs. I didn't figure—"

"I should be carrying." Wyatt stepped closer.

Jack studied Wyatt. "You ever handled a firearm?"

Wyatt pulled a face. "No."

He huffed, frustrated as hell. "You're not using a firearm until you know gun safety and have had some practice."

"Where am I supposed to learn gun safety?" Wyatt sneered.

"You're looking at the instructor right here." Striker gave Wyatt a serious appraisal. "Until then, you call me if there's an issue."

Bill Ramos came to the door and presented an invoice. "All finished."

"Can you stay for food? Burgers are almost ready," Jack offered.

"No, thanks. Got another delivery," Bill said.

"Do you know the guy in that white van that followed your truck in here?" Striker asked.

Bill shrugged. "No. I thought he was a guest of yours."

"He wasn't. Tell you what. If you run across him in your travels, give me a shout, okay?" asked Striker.

Garrick clomped up the steps as Bill was leaving. His gaze moved between them. "Who died?"

Jack got his youngest brother up to speed.

Garrick gaped. "Why are you just now telling me how serious this is?"

"You're never around." Jack tried to keep the anger out of his voice, but hell, they wouldn't have known Garrick lived there if the task log wasn't filled out and his jobs weren't done.

"Let's go after them." Garrick's face hardened.

"Gotta find them first." Striker drew his brows into a dark ledge.

"You know where they are?" Garrick directed that to Wyatt.

"I know where they were," Wyatt said. "But they were talking about leaving."

Garrick extended a hand toward the door. "Let's check it out. See if they're still around."

"Did I hear you saying something about leaving?" Ellie stood a few feet away holding a bag of chips, her expression alarmed.

Jack lifted his palm. "We were just—"

"No," Ellie said with surprising force. "It's Avery's eighteenth birthday party. She doesn't ask for much, and she needs her family here. Whatever you're planning can wait." She headed out to the porch.

Jack nodded slowly. A half-cocked plan to drag Wyatt away from the party and chase down some random criminals could wait a few days. They needed to think it through. And there's no telling where the guy in the van went after he left their ranch. "We'll go when I get back from Ocala."

"You're definitely heading to Ocala tomorrow?" Striker shifted his gaze to where Luke was grilling.

Jack pretended not to notice. "I told you I was heading up soon. There's another horse. I'll send you the information."

"Luke knows?" Striker asked.

He shoved his thumbs in his pockets. "We talked about it a while back."

"And you took in those new minis." Striker's brows formed a solid shelf.

Jack met the foreman's gaze directly. "But I'm breeding full-size horses."

"What does Luke—"

"Luke's busy with his tech business. I'm leaving in the morning."

With the trust he'd inherited from his mother and his savings, he could cover the horses, a new barn, and then some. Their approval wasn't necessary, but it would have been welcome, and they were in business together. He slid his gaze to his younger brother. Did Garrick have an opinion? Did he ever even think about the ranch?

"I'm hungry. She brought chips out back?" Garrick left for the porch.

Striker followed.

Jack found Dani alone in the kitchen, stuffing corn husks into a bag for compost.

"Hey. You're doing it all without me." He took a seat at the table beside her.

"Very funny. You'll pay for saying you'll help and leaving me to do it alone. I haven't figured out your punishment yet."

"I'm gonna be punished?" He chuckled. "Bring it, cupcake. I can't wait."

"You're bad." Dani whipped him with a corn husk. "I'll finish peeling, and you can butter the ears and wrap them in foil. Luke's roasting them on the grill."

"Why don't they grill them in the husk?"

"You know, Luke. He likes things his way."

That was stupid, but being it was Luke's home meant it was his choice. Since Luke and Ellie had the big new house and weren't burdened with caregiving, their place had become the hub of the family.

"Were y'all talking about something interesting?" Dani asked.

Huh? He studied her in that pale yellow dress, all creamy skin and innocent, and his heart did something funny. Why upset her? She didn't need to know OD had been skulking around. "Just talking to Striker and Bill. He filled the molasses licks."

"Before you go out there, I have to tell you something."

"Yeah?"

"Did you know I had a little love bite on my neck?"

Now that she mentioned it, he had noticed last night. "Why?" An odd sensation spread over him.

"Luke knows. Ellie too."

"About?"

"Us."

He exhaled sharply. That explained Luke's mood.

"I never understood why it needed to be a secret."

"It doesn't, Dani. It's not." He cupped the side of her face. "I'm not hiding you."

She turned her face to the side and bit his palm.

"Ouch!" He pulled his hand away. "You're feisty."

"Now we're even."

"You think?" He grabbed her shoulders and ran nibbling kisses down her neck, making her laugh.

"Okay! All right. Stop." She ducked out of his grasp.

They finished with the food, and he offered her his arm. "Porch with Thea or game room with the guys?"

"Easy. Game room with the men."

He shifted her from walking sighted guide to circling his

arm around her waist and led her to a chair in the game room, his expression daring the others to comment.

Bud rounded his eyes. Wyatt grinned like a fool. Brick looked from him to Dani, nodded, then picked up a set of darts. Jack had only taken one turn when they were called to eat.

He placed a hand on Dani's lower back and guided her to where a couple of long tables had been set up on the porch.

Luke gave him the stink eye.

Tension seasoned his meal. He got through it, making small talk with Wren and Wyatt. A buffer of teenage girls separated them from the others. It wasn't enough.

"Jack," Dani asked. "Will you get me another fizzy water from the fridge?"

"Sure." He'd be relieved to get away from Luke's death glare.

Boots clomped the hardwood floor behind him. When he removed the can from the fridge, he found Luke in the doorway. "What's up?" he kept his tone neutral.

"You know damn well."

"You're gonna have to give me more than that." He wasn't making this easy on Luke.

"Dani," Luke practically growled. "I told you to stay away. She's blind. She's ... vulnerable."

"She can make up her own mind."

"She's my sister-in-law."

"You may have adopted Avery and married Ellie. And yeah. You made a show to include Dani in your ceremony. But that doesn't mean you married her too."

"You think you can just take whatever you want." Luke's chest heaved. "Why don't you find a woman in Cedar Bay or Heron Park? Leave Dani alone."

"Maybe she chose me."

Luke scoffed loudly. "That's rich."

"Don't you think it's possible I'm interested in her?"

"An inexperienced woman ten years younger than you?" Luke fisted his hands. "She's family. Don't do this."

Jack fought back the urge to hit something. "I'm done with this conversation." He brushed past Luke and paused. "By the way. I'm going out of town tomorrow, checking on a horse. Be gone overnight." He walked away.

If Luke's look was a pistol, he'd be shot in the back. But Luke would get over it. He had no choice.

16

*J*ack's heart lifted with pleasure when he pulled off the interstate and cruised by grassy pastures lined with white fencing. He could not stop grinning. This day was a long time coming. He was with Dani, and entering Central Florida horse country, Marion County, otherwise known as the horse capitol of the world. And he'd be connected to this prestigious equine scene through the stallion he'd buy tomorrow.

It was nearly lunchtime when they parked in front of the rental in Winter Springs. The back wasn't much to look at—sandy driveway, scrubby grass, and a stucco house past its prime. Probably a good thing Dani couldn't see it. He could afford a nice hotel, but from his research, this was better. The pictures showed a shady yard on a nice bend where the crystal-clear spring-fed river met a darker stream. Inside, the cabin was serviceable, with a big TV, a comfortable couch, and two bedrooms.

They were able to check in early. Later, they had reservations for a pontoon boat eco-tour. He slung a duffle over his shoulder and brought their luggage inside. The guest room had

twin beds, the other had a queen-sized bed, and the view—
that's what it was all about. A sloping yard led to a glistening
river. "You can take the big bedroom. It's got its own bathroom."
He studied Dani's reaction.

She touched his arm. "I thought, maybe, we'd stay in the
same room."

He lit up inside. "You don't have to convince me."

She looped her arms around his neck. "What time is the
boat ride?"

"Two o'clock. We've got time to go out for lunch."

"I brought snacks. If you want to skip going out."

"Are you suggesting ...?"

"I don't want I miss the boat ride. But I can think of something better to do than eat lunch."

This was a side of her he could get used to.

———

They sat at the picnic table facing the river, eating cheddar
cheese and apple slices. Dani trailed her fingers over his
shoulder and down his arm, then leaned over and bit his bicep.

"Whoa. You're a wild one." He laughed and pulled her into
his lap.

She kissed him where his shirt hung open at the top. Then
she used her fingertip and drew a circle on his skin. "Help me
draw a heart."

He positioned her finger on his chest and started moving it
in the shape of a small heart.

"Wait. Go slower." She changed the angle of her finger so
her fingernail pressed on his skin. "Do it now."

He guided her finger, his skin turning pink where she drew.
"That's sharp," he winced.

"There." She kissed where her finger had been. "Now you're
branded with my heart."

"Keep that up, and we'll miss the tour."

"Is that a promise or a threat?"

He cradled her in his arms, carried her indoors, and threw her on the bed, nipping and kissing as he went. She pealed with laughter. And then it got serious.

After all was said and done, they had to rush out of the cottage to make the boat ride in time.

The covered pontoon boat chugged away from the dock on the glassy river. Jack and Dani sat with a dozen other tourists listening to their guide provide a running commentary about the daily output of the spring feeding the river, the cypress trees and wildflowers along the banks, and the multitude of turtles and birds lining the logs. "The state is over twenty percent water, and of the twenty-six types of turtles found in Florida, eighteen are freshwater species."

"Thrilling," Dani mumbled.

Jack studied her. "I thought this might be more fun."

"I think this morning was more fun." She pressed a kiss to his jaw. "But I'm being snarky. I like the ride, the breeze. It smells fresh out here. It's different from the ranch."

"How?"

"All the water wildlife. The turtles plopping into the river, the Osprey. Listen for a minute. I don't remember much about my dad, but he took us camping and taught me different bird calls. He had special training in paying attention to things, and he told me I needed to be like him, a secret soldier, always aware of my environment. When they offered mindfulness training at the yoga center near my house, I signed up. People think if you're blind, your other senses are automatically better, but I've trained mine. And my sense of smell has always been good. Especially when you're around."

"Are you saying I'm smelly?"

Dani chuckled. "I like your scent. There are layers. Horses, hay, whatever you've been cooking, and some kind of after-shave. It's spicy, manly, and makes me want to do this." She nuzzled his neck.

The old man across from him caught his eye and gave him a thumbs-up.

Jack dipped his chin and kissed the top of Dani's head, then stretched his arms wide on the back of the seat, taking in the view. No boulders, no distant mountains, but it was still beautiful in a jungle kind of way. With his eyes closed, he tried to imagine what it was like for Dani. There was the Osprey's whistle, the boat's gentle movement, and the sun on his shoulders. He settled into a peaceful state he hadn't known since arriving last summer. All was right with the world.

Dani snuggled closer, and the realization hit him. He'd been attracted to her from day one, and it'd grown over time. For months he'd chalked it up to her being forbidden fruit. But that wasn't it at all. He knew this feeling. Hadn't felt it in a long, long time.

Jack gazed down at the woman nestled up to him, warmth flooding his chest. He loved her.

Dani shifted on the bench seat, enjoying the afternoon boat tour more than she cared to admit. This was very pleasant, but she needed to dial back her emotions. There was no way what she and Jack had would last. He was older and more experienced, as he'd been more than happy to demonstrate earlier in the bedroom.

And he was sighted. Which meant he probably couldn't be trusted. This was simply a summer fling to wrap up her days at the ranch. There was no point longing for what she couldn't have. She absolutely would not fall in love. Well, anymore than she already was. That was the problem. Right from when they'd first met there'd been something. Something in his voice, in the way she felt when he was around. It was different from anyone else. As though something deep inside of her recognized something deep inside him, and they, who were so different, were meant to be together. It made no sense. But it was undeniable. How could she ever tell him that? He'd probably run for the hills.

Her heart might already belong to him, but she'd play it cool, be more sophisticated and less like an adoring puppy dog. Any other path would lead to pain and rejection. She'd had enough of that for one lifetime.

They cruised into the tannic river part of the tour and the guide spoke up. "Ladies and gentlemen, take a gander over there. You'll want to watch where you're going when there's one of those on your dock."

Passengers in the boat moved around.

"Wow, that's a big one," someone remarked.

She sat tall. "What's he talking about?"

"Holy crap." Jack stood.

Should she stand? She grasped Jack's forearm. "Is everything okay?"

"Yes," Jack answered. "Nothing's wrong. But there's an alligator, he's got to be seven feet."

Tension moved through her arms. "Where?"

"He's up on someone's dock," Jack explained. "Just lying there. Man, I wouldn't want to come out of my house and find him."

"Right. If that were my house, how would I know he's there?" Dani asked.

"How would you know?" Jack asked.

The guide standing nearby answered. "They're typically more afraid of you than you are of them. As long as nobody's been feeding them. You don't want them associating humans with mealtime."

"What a delightful idea. I'd be sure to ask the alligator if he's come for tea or just taking a nap." She groaned inwardly. "That's why I don't swim in freshwater and never will."

"People swim in the river all the time," the guide said.

"I'll stick to swimming pools." Dani shuddered.

"Good plan," Jack agreed.

That was another thing. Jessica's condo had a swimming pool. She laid her hand over Jack's, the bittersweet moment tightening her throat. For now, things were wonderful, but soon, it would end. She didn't like it, but she was a grown-up and could accept the ups and downs of life.

Jack laced his fingers through hers, and she squeezed his hand in return. It would be a shame to waste what time she had with him. Even if it hurt when she left.

The meeting at the S bar C horse ranch wasn't until the afternoon. Jack and Dani drove to downtown Ocala and tried a little breakfast place on the square. After eating, they sat in the gazebo and talked, then strolled around.

"Tell me about the shops," Dani said.

Jack scanned the area. Few interested him. "There's an antique store ahead." His mom had always loved those.

"Let's go in. They might have vintage handkerchiefs."

He led her into the store.

"Do y'all have handkerchiefs, old ones with embroidery?" Dani asked.

Jack browsed the old tools while the shopkeeper led Dani to a drawer full of handkerchiefs.

In the back room, beside a bin of hinges and handles, a basket held old branding irons and newer wrought iron brands for steaks. Smaller ones, novelty items, sat in a dish on a table beside them. One was shaped like a horseshoe, another like a cowboy hat, and there, among them, was one in the shape of a heart. He chuckled. After what Dani said about branding him, he had to buy it.

When he paid for the handkerchiefs, he had the saleslady ring up the heart-shaped branding iron and package it separately. He'd find just the right time to surprise her.

Jack drove them back to Pine Crossing with a beautiful buckskin stallion in the trailer.

"Am I wrong, or is that horse bigger than the ones we have at the ranch?" Dani asked.

"He's about the same size as our tallest. But you're right. He's a big guy." The American Quarter Horse was even better in person than it looked in the pictures.

"How much did he cost?"

Jack huffed. "He has titles and an excellent pedigree. He set me back well over what this truck cost brand new."

Dani gasped.

"I got an excellent deal. The owner died, and his widow wanted to sell." He and Dani had toured the horse ranch in a golf cart while Adam described the new equipment and state-of-the-art therapeutic services available for the horses. A top-notch equine operation. If he didn't have the Tall Pines to run, he'd consider the manager position opening when their man retired.

He brought his attention to his own operation with renewed enthusiasm. If they were breeding, he needed to start building that new barn. He had just the spot picked out. While originally, he'd planned to build in the east pasture, it made more sense to keep the pricy animals closer to his house in a place where Dani could easily walk over and find him. The thought made the corner of his mouth hike up. He was planning for a life with Dani. He'd be busy with the new horse for a few days, but soon he'd talk to her about the vision he had for their future.

Jack was feeding the new stallion when Striker's boots clomped down the aisle of the big horse barn.

Striker whistled. "Man, he's a real beauty."

Jack's chest opened with pride. "Right?"

"You're taking the breeding thing seriously. A horse like this will—"

"I know." Jack leaned on the stall. "He's already sired a couple of fine foals. One's gone to Kentucky for racing. They've been selling his semen too. He'll earn us a dollar or two. I knew you'd get it."

"What do Luke and Bud think?"

Luke appeared at the end of the barn and walked their way.

The muscles in Jack's face hardened. "We're about to find out."

"Weren't we meeting in the—" Luke came to a stop "—whoa, what's this?"

Jack shoved his thumbs in his pockets and got his chill on. "He was available, and there was a short window. I jumped on it."

"You bought the stallion?" Luke gaped.

"Sure did. He's got an impeccable pedigree." Jack's teeth clenched, and he worked to keep a neutral expression.

"What'd he cost?" Luke asked.

"That's irrelevant. I used my own funds. The business can pay me back over time when he starts bringing in income."

"You went to Ocala?" Luke narrowed his eyes.

That wasn't really the question.

"Yes. *We* went." He met Luke's gaze, waiting for the word *we* to sink in. He'd promised Dani they wouldn't be a secret. This moment was bound to come.

Luke's gaze sharpened. "We as in—Dani?"

He forced himself to wait a beat before responding. "That's right."

Luke moved closer, standing taller, more tense.

Jack went on alert. Dani was a grown woman and not Luke's property. But based on Luke's attitude, the prudent thing right now was putting distance between him and his brother. He strode to the other end of the barn and opened the desk drawer like he needed something.

Luke came up behind him. "What the hell? I thought we discussed this."

"You're in my personal space. Step back." He shut the drawer and turned around, giving his brother a hard glare.

Luke's nostrils flared. "I asked you a question."

He scoffed. "Are you for real?"

Wyatt entered the barn and hung back at the other end with Striker.

"Dammit, Jack," Luke bit out. "You need to back off before you mess everything up."

"Drop it. Now." He stared past Luke to the stalls along the opposite wall. It'd be too easy to grab Luke by the collar and toss his smug, self-righteous ass to the floor.

"You're gonna screw up everything, if you haven't already." Luke stepped forward, crowding him. Jabbing at him with a finger. Connecting with the center of his chest. Hard.

He lunged at Luke with a jab to the face, then took him down.

They tumbled around the floor grappling, Luke's nose gushing blood.

Luke surprised him with a hook to the jaw.

His head snapped back.

Luke tried to get in another punch.

Jack blocked it. His right hook connected with Luke's shoulder. Luke grunted and grabbed his shirt, tore it.

They rolled. He angled Luke's arm behind his back.

Luke groaned.

This was Luke's bad arm. If he applied more pressure, Luke would be in a world of hurt. He eased his hold.

Luke bucked. Got in another punch.

They tumbled around again.

Hands grabbed his shoulders. Jack started to take a swing and saw Wyatt's shocked face.

Wyatt. He'd almost hit Wyatt.

Striker pulled Luke to his feet. "Are you about done here?" Striker's voice boomed through the barn, powering between them like a semi-truck.

A tense silence blanketed the room.

Striker swung his gaze between Luke and Jack. "If you go at it again, I'll throw a bucket of water on you like I would the damn dogs."

Luke blotted his face with a bandana.

"Come on." Striker gestured to Wyatt, and they returned to the other end of the barn.

Jack jammed a hand over his short hair, panting, his mind reeling, shame washing through him. How the hell? After all those anger management classes and months of therapy. "Are you happy now, golden boy?"

Luke rubbed his arm. It had to hurt. "You threw the first punch."

"You poked me." That sounded weak, even to him. He brushed bits of hay and wood shavings from his ripped shirt.

"What's with the *golden boy*?" Luke asked.

Jack retrieved his hat from the floor. "Nothing." His heart still crashed around inside his ribcage as he caught his breath.

"I'm stuck taking care of Bud while you fly off whenever you want and come home to a wife and kid. He thinks you fart roses and has since day one." Ah, hell, this wasn't the time to dredge all that up.

Luke's eyes narrowed. "Think I could help how things went down? Must've been nice having two parents from birth."

"Everything went to hell after you came to live with us."

"Like I had a choice where I lived?"

"My mom was happy. Then you ... She cried all the time. You ruined everything." He sounded like a whiny little girl, but he couldn't help it. This was Dr. Dave's fault.

Luke's face screwed up like he was in pain. He probably was. "Your mother hated me."

Jack chuckled. "She did."

Luke's chest heaved. "I went from getting beat up by my stepdad to getting beat up by my half-brother."

The truth of that statement settled over Jack. No arguing. He'd been jealous and had treated Luke like the enemy. Of course, Dr. Dave had said the same thing, but it sounded different coming straight from Luke. "It sucked for you."

"It sure did. But I had to let it go and move on."

"I'm moving on." He practically spat. Couldn't Luke see it? "You think I haven't changed since I got locked up? I learned a few things. Went to a program. Met with a damn therapist."

"You ought to get your money back."

"It's working." Jack ground his teeth and glared at Luke. "You're still standing, aren't you?"

"You're a dog," Luke sneered.

"Look who's talking," Jack shot back.

"That was a long time ago."

"Same here."

"Bullshit." Luke huffed. "And you're twice divorced."

"You're divorced."

That took a little wind out of Luke's sails. "You can't hurt Dani. She's family."

"She's not my family." Jack sat on the old desk chair and rubbed his face. "I care about her. For real."

Luke gaped. "Come again?"

A moment of silence stretched between them.

"I've got feelings for her." It was true, but he hadn't intended to go telling everyone.

"This is something serious?"

"Maybe."

Luke walked over.

Jack braced himself. If Luke wanted to go another round, he was game. But he wouldn't take the first swing.

"What if this goes south?" Luke stood inches away, his hands on his hips, but his voice had softened. "It'll mess up everything."

Jack understood his brother's point. That had been his own concern, and he had a long history, a reputation to erase. But Luke hadn't been there when he'd sat in jail with too much time to think, or when he'd been ordered into anger management classes and therapy. Luke didn't know how much he'd chafed at being locked up. Had no idea how hard he was trying to be a different man. Luke didn't understand how Dani brought out the best in him.

"Why do you think I waited nine months to act on it?" Jack exhaled loudly. Luke was right. Things could get ugly. "I waited until I ran out of willpower. Until I couldn't not have her. To you, she's a sister-in-law who's blind. I see her as a woman. Smart, kind. And yeah, smoking hot. I could find another smokeshow in town. But they wouldn't be Dani."

Luke extended his hand.

Instinctively, Jack pulled back.

"Shake?" Luke tilted his head.

He gripped Luke's hand and looked him in the eye. Instead

of finding anger, he saw hope. Which was even more unsettling. Luke was giving him a chance to prove himself.

They shook hands.

Luke tightened his grip. "Don't hurt Dani. Ellie will have my ass."

"Hell, she'll have mine too." Jack pulled his hand away.

"When she sees this blood." Luke shook his head.

"Can you not discuss this with her?" Jack asked.

"That's not how our marriage works." Luke angled his head toward the new horse. "Don't expect the business to rescue you if the horse venture doesn't pan out."

He lifted his chin and said with false confidence, "It will work out. All of it."

Jack sat in front of the computer and folded his arms across his chest. "He had it coming." Twenty-four hours after the fight with Luke, he'd figured the therapy session would be a chance to vent. But Dr. Dave had him on the hot seat.

Dave's eyebrows arched, but he remained silent.

Jack pled his case. "Nobody got seriously hurt. Both of us walked away."

"And?" Dr. Dave was giving him that look, using his Jedi mind powers to make him squirm.

"Okay. I regret it. Dammit. I've been doing good. For real."

"I know. You and Luke needed to have a talk." Dr. Dave rubbed his forehead. Damn, his arms were big. How many hours a day did the man spend in a gym?

"You're not gonna report me or anything?"

"It doesn't work like that."

"Huh?" He wasn't entirely convinced the doc was keeping it all confidential. At the start of the court-ordered therapy, reports had been filed. But they were in the home stretch now.

"He poked you," Dr. Dave said. "There was a moment when you could've pulled back, but you threw the first punch."

Dr. Dave got quiet, and Jack shifted in his seat while the facts sunk in. Uncomfortable shame washed through him. He'd been doing so well. "Maybe I oughta keep seeing you for a while longer."

"Probably a good idea."

Jack nodded. "All right."

"In your defense, Luke was probably spoiling for a fight, and it's been a long time coming. Sounds like you got a few things off your chest." He stretched his fingers and tilted his head. "What's going on with Dani? It has nothing to do with thumbing your nose at Luke?"

He nearly lifted off his chair with indignation. "No. I really like her."

"That might not be good enough. Not in a situation like this. Luke has a point. You know that. In addition ..." David paused. "You might want to think about how much of this has to do with how your relationship with your mom changed when Luke came to live with you."

Jack exhaled hard. He wanted to tell the doc he was wrong. Was he? He'd tried to comfort his mother, to take care of her. She was hurt.

"An eight-year-old kid shouldn't have to take care of his mom. Who was taking care of you?" Dr. Dave stared at him for a long moment.

Ah, hell. He hated it when the doc wanted to dredge all this shit up. "Maryann. Sometimes." Except he'd looked out for his sis too. A couple years older, she was sensitive and small for her age. Jack shook his head in frustration. He'd no longer been his dad's favorite, but he was able to protect his mom and sister.

The doc softened his tone. "I'm not saying your feelings for Dani aren't real. I'm suggesting you examine your motives. Be honest with yourself."

"I am being honest." Jack ground his teeth. For months, he'd kept his distance from Dani. But even before he'd slept with her, she was like a drug—compelling, appealing, forbidden. Now he couldn't get enough. And when he'd tried to stay away, his gut had twisted in knots.

"How do you see this going down? You plan to marry her?"

Jack scowled. "You know about my marriages."

The doc steepled his fingers and did that Jedi thing, or possibly it was something he learned training for the SEALS. Either way, it made him squirm, made him question himself.

They sat in silence for a few beats. Jack checked the time. Almost up. And he wasn't sorry. This had been a grueling session.

"And your dad?" Dr. Dave asked mildly, as though he were inquiring about the weather and not a man as ornery as rough stock in a chute.

"Is doing better." Now that he thought about it, Bud had been speaking more clearly and actually smiled this morning. "He laughed the other day."

The edge of the doc's mouth curved up. "Which will make life easier for you. When you have that talk with your dad."

"What?" A heart-to-heart with his dad? No way.

Dr. Dave chuckled. "And Jack. Get clear on what your goal is with Dani. Do some journaling about your marriages."

Right. Jack gaped. "Next, you'll tell me to buy a little pink diary."

"I have a journal. Mine's black leather. But if you want pink, go for it."

He stared at the doc, speechless.

"Our time's up. See you next week." Dr. Dave fist-bumped into the camera.

"Okay." Jack fist-bumped the camera in return, which was weird as hell if he thought about it. His fist was what had gotten him into this mess. That and his temper.

The doc ended the session, and he sat there, his brows drawing tightly together. Journal? On actual paper? That was never going to happen.

And then he spotted that notebook, the one Louise—the previous ranch owner—had used. Instead of returning it to his desk in the barn, he'd stuck it on his bedroom shelf. About half of it was just empty pages. He pulled it down and reread the parts about the horses. Then he read the parts about her dreams. He picked up a pen and turned to a blank page.

Jack strode to the bunkhouse holding the cast iron heart in one hand, a bottle of Maker's in the other, and his mouth set in a determined line. It was after midnight. He'd written for hours. After pouring it all into the journal, he had more clarity. Finally.

He knew what he wanted.

Striker was already waiting behind the bunkhouse at the charcoal grill. Flames from the fire licked at the edges of the grill.

Striker gave him the hairy eyeball. "You sure about this?"

He nodded.

"You can't get a tattoo like most people?" Striker's tone of voice made it clear he doubted Jack's sanity.

"No. For obvious reasons." A tattoo wouldn't work for a blind woman. She had to be able to read his chest like Braille. He handed Striker the miniature branding iron. A souvenir, it wasn't meant for this.

"Where in hell did you find this thing?" Striker turned the piece of metal in his fingers.

"An antique shop. It'll work."

"Probably. But you have to heat it." Striker handed it back.

"Let me know when it's ready. And here. You'll want this to bite on." He gave Jack a wadded-up kitchen towel.

Jack took a swig of whiskey and sat the bottle down. He held the heart end of the iron in the flames until the end glowed red.

Holding the end with a pad, Jack handed the iron back to Striker.

Striker pressed the red-hot poker to the spot Jack pointed to on his chest.

The pain was instant. The odor of burning flesh briefly filled his nostrils.

Jack bit down on the kitchen towel. His eyes watered.

He groaned. Cursed into the towel. Bent in half and straightened. Then he ditched the towel and took another slug of whiskey.

Damn! That hurt.

But it would be worth it when the wound healed, and he could show Dani.

*T*he end of the workday couldn't come soon enough. For the first time since she'd lived in Pine Crossing, Dani was having a friend over. She was practically giddy with excitement. They'd tour the ranch and she'd get to show Lita the miniature horses. This morning she'd assembled her delicious bean salad. Jack was grilling steaks and making potato salad, and Lita would stay for dinner.

She was handling the tasks required to close the produce stand, when a vehicle pulled into the parking area and the doors opened and shut. Her heart leaped in anticipation. "Lita?"

"Hey, Dani!" Lita greeted her from the parking lot.

"Howdy, Dani." Noah led Lita over. "Wren's truck is gone?" He'd come to pick up his daughter who'd been helping in the honey house and goat barn.

"Wren had to run to the feed store," Dani explained. "She'll be back in a few minutes. Maya is finishing up with the goats."

"Do you need help closing down?" Noah asked.

"No, thanks. Wren will be back soon, and Wyatt's working in the barn. He'll help."

Wyatt had been earning extra money doing odd jobs for Wren. It was good, because he'd take breaks and visit with her, which helped pass the slower hours. But it was bad, because sometimes he drove her to work instead of Jack.

"Okay. I guess we'll go on into town." Noah was taking his daughter to the craft store and the diner while Lita visited Tall Pines.

Maya joined Noah and they drove away.

"Well, it's come to this on a Saturday night," Lita said. "We should have Wyatt drop us off in town at Lone Star Pete's and get us a couple cowboys."

"Weren't you dating someone?" Dani asked. Lita had mentioned going out with a detective who worked undercover.

Lita scoffed. "Not anymore. He spent too much time in the field. They offered him an extended assignment, three months with no contact. No thanks, honey. I'm not putting up with that. In this case, the other woman was his job. He's married to it. I need more."

"I'm still with Jack. We went out of town and stayed on this river. It was ... really nice."

"Oh, girl. I can tell by that tone." Lita touched her arm.

"Yes. Very nice. But...." She sighed. "Since we've been back, it's been ... well, he's so busy. He got this new horse. You might get to pet it. But he's been meeting with contractors and I've hardly spent more than an hour with him this past week."

"He doesn't stay at your place? I mean, with y'all living near each other?"

"That would be nice. Unfortunately, he has to help his dad. Bud is better, but they don't have anyone to stay overnight. That's usually on Jack. His brother lives there, too. But honestly, Garrick seems a little wild."

"I like my men wild," Lita said, chuckling.

"No. Not that way. More like unpredictable. I didn't know him before he went in the Army, but Garrick gets up in the middle of the night to do chores and then goes off, just disappears."

"Where to?"

"I have no idea. But it creates more work for Jack."

A vehicle rolled into the parking lot.

"We have a customer." Dani stood.

The car sat for a long moment, engine running. After a couple of minutes, a door shut and someone approached.

"Afternoon, ladies." That voice! It was the man from the diner.

"Can I help you?" she asked warily.

"It's just the two of y'all here today?"

A chill moved over her arms. "I can ring up your order if you want produce." She brushed away the niggling sensation he wasn't there for vegetables. "Everyone loves the tomatoes. And the green beans have been good."

OD huffed. "Working here, I'll bet you meet a lot of people in the area."

"Sure." She put false confidence in her voice. "In fact, we get a late afternoon rush, usually right about now." Dani felt for the cell phone in her pocket, but there was no way to send a voice text without OD hearing. She couldn't text Wyatt without giving him away. Should she go ahead and text Jack? Would it be better to try to get rid of OD? Would he hurt her if she called for help?

OD stepped closer. "Have you seen a kid? Goes by the name of Wyatt."

"Well, no ..."

"He hasn't applied for work here?" His voice had a sharp edge causing the hairs on the back of her neck to stand up.

"No."

The man came a little closer.

There it was. The odor. Faint. But detectable.

"We met at the diner. You were gonna go out with me."

"I think we had a misunderstanding." She took another step back, tension buzzing through her. "I'm working and my ride will be here soon. If you want something, you need to pick it out. We're about to close."

He drew closer. She backed up and clutched the side of a bin. Sweet potatoes. Her heart slammed against her ribs while her fingertips skated over the oddly shaped tubers, and she took hold of a large one. As weapons go, it left something to be desired, but it's what she had.

Behind her, Lita made a sound.

"Lita, weren't you going to call Noah?" Dani asked.

"I'm calling him now." Lita said.

"I'm leaving." OD's heavy footsteps moved away.

Dani released the potato and exhaled a hard breath. That man gave her the creeps.

"That was weird," Lita said. "Do you get many oddballs like him here?"

"No. Thankfully, we don't. But how about we don't mention it to Jack?"

"Seriously? That guy seemed kind of dangerous."

"I'll tell him later tonight." She knew OD was a danger to Wyatt. But, dang, she'd been looking forward to Lita's visit. "If I tell Jack, he'll get upset. It will ruin our evening."

Dani went on to relay the story about meeting OD in the diner, but she held back about Wyatt's involvement. After dinner, she'd let Jack know about OD's visit. And she'd talk to Wren. They needed a plan, one that included installing some kind of security system. Tonight, when Lita left, she'd tell Jack.

Dani sat back in her chair and stretched. This pleasant evening was exactly what she needed after that creepy incident at the produce stand. She'd shown Lita the big horses and taught her how to brush the minis. Then Jack had grilled steaks. They'd had a wonderful meal filled with good conversation and laughter. Lita told funny stories about people who stayed at the inn where she worked and, for dessert, Thea had baked a delicious carrot cake.

Bud and Thea had just gone inside and were watching another nature show, while Garrick, Jack, and Wyatt sat with her and Lita on the porch. The visit had been a huge success.

"I'd like to do this again," Lita said when Noah came to get her. "Does Jack have a rancher friend he can invite over? Or maybe that Striker fella."

She laughed. "I doubt you'd want to live way out here."

"I'm serious. Tell Striker I'm available, or even Brick. His guitar playing was amazing."

Lita left with Noah.

Dani could go home now, but she cued Lucky to take her to Jack's porch. Now that Lita was gone, it was time to ruin the evening and tell them about OD stopping by the stand.

Jack, Garrick, and Wyatt were still there, arguing about whether the Broncos or Vikings were shaping up to have a better team this fall.

When they paused, Dani broke in. "We had a customer at the end of the day." She chewed her lip, hating to be the bearer of bad news.

Jack placed a hand on her arm, alert to her tone. "And?"

"It was the man from the diner, possibly OD."

Jack's hand whipped away. "This afternoon?"

"What?" Wyatt asked, alarmed.

"We were getting ready to close," Dani said. "You were still in the barn, Wyatt."

"Why didn't you say something sooner?" Wyatt demanded.

Dang, she hadn't expected to be attacked like this. "I didn't want to ruin dinner." Maybe she should've mentioned it earlier.

Garrick huffed. "Dammit, Jack, I told you we shoulda—"

"You're right," Jack interrupted. His boots thudded on the porch as he paced.

"It gets worse." Dani clenched and unclenched her hands. "He was asking about Wyatt."

The breath whooshing from Wyatt's lungs could've formed a tornado. "What are we gonna do?"

"It's time to handle this," Garrick said.

"Right," Jack said. "I'm calling the sheriff."

"No!" Wyatt moved from his chair. "They'll blame me."

"What do you mean, blame you?" Jack had that tone he usually reserved for Luke.

"They ... might have a photo or two of me." Wyatt sounded panicked.

"What's in the photo?" Jack asked.

"I had a box in my hand. It was ... a delivery. They called it insurance. I didn't understand what they meant. I mean, now I do. The cops will think I was one of them."

Jack growled softly. "Shit."

"We're dealing with this. Now." Garrick's chair moved.

Dani wrung her hands, her dinner threatening to come back up. This was her fault. She'd ruined the evening, and now they were going to do something dangerous.

Jack swung his gaze from Wyatt to Garrick. "I'm in. But what are we doing?" The words tasted sour on his tongue. This situation had disaster written all over it.

Garrick turned his palms up as though the answer was obvious. "Wyatt shows us where these assholes are, gives us the lay of their operation, and we take care of them."

"That's it? No! Hell, no." Jack rubbed his neck. "Wyatt said they're armed."

"Are they cartel? What are their connections?" Garrick pinned Wyatt with a *don't lie* glare.

"No. They weren't connected to any cartel that I knew about. Once I realized what they were doing, I paid more attention to their conversations." Wyatt lifted his shoulder. "I can draw you a map of their camp. It was out in the brush where nobody could find them. I think that's why they stayed so long. But they were talking about leaving."

"If that was OD today, some of them are still around." Garrick winced. "We can't have them coming by. Not when there're vulnerable women around here. They're searching for Wyatt and OD was already here once."

"And they have guns," Wyatt added.

Garrick lifted a brow. "What kind?"

"Mostly rifles," Wyatt said.

"A bunch of meth heads into firearms? Not likely." Jack dismissed him with a wave.

"Seriously. In crates," Wyatt continued. "I think they were doing some deal with weapons." Wyatt's expression morphed into something resembling panic. "There were some other men. Didn't come around much. They picked up the guns."

"I guess it's possible they could be involved in weapons trafficking." Jack rubbed at the tension gripping his neck. This was a bigger deal than he'd initially thought. "We don't know what we're walking into. I'm not in the mood to get shot. Or go back to jail."

"Understood," Garrick said. "We'll get Flash and Tate to help."

"Do they want to get involved?" Dani asked.

Garrick huffed. "They live for this stuff."

Oh, crap! Jack put a hand on his head. Dani was still sitting there listening. He grasped her arm and lowered his voice. "Take Lucky and go home. I'll come by later. You don't want to hear this."

"No. It's interesting. I'm fine."

"He's right," Garrick added. "Plausible deniability. You need to leave." He made a call.

"But I care about Wyatt," Dani said.

Wyatt circled Dani in a side hug. "Thanks, *Mom*. But the less you know, the better."

"You take that back. I'm not old enough to be your mother. But you're right. I don't think I want to know what you're planning. I'll worry." Dani gathered her things. "But Jack, text me as soon as you're back." She headed to her cottage.

Garrick was already finished with his call. "They'll be here in an hour. We'll make a plan and move out. Are you armed?"

"No. I just got off probation. I don't carry firearms and ...." His words evaporated. That was about to change. He had to get involved. And suppose it went sideways. He'd probably be facing more than a month behind bars this time.

Could the legal deal he'd made in Montana evaporate? Their attorney had pulled a lot of strings to get him leniency. He didn't want to blow it. But this was about protecting Wyatt and Dani. He had to help.

Jack was crammed into the back seat in the center spot between Tate and Flash.

Garrick's Jeep Wrangler sped east.

The five of them had met at the picnic table behind the house and reviewed a map of the area. They hashed out Plan A and Plan B based on Wyatt's explanation of the layout and probable location of the men.

"Be ready. Plan B is what usually goes down." Tate, the most experienced of them, had taken charge and openly studied him, assessing, and likely found him lacking.

There was brawling. There was boxing. And there was this.

The Jeep was outfitted with extra storage pockets, now holding handguns, and they'd stuffed a duffle of what might be weapons in the cargo hold. Jack's pits were soaked, and his heart pounded in his ears. He had his hog rifle, and right about now wished he'd gotten in more hours of target practice. What in the hell were they doing?

Jack's gaze fell on Wyatt, riding shotgun, reiterating the typical routine of the group given the time of day.

His chest tightened. The kid had to come because he was the one who knew the location. But despite Wyatt's bravado, the teen was softer than he appeared. Jack felt a strong urge to protect him.

He wiped his sweaty palms on his Wranglers. In the past, his tangles had been explosive bursts of losing his temper. This was premeditated. Even though they'd devised a plan, it felt like he was riding to his execution.

Garrick and the other two men were well-trained soldiers with a lot more experience. He was born tough, got into more than his share of scrapes in his youth, and had a few too many as an adult, but these men were in a whole different league. And his skills with a firearm weren't even in the same ballpark. Other than shooting a few bucks and hogs, the only shots he got in were whiskey.

Yeah. He was screwed.

If he weren't so concerned for the safety of the people on his ranch, he wouldn't be here. He wasn't a gun guy. And right about now, having had time to think, he couldn't shake the feeling they should've called the DEA, FBI, or whoever handled drug dealers. Call them and get Wyatt a damn good lawyer. That seemed like the more rational approach.

Luke was at home with Ellie, oblivious. Which was better. Someone had to stay back in case things went sideways. He had to be here for Wyatt. The kid had gotten under his skin. He felt responsible for him. Maybe even fatherly.

"It's gettin' dark soon," Jack stated the obvious.

"We brought the NVGs," Flash replied, never shifting his gaze from the landscape outside the window.

"En what?" Jack asked.

"Night vision goggles," Tate said, studying the terrain on his side of the road.

"Huh." Yep. He was in over his head.

"Good ones," Flash added.

They had just passed the main gate to Whitehall's Ranch.

"There. That's the tree." Wyatt sat forward and pointed. "It's not far. There's a road on the right."

Garrick slowed the vehicle.

Wyatt whipped his head to the right. "That was the service road. The dirt road is coming up in about a quarter mile."

The dirt road was little more than grassy tracks traversing uneven terrain.

Garrick turned the Jeep onto the path.

"Careful," Wyatt said. "There're low areas where you can get stuck. That's why they didn't use this one."

They bumped down the uneven path. Garrick took a hard left, narrowly missing a muddy patch, managing to pull back onto the track.

A moment later, Garrick stopped the vehicle behind a thicket to the east of the road. "This is where we get out."

The men climbed out and unloaded the cargo hold. Garrick, Tate, and Flash wore hands-free walkie-talkies on their belts and headsets that wrapped around their ears. Garrick handed Wyatt a walkie-talkie. "Stay. Don't leave the vehicle. Don't follow us. Keep quiet. Be ready so we can beat it out of here. Keep listening in case you need to leave without us. Use that shotgun if you have to."

Jack scoffed.

Wyatt was no match for any of those criminals. And the kid looked half-crazed with fear.

"I still don't get the plan," Jack said to his brother. "We look for the guy Wyatt described and get his phone?" He was itching to call for help. "Even if we get his phone, the photo is probably backed up. Then what?"

"I'm going to break this down Barney style. The plan is, be ready for anything," Garrick huffed, impatient. "We find the guy who took the photo and take his phone. One way or another delete the photo. But there may be obstacles."

"We can't leave a bunch of bodies in a pasture," Jack balked. "It's not the old west."

Garrick scoffed. "Quit worrying, Grandpa."

"Last time I checked, murder is illegal."

Garrick gave him a hard look. "After OD showed up at Avery's birthday party, Flash and I did a little digging. He's a real psycho. A felon with an active warrant. Part of a nasty group."

"Wyatt said they weren't cartel."

"There are other groups. Real scumbags."

Hell. This was bigger than— "Shit! My boot." Jack pulled his Ariat from a mucky wet patch. *Dammit!* These were his favorites.

"No more talking." Flash scowled. "Use the hand signals we showed you."

Flash and Tate stole into the woods ahead of them, east of the camp, moving behind trees and thickets. They'd radio when they were in position. Flash, the best shot among them, would find a place to provide overwatch and cover them if needed.

Jack and Garrick were assuming a position to the north. They snuck into the woods, creeping from tree to tree, alert to sounds and movements. At least they had the element of surprise.

Jack's stomach churned. Sweat streamed from his face and

trailed down his neck to his chest where it stung the burned area.

Despite the plan, the *figure it out on the fly* aspect of this operation had him on edge. They weren't certain how many men they'd find and how heavily they were armed.

They stalked forward, then waited for Tate's signal, four clicks over the walkie talkie.

Jack felt disembodied, outside of time, yet alert, like pure adrenaline was pumping through his veins.

Garrick motioned with his hand. All set.

The men crept forward, listening hard.

The trees thinned.

In the dim light, he made out the clearing ahead, just as Wyatt had described.

And the shed.

No trailers.

No trucks. No RVs. No men. Nada.

"Shit!" Garrick hissed.

They checked the shed. Empty. They studied the area. Flattened and dead patches of turf. Evidence of recent camping, charred earth.

Garrick laid a palm on the burnt area. "It's barely warm."

"Dammit. We're too late." Tate ran a hand over his head.

Flash strode out of the woods and joined them.

They divided the scene into quadrants and searched.

Jack found a short length of hose and empty antihistamine boxes discarded in the weeds. He pulled a bandana from his pocket and collected the trash.

Garrick looked at him like he was nuts. "You don't want that on you."

"The cattle could get it."

"Now you're a Boy Scout?"

His younger brother was giving him shit? When did the tables get turned?

"Looks like tire tracks leading to the service road," Flash said.

"Which takes them to the state road we came in on," Tate added. "They could be miles away by now."

Discouraged with their results, they hiked back to the vehicle.

Wyatt leaped from the Jeep. "What happened? I didn't hear anything."

Flash stowed his ruck in the cargo hold. "No joy."

"They're gone," Tate said to Wyatt.

The tension bled from Wyatt's face. "Good. They'd said they move every few months. Maybe they left."

"Right." Jack didn't want to pop Wyatt's bubble. But what was OD doing at the produce stand if they'd left the area? Those jerks were still out there, somewhere. How far had they gone?

Garrick rode into town with Flash and Tate, leaving Jack and Wyatt on the ranch.

Jack trudged inside and thanked Thea, then begged her to stay so he could spend the rest of the evening at Dani's.

Dani welcomed him with open arms. "Hey there, handsome cowboy. Did you take care of the bad guys?"

Dani was so cute when she flirted with him like that. He tipped her face up for a kiss. "They were gone. Cleared out. They must've done this a time or two." He poured himself a few fingers of Makers from the bottle he kept at her house, then poured her a glass of wine and joined her on the couch. He leaned his head back. "What a night."

"They were just ... gone?"

"Looks like it. Wyatt said they move every three or four months. OD showing up today could've been his Hail Mary before leaving." He wanted to believe it, but the timing felt off.

"That's a huge relief." She planted tantalizing kisses on his neck and jawline. "You're my hero."

"I am, huh?" The corner of his mouth tugged up.

"Yes. And heroes get rewards." She climbed onto his lap and straddled him with her bare legs, her dress hiked up around her hips.

He ran his hands over her smooth skin, under the fabric of her dress, and kept going until he could cup her hips. "I think I'm gonna like my reward."

She pressed forward and whispered in his ear, "You're gonna love it."

Fire charged through his veins. He placed his hand on the nape of her neck and pulled her in for a kiss, his mind fuzzy with desire.

Dani nibbled her way across his cheek and down his neck. "What's this?" She fingered the bandaged area on his chest.

"Just a scratch." He growled and rolled her onto her back, his breathing ragged, heart thundering. He couldn't get enough of Dani Tremont. This was exactly where he wanted to be. In the arms of the woman he loved, showing her just how much he adored every inch of her.

18

*J*ack filled a grocery tote with ingredients to make dinner, placing the tomatoes in last. Nearly a week had passed since searching for the meth dealers' camp, and he hadn't spent enough time with Dani. Tonight, he'd make it up to her.

"Someone has the fixings for a good meal." Thea stood in his kitchen doorway, arms folded, eyes sharp.

How long had she been there? The woman was stealthy.

"Yep. Pasta primavera. With meatballs." He pulled the container of meatballs from the fridge. "I've got Dad's dinner ready on that plate."

"I brought my vegetable soup. He asked me to make it," Thea said.

"He's giving you special orders now?"

"I don't mind." Thea's gaze moved from the tote back to him. "You're cooking dinner for Dani?"

"That's the plan." He double-checked that he had every-thing and grabbed the totes. "Appreciate you helping like this."

"So you can spend time with Dani." She tilted her head, studying him.

"Right ... is there a problem?" he asked, a little too defensively.

She pursed her lips as if weighing her words. "You've been busy. May as well spend time with her while you can."

"What's that supposed to mean?" True. Lately, his days were spent researching his new horse breeding operation, meeting with Striker about the cattle, and going over plans with the architect and the contractor. Since bringing in the stallion and working on expanding the business, Striker had been giving him more respect, checking with him instead of Luke. It was a busy time, but today he'd made a point of stopping early so he could spend the evening with Dani.

"Before she goes," Thea added as she moved past him and retrieved a soup container from the fridge.

"Goes?"

"Dani's leaving sometime in August." Thea's face was a mask of innocence, but she was sly and was probably well aware Dani hadn't said anything to him about it. "We've been planning how she can continue with herbs and creams and even partner with Wren. She'll continue the business, expand it into where she plans to be in Jacksonville."

"Come again?"

Thea studied him for a beat. "She really didn't tell you her friend invited her to move back? Jessica needs a roommate, and Dani plans to go."

Heat climbed up his neck. Dani hadn't said one word to him about leaving.

Thea sighed loudly. "It's a shame. She has a knack." Thea opened the freezer and removed a bag of rolls she'd stashed there, moving around his kitchen like she owned the place. Since when had Thea become such a fixture?

"I suppose, if Dani had a good reason to stay, she might. But apparently, learning the herbal healing business from me isn't enough." Thea gave him a pointed look.

Jack hauled the totes of food from his house and stormed toward Dani's cottage, ready to confront her.

And say what?

If helping with the horses and working with Thea and at Wren's Organics wasn't enough, why should she stay? *Because you love her, dummy.* But did she love him? He was pretty sure Dani loved Thea, but it seemed the old woman and the herb business weren't enough to make her stay.

Jack paused on the trail and studied the red-shouldered hawk sitting on the fence. A pang of sadness pinched his heart. As close as they'd become, Dani hadn't seen fit to tell him her plans. Ellie hadn't mentioned it. Did Ellie and Luke know? Had they encouraged her to leave? Did he look like a fool to them? Was this Luke's doing? The thought sparked the nuclear power plant in his chest.

He could ask Dani to stay, but what kind of life would he be offering her? Nothing she didn't already have. And she wanted to leave.

"You need to get clear," Dr. Dave had said. "Are you planning to marry her?"

Jack's first and second wives came to mind in a slideshow of hurt. The doc had said a lot of marriages dissolve when a child dies, but his second marriage hadn't worked either. And then there were his mom and Bud, who hadn't made marriage look like a picnic.

There was an unscalable wall between him and marriage. It didn't feel like something he wanted to risk again. And if he couldn't offer Dani marriage, she may be better off leaving. Better off somewhere else.

Without him.

Crap. His chest felt heavy. The still-healing brand on his chest stung. Everything seemed pointless.

The hawk flapped to the ground and came up with a lizard.

He turned away and resumed his hike to the cottage.

They still had now. This month and part of the next. He wouldn't waste it.

Dani opened the door. "Why did you knock when it's unlocked?"

"First, you're supposed to lock your doors. And second, my hands are holding two totes of food."

"You said you were bringing dinner."

He set a bag of groceries on the counter. "No, I said I was bringing food. We're cooking together."

"I have to cook? I worked with the minis this morning and in the garden all afternoon." She pouted.

"And I worked cattle all morning and was in meetings all afternoon. You're not getting out of it that easy. You can dice the onions and chop the tomatoes. We're having pasta. I already made the meatballs. C'mon, let's wash up."

"I'm too tired to wash up."

"Get over here, you gorgeous slacker. Cup your hands." He squirted lemon soap into her palms, ran the water, and lathered it up, rubbing every finger and the back of her hands.

She leaned into him. "That's so nice."

His chest opened as the unexpected intimacy of the moment choked him up, stealing his ability to respond. Instead, he dried her hands and kissed her palm, then planted a featherlight kiss on each fingertip.

Dani whispered, "If this is how cooking starts, I believe I could get used to it."

As they worked side by side in the kitchen, he flashed on the pleasant moments when he'd helped his mother cook. It'd begun when he was young, when Luke had shown up, and his mother had been devastated. He'd wanted to help, to make her feel better, and then he discovered he liked it.

This was even better because he could steal a kiss whenever he wanted.

His heart twisted. It wouldn't last.

They sat down to dinner and talked and ate while a shower moved through, the rain pelting the windows. When the pattering let up, Dani pushed her plate away and stood. "Let's go for a walk. It's probably cooled off from the rain, and I need to burn off that pasta. I'm not used to being so sedentary. Aside from the riding, I feel like a slug." She fetched Lucky, and they stepped outdoors.

Jack enjoyed boxing and, back in Montana, had kept a bag in one of the barns. Here he preferred the boxing gym because they had a decent free weight area, but it was quite a drive. "How did you exercise before coming to the ranch?"

"I swam. I had these little foam weights you use in a pool. My Aunt Pat had a pool at her condo, and Jessica's complex had a pool and a room with exercise machines. I learned the circuit. I was in much better shape."

His gaze skimmed her body. Her shape was exactly right if you asked him. "You want to exercise?"

"Yeah, that's not easy here, but—"

"Hey, Dani." Wyatt came jogging over.

Jack shot him a glare. Couldn't the kid see they were having alone time?

"I can take you tomorrow." Wyatt shrugged. "Striker says he doesn't need me in the afternoon, and Wren can use me. She's got some repairs out in the barn."

"Sounds good. Now, weren't you leaving?" Jack angled his head toward the bunkhouse.

Wyatt pulled a face, then grinned wickedly.

Jack laced his fingers through Dani's, and she held Lucky on a leash like a regular dog while they circled the ranch's main area twice, returning to her cottage sweaty and hot.

"Good enough workout for you?" he asked.

"Yes. This is when a nice dip in a pool would feel great." Dani poured them each a tall, iced tea. "I guess I'll have to be satisfied with a cool shower."

Jack stood behind her and nuzzled her salty, damp neck. "I think a shower sounds great."

The heat of summer was upon them. Dani left Lucky at Ellie's to hang out with their dogs while she went to work at the produce stand. Her dog would have more fun with Ellie's pups and stay cooler. But it made for a lonelier day when business was slow. And it was slow. Fewer tourists passed through in the summer, and locals weren't as apt to visit a produce stand with no air conditioning when it was sweltering.

Wyatt dropped her off in the morning, returned to the ranch, and came back at noon to work in the barn.

"Hey, Dani. Got anything to drink?" Wyatt strolled into the stand.

She'd just finished the afternoon snack she'd packed. "Do I look like a convenience store? Wren might have water if you ask her. But she won't be home from the vet for a while. Macy's sick." Macy was one of the puppies from the litter Ellie's dog had the previous year. The rambunctious border collie was getting into all kinds of mischief on Wren's farm.

"Can you even work here without Wren?" Dani asked.

"She told me what to do when she texted. You usually bring something to drink. Got extra?"

Without waiting for her answer, Wyatt opened the cooler by the register. "This tea looks weak." There was a thunk and a second thunk as Wyatt rummaged through the cooler.

"Wait. Wyatt. Don't be grabbing my jars. What do you have there? It's not all tea. The jar with two ribbons is a valerian infusion, and it's concentrated. Please don't drink it. It's a sedative. You wouldn't get any work done. Good grief, I'm not sure what would happen if you drank too much. You'd probably pass out and might not wake up."

"Why do you even have that here?"

"Wren and I are developing a honey tea product for drinking before bed."

"What's this other one with one ribbon?"

She stood, alarmed. "Don't even open that. It's made with ghost peppers."

"Those hot chilies?"

"Yes, we're making sweet and spicy tea. And those dang things are so hot I use gloves when I handle them."

"What would happen if I drank it?"

She huffed. "You'd be sorry. It's diluted with tea, but it's still strong. It's only diluted to make it safer for me to handle. But if it gets on your skin, it'll still burn."

"Damn, Dani. That's evil."

"No. Capsaicin can be healing when used appropriately. We use it in pain relief creams. But they also use it in pepper spray. You have to know what you're doing."

"Huh. What do you have to drink?" Wyatt asked.

"I have a small bottle of water and the rest of my tea."

"Can I take the water?"

"Go ahead." She snorted. Later, she may regret giving it to him. "Next time, don't forget to bring your own. And hand over my tea. The one with a rubber band and no ribbon."

She accepted the bottle, checked the rubber band, opened it, and sniffed. Not that Wyatt couldn't be trusted, but it seemed prudent. She poured tea into her glass and set the ball jar on the counter.

"I'll be back up at four, possibly sooner, to help you close."

"Bless your heart. I don't know what I did to deserve you."

"Me neither." Wyatt chuckled. "There's not as much to do as I thought. I may as well earn my pay. Text me if you need something. I'm heading back to the barn." Wyatt left.

She slid her fingertips across the counter and ran into the jars. Darn that Wyatt, leaving them out. An engine sounding a lot like a motorcycle pulled in.

"Howdy, Dani. Whatcha got good today?"

"Bear!" She perked up and left the jars to greet him. "We still have peaches from Wren's cousin in South Carolina, and we have some nice tomatoes. They talked for a while before he bought a sack of produce and left.

The afternoon stretched long and quiet with the occasional car driving by or plane buzzing overhead.

She got out her phone, listened to a podcast, and tried to resist nodding off.

Tires crunching in the parking lot jolted her awake. She willed herself alert. What time was it?

The vehicle stopped in the parking lot.

The door shut.

Footsteps approached, something familiar in the sound.

"Lookie who's working all alone today."

A chill shot up her arms.

When Jack had driven by Wren's Organics, Wyatt was there talking to Dani. He'd fought the urge to turn in but had needed to get to the diner where he'd met with the contractor. There were changes he needed to make to his plans. Big changes. And the man had worked him into a very narrow window of availability in his schedule.

The meeting had ended, and he was leaving when Bear approached the diner's entrance. "Howdy, Jack."

"Bear." Jack liked the biker. He was a damn good mechanic. Bear had resurrected the golf cart from what had seemed to be its final death.

"That creep driving the white van is still around," Bear said.

"Come again?"

"White van. You know. The low life who was here, bothering Dani? I thought you'd want to know."

Adrenaline shot through his veins like electricity. "Where was it?"

"He was heading east." Bear lifted his chin toward the road. "I stopped at the stand, picked up some peaches, and spotted him on my way into town.

The hair on Jack's neck stood on end. "Just now?"

"Yeah."

Jack flew down the steps.

Bear was right behind him. "What's going on?"

Jack started the truck.

Bear pulled open the passenger door and jumped in. "You look like you saw a ghost. Want to tell me what the hell's happening?"

"He's come around a few times. Looking for Wyatt."

"That kid who works for you?"

"Yeah."

"I thought he wanted Dani."

That statement didn't help.

Jack clenched his teeth so tight he might break one.

He floored it.

Dani wasn't one hundred percent sure the man was a danger to her, but she needed to warn Wyatt. She felt around the counter, bumping into those jars. No phone. Dang!

The sound of each approaching footfall made it more difficult to breathe.

She tried giving OD the benefit of the doubt. "We have some sweet peaches today."

He chuckled. It was an ugly sound. "Later."

Her nose wrinkled as he drew close enough to smell his stinky clothes.

Where had she set her dang phone?

Bile climbed up her throat.

She backed up another step, sliding her hand along the counter. She grabbed a jar. If nothing else, she'd smack him upside the head.

"I'll take that." He snatched it from her hand and cracked the lid. "What's this?"

"My tea." It couldn't be her tea, she'd drunk it all.

She heard the glug, glug, glug.

He spat. The bottle hit the ground. "Damn stuff's bitter."

That had to be the valerian.

He moved closer.

"If you want money, it's in the drawer. Let me—"

"Yeah. I'll take that too."

"Wren will be here any second. I'm not alone."

He huffed. "Nice try. We're leaving." He grabbed her wrist.

"Wait." She pulled back. Stumbled. Caught herself.

"Let her go!" It was Wyatt's voice. "Now."

A deep sound filled with malice emanated from OD's chest. "Look who's here. You think you can protect her?"

"I said let her go." Wyatt's steps came closer.

"Like a stick's gonna ..."

Something smashed. "I said let go." Wyatt demanded.

"I'll hurt her if you don't put that down." OD grabbed her wrist and twisted her arm.

"Ouch." She reached out with her other hand, searching for something, anything, to slam against this monster's head.

Wyatt's footsteps approached.

Dani called out, "No, Wyatt."

Footsteps moved faster. Something hard crashed into something wooden.

OD released her.

It sounded like they were grappling.

Bumping into crates.

She stepped farther back.

Grunting.

There was the sound of the stick hitting the ground.

"Ouch," Wyatt cried out.

Then smacking.

Tumbling.

Wood scratching, crates of produce spilling. Things dropping.

With icy fingers, she groped for her phone. Found it!

There was a loud smack.

"Ugh." Wyatt moaned. Clunk. It sounded like he fell.

Panic gripped her chest. "Wyatt. Are you—"

"Drop the phone, or I'll finish off your friend." OD's tone, so venomous, made her freeze.

She set her cell back on the counter.

Then there was silence, followed by grunting.

"Wyatt?" she called out.

"Quiet. Don't move, or I will end him." OD chuckled.

There was a sound of dragging as if OD might be pulling Wyatt along the ground.

The door to the vehicle opened and then slammed.

What was he doing?

Wyatt was hurt. That much she knew for sure.

She grabbed her phone, opened it, commanded, "Call Jack."

"Calling Jack," the mechanical voice replied.

Jack's phone rang.

Jack clutched the steering wheel. To hell with the speed limit. They were almost there.

What was that sound?

His phone!

Dani flashed on the screen in his truck.

He glanced at Bear. "Press answer."

Bear raised an upturned palm. "The call ended."

Jack didn't answer. Why hadn't she called the sheriff first? "Call 911," Dani commanded. The phone didn't respond. "Call 911."

OD snatched her phone and it hit the ground. "Your turn."

"Calling—" the mechanical voice on the cell phone responded to her voice command.

"Shit!" OD released her. Took a step.

While he was smashing her phone, she grabbed the other jar on the counter.

The bottle with one ribbon.

Pepper tea!

She quickly unscrewed it, spilling some. Ouch. It stung.

Thank God it wasn't full strength.

"You're coming with me." OD grabbed her elbow, and she spun around, aiming the liquid in his direction.

"Ahhhh!" he screamed. Moved around. "You bitch—"

The white van was at the produce stand.

As they pulled in, Dani hurled something at OD. He held his face, screaming.

Jack and Bear leaped from the truck.

"Dani! We're here," Jack called out.

Dani backed into the corner by the cash register.

Bear went right for OD, hiked his knee into his torso, and took him down. He landed a fist in the man's chest, pinning him to the ground. Over two hundred pounds of biker rage was no match for that scrawny scumbag.

Jack ran over and circled Dani in his arms. Her dress was damp.

"Holy shit! What is this stuff?" Bear winced. "It burns."

Dani called out, "Try not to get it on you. It's pepper tea, very hot. Like pepper spray."

"Now you tell me." Bear wiped his hands on his pants. OD hardly moved. It looked like the fight had gone out of the creep.

"Are you okay?" Jack held Dani's arms.

"Yes, I'm fine. I'm good. But Wyatt. OD hurt Wyatt."

He scanned the area, panic rising all over again. "Where is Wyatt?"

"I think he's in the van."

Jack sprinted over to the vehicle.

Wyatt lay still in the back of the van, his face and arms covered with blood. It reeked of chemicals.

He gave the kid a shove. "Wyatt? Hey, buddy, are you okay?"

No response.

He pulled Wyatt out of the van, carried him to the grass, and checked for breathing. Crap. Here goes nothing. He sucked in a breath to administer rescue breathing when Wyatt coughed, and his eyelids fluttered.

"Jack?" Wyatt sat partway up and grabbed his head. "Oh. That hurts." He collapsed and passed out again.

Jack dialed 911. "We need an ambulance and a deputy." He

gave the operator the short version, talking while he fetched Dani.

"I need to get out of my dress because this stuff burns." Dani was holding the fabric away from her body.

Wren pulled into the lot and jumped from the car, her dog, Macy, yapping at her heels. "What's going on?"

Bear came strolling out of the produce stand, dragging OD behind him like a half-full sack of potatoes.

"Is he ...?" Jack asked.

"He ain't dead. I think he's sleeping. Conked out. Damndest thing."

"OD drank the valerian tincture. It was concentrated," Dani said. "He needs a doctor."

"Be better if he needed an undertaker," Jack mumbled.

"Will someone explain to me what's going on?" Wren swung her gaze from one to the other.

"I got the ghost pepper tincture on my dress, and Bear has it on his skin," Dani explained. "OD, that guy with Bear, he came to hurt Wyatt and maybe..."

Jack could see the moment when the enormity of the situation hit her.

Dani's face scrunched up.

"Oh, no," Wren said. "Come in and let me give you some different clothes. I have a paste for the burns. I use it for bee stings. Fill me in while you change. And you might have some explaining to do. The deputy just pulled in and there's a fire truck and a rescue behind him."

Jack directed the EMT to Wyatt and brought Deputy Kurt up to speed on the situation. They called for another ambulance. This was a shitshow, but at least help had arrived and Dani was okay.

Would Wyatt be all right? A nasty gash along Wyatt's cheekbone might require stitches. His face was already swelling up, and the kid had regained consciousness, but seemed delirious.

Blood covered Wyatt's arms. He probably got all cut up when he was dragged across the shell parking lot. Unfortunately, Dani couldn't have seen what happened, but she was an astute listener.

OD lay passed out in the grass and eventually the EMT's loaded him into one of the rescues. He was the sheriff's problem now.

When Dani returned with Wren, he took hold of her hand. Along with Bear, they gave Kurt statements, promising to come down to the station tomorrow and answer any additional questions.

Jack's pulse still thudded in his ears. He'd almost lost Dani today, and it made him sick to his stomach. She meant the world to him. And he needed to let her know, to convince her to stay. He had a plan in place, but he needed to step up his game —fast.

"*H*ere's your drink, milady." Jack moved the strawberry daiquiri on the table closer to Dani. They'd come directly from buying her a new cell phone to the gathering at Lone Star Pete's. He sat on one side of Dani while Ellie sat on the other.

"Thank's, Jack." A small smile curved Dani's lips. It appeared she enjoyed being treated like a princess, and rightly so. She'd helped bring a wanted felon to justice through her fast work with the pepper tincture.

"I feel kind of guilty enjoying a celebratory evening while Wyatt's recovering in bed." Dani's forehead wrinkled.

"He's okay." Jack was in the mood to celebrate and had convinced Dani to be there. After all, she was a huge part of the occasion. Now that they knew Wyatt was going to be alright, and OD was in custody, everyone wanted to talk about what had gone down the previous day.

Thea and Avery were with Wyatt. He'd spent the night in the ER, had a thorough exam and IV fluids, and had been released to recover at home. Tomorrow he'd go to the sheriff's department and speak to a detective.

"Him being only eighteen, and getting over a concussion, he wouldn't be able to join us here." Jack took a long drink of his beer and let out a satisfied, "Ahhh. Wyatt's good right where he is."

"The kid's got a helluva shiner. It's gonna hurt for a while." Garrick offered a slow, solemn nod.

"You know it," Jack agreed.

"How much trouble is Wyatt in?" Garrick asked.

"The sheriff has a lot of questions, but as of now, he's not under arrest." Jack turned his beer in his hand and snorted. Wyatt was a good kid who got mixed up in something big and bad. But he was a victim and underage when they'd used him. If the detective didn't get that, he'd go in and give the man a talking-to.

They continued discussing the big capture, speculating where the others in the group had gone.

"I hear they were heading closer to Homestead." Tate set his beer on the table.

Flash shook his head. "My source says they're probably heading to Arcadia."

Garrick raised his hands in the motion for stop. "I just came from seeing Wyatt. He thinks they mentioned the Okeechobee area."

"Hell." Striker took a big swig of his beer. "They coulda stayed close by and moved to a different part of Whitehall's place."

"Or somewhere on ours." Brick lifted his index finger. "Or the McClure's place."

Jack whipped his gaze to Striker. "Tomorrow, we cover every inch of the ranch and the property next door."

Brick glanced at the jukebox. "What do you want to hear next, Dani?"

Jack studied their interaction. If he didn't want Dani for

himself, Brick would be waiting in the wings. The woman had a spell on their cowboy.

"Play me one of Toby Keith's." Dani reached for a tortilla chip from the basket on the table.

They'd chosen the Lone Star to celebrate since Sunday evening was typically one of the quieter times of the week. But people streamed through the entrance like they were giving beer away for free.

"What's that crowd over there?" Jack asked the server when she returned with more drinks.

"Oh, a big family birthday party. That's Judy, who owns the craft shop." The server tipped her chin toward the growing crowd.

"I thought Sara-Lynn owned it," Ellie said.

"No," the server continued. "She runs it. Judy's her mother, and as you can see ... it's a big family. Occasionally, she throws one of these shin digs for her birthday and invites all her kin. But y'all have had dibs on the jukebox because Dani's the lady of the hour."

"She sure is." Jack reached under the table and squeezed Dani's hand.

"It's fixin' to get loud in here now. They have a DJ, and the dance music is about to start." The server took their food order and left.

"Dani, I'll bet you're relieved that low life is in jail," Brick said. "You must've been pretty shaken up."

"You can say that again." Dani shuddered.

OD had nearly overdosed on the valerian tea, but they'd brought him around. After a night in the hospital, he was now in custody. Jack ought to feel peaceful but couldn't shake the odd discomfort nagging him. Probably just nervous about later on. He had big plans for this evening.

Dani swallowed hard. Shaken was one word for it. She still felt raw, composed on the outside, but rattled to her core inside. Drinking a daiquiri at Pete's with the group was just the kind of fun she loved, but part of her wanted to curl up in her bed and listen to calming music while petting Lucky. Or even better, sit with Wyatt and hold his hand. Make sure he was okay. He'd gotten hurt on her account.

"Try this guacamole. It's really fresh." Ellie's voice broke through her thoughts.

"Thanks." But for once, she had no appetite. She simply wasn't herself yet.

"With OD in custody, you'll feel safer working at Wren's," her sister continued. "And you'll be one busy lady with the new horses arriving and Jack's expansion."

"By the way, El, about that." She started speaking, but it was no use trying to have a serious conversation above the music. At some point, she needed to bring up the topic of leaving again. She was going to Jessica's in less than a month. After the ordeal yesterday, it felt like a safe place to land, and her friend was excited to have her returning.

Tonight, she'd discuss it with Jack. She couldn't postpone the unpleasant talk any longer. It made her heart ache to think about leaving him, but they'd never discussed the future. He'd never said he loved her, that he wanted her to stay and make a life with him.

Once or twice she'd overheard him say something about never getting married again, and Luke used to call him Good Time Jack. This had been a good time. She'd been his good time, and she'd enjoyed it too. It's not that she was complaining, but didn't she deserve something more? A bigger life with someone who loved her?

A long-distance relationship wouldn't work because Jack's life was on the ranch. Perhaps he could visit her when he drove to Ocala for horses. Jacksonville wasn't that much farther. And she'd come back to the ranch for holidays. If she left on good terms, it wouldn't make things weird the way a bad break-up might.

"Where do you want these plates of nachos?" The server was back.

"Did we order those?" Ellie asked.

"That big group sent them over. Enjoy. I think it's a peace offering because of the loud music."

"I don't mind music," Dani said, "but it is getting loud." She wrung her hands, ready to leave. To have a little peace. Maybe she and Jack could get their orders to go.

Jack drew down his brows. What was wrong with Dani? This gathering was her kind of thing, but she didn't look happy. She'd seemed okay earlier. Maybe they should've gone home like she'd suggested after buying the cell phone. She'd been through a lot and was worried about Wyatt. His chest warmed. Dani was like a mother hen with that kid and caring behavior looked good on her.

"Who's up for darts before dinner?" Luke asked.

"I'm in," Garrick replied.

"Me too," Bud said.

Jack looked at his father, astounded. "You sure?"

"I'm feeling lucky. Gotta throw darts with my boys. Ready for me to stomp you?" Bud grinned.

His father actually grinned. If Jack hadn't seen it with his own eyes, he wouldn't have believed it.

Now he was torn. Dani was too quiet. Something was off, but this was the first opportunity in years to do something fun with his father. And he and Luke were getting along. "I'll toss a few."

The edge of Luke's mouth tugged up. "Okay, bro."

Jack leaned toward Dani. "I'll be back in fifteen minutes."

A short time later, Bud stood before the target, holding onto his cane and aiming with the other hand. The pointed tip of the dart lodged in the center of the bullseye. "Eat my dust, suckers." The wrinkles around his eyes crinkled upward.

Jack exchanged a glance with Luke. This was the first time, since the stroke, they'd had their dad in public. "He's almost like his old self."

"Maybe a better version." Luke gave Jack a wry smile. "Bud 2.0."

Garrick took his turn and sealed his win.

Jack was following the other three men back to the table when a woman intercepted him. A hot woman, standing tall and proud in knee-high boots and a top that left nothing to the imagination. "Serena?"

"Hey, Jack. How about that—running into you here?"

"What are you doing in Pine Crossing?"

"It's my grandmother's birthday." Serena grabbed his hand. "Dance with me, Jack."

He glanced at the table where the other men were taking their seats, and he longed to join them. To get back to Dani. But this was the woman who'd come through with help for his dad. "I need to—"

"One dance. C'mon. Didn't I make a special effort to find you someone perfect for your father?"

"You did." He didn't see a tactful way out between Serena tugging his hand and the other couples coming onto the dance floor. One dance. That was it. He did kind of owe her. And he didn't want to make a scene and embarrass her. Bud was doing better, but if Hetta quit, he might need Serena's help again. He held Serena's hand and twirled her on the dance floor.

Dani was ready for another daiquiri. She leaned toward her sister. "Do you see the waitress? I'd like—"

"Who's she?" Ellie asked, sounding irked.

"Who's who?" asked Dani.

"I don't know," Luke said from the other side of Ellie.

"She's hot," Brick said from across the table.

"Kinda young," Garrick added.

The chair beside Dani was still empty. "Where's Jack?" she asked no one in particular. Why was he the only one who hadn't returned from playing darts?

"Uh ..." Brick said, "he's—"

"He's dancing," Ellie bit out. "Why is he dancing? With her? It seems like Jack knows her."

"I've got no idea." Luke's tone had taken that familiar edge he used with Jack.

Dani shrank into her chair, her stomach gathering in knots, the kind of knots she was well acquainted with. The type of sick she'd felt when she'd been dating Parker and had caught him in lie after lie. *This is what happens when you date someone sighted. What did you expect?*

Not this. Not Jack out there with another woman in front of his family and everyone who lived at the ranch. Unless. Unless she'd mistaken their entire relationship. Unless he hadn't been honest after all, and she was a stupid fool like she'd been before. It shouldn't matter. She was planning to leave next month. But it hurt. *He's dancing with someone else.*

Jack had left her at the table and, without even saying a word to her, had chosen some pretty sighted woman for a dance partner.

Memories of Parker flooded her mind.

She would not be made a fool of again. Jack couldn't play around and treat her like a back-burner booty call.

Jack glanced over at the table and locked eyes with Ellie. She seemed furious. Luke sat beside her with a puzzled frown, his gaze hard.

He shrugged slightly. Later he'd explain. He wasn't disrespecting Dani. And Serena did know how to dance. The old Jack would've eaten this up and segued into a more exciting evening from here.

He had a different kind of nice evening in mind, back at Dani's cottage. A private celebration. After the events yesterday, he'd found clarity. Back at the house, he had flowers. They'd been delivered earlier. And a box with a ring was stuffed in his pocket.

———

Dani sat tall, filled with resolve. There'd be no waiting around for Jack to dump her. Or lie to her like Parker. No. She had more backbone now. She had options. She was in touch with her inner strength. She wasn't some frail blind girl waiting for a crumb.

Jack couldn't play this game with her.

"Brick, honey." Dani pulled her shoulders back and forced confidence into her tone. "Can you give me a lift?"

"You want a ride?"

"Yes. I need to go home. I have a headache starting. And this music ...."

"Now? I'm sure Jack will be back in a minute."

"No! Now. I have to go now."

"Dani, wait." Ellie placed a hand on her arm. "I'll take you."

"No."

Ellie had been right and might lecture her. Ellie would be disappointed that she was going to Jessica's. She couldn't deal with her sister's hurt feelings right now. This was her life. She needed to be alone. "Please let go. I'll text you later. I have to do this."

The number seemed to go on forever. When the song finally ended, Jack unglued himself from the young woman before him. "I'll be getting back to my group." He tipped his hat and strode toward the lot of them. "Where's Dani?"

"She left." Luke's gaze was lethal.

"Left?" He scowled, ignoring Ellie's venomous glare. "How?"

"Brick took her," Luke bit out.

Brick's chair was empty.

"Why? Is she okay?"

Luke narrowed his eyes. "No dummy. She said she had a headache, but I didn't buy that excuse. It's something else." A muscle in Luke's jaw ticked.

Everything inside him tightened. Dani had left with Brick. He stared ahead. Instead of seeing the room, all he saw was devastation—the ashes of his life if Dani wasn't in it. Why hadn't he been more tuned in to her needs? "I've gotta go."

Luke's gaze softened a degree. "I'll cover you. Go on."

He flew out of there and sped toward the ranch, bile climbing in his throat. Was this about him dancing with Serena? How would Dani even know? Guilt tightened his chest. Someone must've told her. *Dammit.* He would've told her himself.

Dani had barely gotten inside when Thea knocked.

"You hoo. Dani. I saw you come back. Why are you home so early?" Thea's soft steps approached.

"I'm leaving." Lucky nosed her leg as she stood at the end of her bed opening her large suitcase.

"Why?" Thea asked.

This was no time to sit and have a chat. She yanked her clothes out of the closet.

"What's wrong, Dani? Why are you packing? You weren't leaving for another month. Things were good with you and Jack. I was hoping you wouldn't go."

Her lips trembled, and she sucked in air, trying to maintain her composure. The entire incident at Pete's had been so triggering. "It's time I leave." She was independent. Taking a stand for herself and the life she wanted. And if she couldn't have it here, well, why wait around?

"If this is because of yesterday or because you don't want to work at Wren's, we'll figure something out. She's getting a security system. I thought working would make you happy."

"It's not that. It's just time." Her eyes burned, but she would not break down.

"You were in such a good mood when you left."

"Is Wyatt up?" she asked.

"Yes."

"Can you please ask him to come over? I want to say goodbye." Her stomach clenched, and a nearly unbearable ache formed in her chest. Wyatt. She loved him too.

"You're leaving right now?" Thea asked.

"As soon as I get packed."

"How?"

"I'll ask Brick to take me to the bus station in Heron Park."

"I think he went back to the Lone Star."

Dani folded her arms against her stomach. "I'll call for a ride-share."

"You can try, but it's difficult to find someone to come way out here."

"Maybe Wyatt can take me."

"Wyatt had a concussion. He can't drive yet."

"Avery will take me," she choked out. "I just want to be gone before Jack comes back." A wave of helplessness washed through her before she shored herself up. "I'm finding a way to leave. Now if you'll excuse me—" And then she couldn't hold it together any longer. Tears streamed down her cheeks. She grabbed one of the small handkerchiefs from the pile of clothes on the bed and blotted her face. Then cried harder. Jack had bought her the embroidered handkerchief.

"Did Jack—hurt you?"

"Yes." She dropped to the side of the bed and wiped her face.

"How?" Thea sounded alarmed.

She shook with despair. Memories of Mark and Parker, and now Jack. "He was dancing with some other woman. He's a liar like Parker. He says he wants me, then he's out there with some sighted girl. He's ... he ... he doesn't love me. I'm not who he wants. I can't be that."

"Why? Because you're blind? Do you need to be so dug into the belief that he can't love you because he's sighted and you're not?"

She wiped tears from her cheeks. "That's how it's always gone."

Thea encircled her in her arms and stroked her hair. "Honey, you know the past doesn't have to determine the future. You and Jack are different. Every relationship is unique."

Dani inhaled a shuddering breath.

"There, there. I know you've had a rough time. But I happen to know Jack's worked very hard on becoming a different man over the past year, and you've been instrumental in that."

"I have?" she sniffed.

"Yes. You showed him a person can be both vulnerable and strong."

"I'm strong?"

"Stronger than you know. It takes true strength to be vulnerable and power into life anyway. You hold it all—love and sorrow, vulnerability and strength."

She breathed a little easier. "That's nice to hear. But Jack hasn't said he loves me. He's ... I should've never gotten involved with him. I'm going to Jessica's. She wants me. I told her I'm coming. I can make a life there."

"Jessica can find another roommate. You can make a life here." Thea kissed the top of Dani's head. "The person you shouldn't let down is you. Remember when I talked about the Jell-O-mold? You have some control here. I think now's a good time to be clear on what you really want and take steps to make that happen. Why not tell Jack what you're thinking? What've you got to lose?"

Her pride? What was left of her heart after what she'd been through with Parker and Mark? Dani chewed her lip. "Can you send Wyatt and Avery over?"

"If you're sure that's what you want." Disappointment softened Thea's tone.

"I'm sorry, Thea. I appreciate everything you've done for me. I love you."

"I love you too, honey."

A moment later, the door clicked. She was alone.

The tears started up again.

Dani palmed them off of her face, then stuffed her cosmetics into her smaller suitcase and gathered her composure. She needed to appear strong for Wyatt and Avery.

Traffic ahead of Jack slowed. The truck turned off and, shit! A large, slow-moving tractor had pulled onto the roadway ahead of him.

Jack steered to the right. Big ditch. Figures.

He pulled to the center to pass—but what?

Traffic on the other side had stopped.

He drummed his fingers.

What was the issue?

Oh, hell. It was one of those turtles, no. Make that two. Two turtles were taking their sweet time crawling across the road.

He banged his fist on the steering wheel and crept along behind the tractor.

Dani sat in the passenger seat clutching her hands together so hard her fingers hurt, refusing to break down in front of Avery and Wyatt. She had to go. Didn't she?

"I think I might be getting carsick," Wyatt said from the backseat of Avery's vehicle.

"You'd better not. I told you not to come," Avery said, growling.

"I had to make sure Dani got off safely," Wyatt barely croaked out.

"Like you can protect her? I'd be protecting the both of you." Avery released a huge sigh. "Oh. No. The traffic ahead is stopped."

The car rolled to a standstill.

"Thank you," Wyatt said.

"I didn't stop for you. I think there's a turtle ahead. I'll go move it." Avery's door slammed.

They were stopped.

In the middle of the road.

It would be difficult to make it to the bus station on time. Was the universe nudging her? What did she really want? She loved Jack. Loved him differently, deeper than she'd ever loved Parker or Mark. Loved him so much it scared her. Did he, could he, love her?

She could imagine life on the ranch. A life with Jack and the horses, having Lita out to visit and selling herbs. Helping the locals with their aches and ailments. Would that be enough? Could she make a life being stuck way out on the ranch? She didn't want to be a burden asking others for rides all the time. And bumming rides from whoever was going to town didn't work because it was impossible to plan anything that way.

Did she have the courage to reveal her feelings to Jack? To explain her fears? Wasn't opening her heart worth the risk? If life were like a Jell-O-mold, then she'd choose the shape of Jack. The shape of the horses. Of Pine Crossing.

Avery climbed back in the car.

"Did you save the turtle?" Wyatt asked.

"Somebody else is carrying him across the road." Avery revved the engine. "We need to get going or you'll miss your bus."

Go slow to go fast. One of Dr. Dave's cryptic Jedi phrases played in Jack's head. He willed himself calm and slowed to create space between himself and the tractor. As soon as there was room, and the roadside ditch became shallower, he steered into the weeds on the side of the road and hauled ass around the tractor. Thank you, Dr. Dave.

He floored it to the ranch and pulled right in front of Dani's cottage. Jack stormed to the door and had his hand on the knob when he paused. Was Brick in there? Nah. His truck wasn't even here. He opened the door. "Dani. I'm here."

The cottage was empty. Lucky was gone. So was her stuff.

He stepped outside and found Thea. "Where is she?"

"Heading to the bus station. In Heron Park. Avery's driving her."

Jack peeled away from the ranch and sped down the road toward town. Traffic was moving again, and with luck, he'd get to the bus station before Dani boarded.

He approached the traffic light in Pine Crossing. When the pickup in front of him turned right, his heart jumped to his throat. The car ahead of him was Avery's.

He laid on the horn.

Avery's vehicle turned into the grocery store parking lot.

Jack leaped from his truck and ran to the car's passenger side.

Avery opened the driver's side and stood facing him. "What do you want? We're late for the bus."

He leaned on the roof of the car. Dani was right below him. So close. "If you're late, why'd you stop?"

Avery looked away, and a hint of a smile tugged at her mouth. She opened the door to the back seat. "Come on sick-o. We need to give them some space."

Wyatt climbed out. "Hey, Jack."

He dipped his chin. "Wyatt."

"Let's go." Avery grabbed Wyatt's arm and pulled him toward the store.

Wyatt glanced back, his face a bruised mess, but he still managed to narrow his good eye, and point at Jack.

Seriously?

Jack climbed into the back seat behind Dani, beside her large dog. "What the hell is going on?" Hearing himself, he gentled his tone. "Why did you leave Pete's? Why did you take all your stuff?"

"Why are you here, Jack? I have a bus to catch."

He scoffed. "No." Was she serious? "Stay. I thought we have something good." Jack leaned forward, his heart aching. He'd never expected to feel love like this again.

"Part of me wants to stay. But it was always going to end," she said flatly.

"Does it have to?" He traced a finger up the side of her arm. She didn't flinch.

"Why wouldn't it?"

"Because ... because dammit." He was quiet for a moment. The language of emotions was still new to him. "I'm bad at this. I should've said something sooner. I want you to stay because you light up my day more than the sun. I love how the horses sense your gentleness and walk right over to you. How you can listen with your heart and make people just the right cream or tea to help them feel better." He leaned closer. "You always notice things I don't even hear, all the different birds, the wind in the trees. You taught me how to listen to the rain. And just when I think you're the sweetest person I know, you say something snarky and make me laugh. My life is better with you. I'm better with you. I want you to stay. I love you."

"You ... love me?"

"Yes. Can we get out of the car, so I don't have to keep talking to the back of your seat?"

Dani stepped out of the car.

He climbed out and pulled her into his arms.

She placed a hand on his chest, a tentative smile curving the corners of her lips. "You ... love me?"

Would she say it in return? He hadn't said those words to a woman in a long time. "More than anything."

Dani began sniffling. Her chin trembled.

"What? This is what happens when I say I love you?"

"Parker said he loved me too. And he hurt me. It was awful. And, this sounds stupid, but you were dancing with someone...."

He cupped her face in his hands and kissed her forehead, her cheeks, the tip of her nose. "I was being polite. That's the woman who sent Hetta to help with my dad. It was a bone-headed move. I should've turned her down. Or come back to the table and let you know. I'm not Parker." He ripped open the snaps on his shirt and brought her fingers to his chest. "Feel this. Where I had the bandage. I'd planned to show you when it was completely healed."

He traced her finger over the scabbed outline of a heart on his skin. "It's where you branded me."

A look of confusion came over her face. "I don't understand."

"When we were at the river and I helped you trace a heart on my skin. Then we stopped in at that antique store where you got handkerchiefs. I found a little heart-shaped branding iron. A souvenir. I was planning to give it to you tonight."

"I can't believe you did this." She skimmed her fingertips over the healing area on his skin.

He laid his hand over hers, then brought her fingers to his lips and kissed them. "You'll be able to read my love for you on my chest, like Braille. And...." He pulled the box from his pocket and placed the ring in her hand. "This is for you. An engagement ring. If you'll accept it. Because I am yours, woman. Branded. Now and forever. Marry me, Dani. Wear the ring. Marry me and stay on the ranch. I promise I'll make you happy. I love you." His breath stuck in his throat, and he searched her face, impatient for the answer.

Dani bit her lip. "I love you, Jack. I do. I have for a long time."

Joy expanded his chest. He tipped her face up and dropped his lips to hers, kissing her there in the parking lot, long and slow, letting the traffic sounds fade away. "Is that a yes?"

Her forehead drew together. "I want to stay. I really do. But I can't even go into town on my own. It takes more than love to make a marriage. I can't exercise. The Y is all the way in Heron Park. And I can't get to town to visit friends. I love you. But I need to be able to have a life too."

"You'll have your life. We'll make a schedule and get you into town wherever you want. I'll hire you a chauffeur if that's what it takes. I have the money. I can take care of you. And what if you could exercise on the ranch?"

She huffed. "How?"

"Tomorrow, they're starting construction on an Olympic-sized swimming pool." He rubbed his neck, frustrated. "I was going to tell you tonight. It was a surprise."

"You're putting in a pool?"

"*We're* putting in a pool. For you and everyone else who wants to swim. Set back between Thea's cottage and the house."

"But ... that's where your new horse barn is going."

"Not anymore. You're more important than the new horses. I'll find another spot for the barn. What matters is that we both have what we need. And number one, I need you. I've never said those words to another person before. You make me a better man. Say you'll stay. Say yes."

"You do know how to lay out a sweet deal, Mr. Stone."

"Are you saying you'll only stay because I'm giving you a swimming pool?"

"No. But it doesn't hurt." She chuckled, more like her usual teasing self. "Yes, Jack, I'll stay and marry you."

"Good. Let's do it soon. How about you move up to my house? Or I'll pay Brick extra to stay with my dad, and I'll move into the cottage with you. Or hell, I'll move Bud into the bunkhouse. I want to spend every night with my wife. You. I want you, cupcake. You're what makes my life sweet."

*T*en weeks later...

Dani leaned her head back and kicked her feet, drifting across the water in the mesh pool chair. It was her favorite pool float, the one with a place for her drink. This was absolute bliss, especially after a day brushing horses, helping Thea in the garden, and topping it off with a hard workout using the aquatic dumbbells. Her arms felt like wet noodles.

The gate to the pool area opened and shut.

"Think fast!" Wyatt called out before a huge splash covered her with water. A moment later, he came up behind her and held onto her chair, rocking her, and laughing mischievously.

"Dang it. Wyatt. Stop. I almost spilled my drink." She couldn't help chuckling. "Don't think I can't get even with you."

"Sorry." Nothing in his tone said he was sorry.

"No, you're not."

Wyatt scoffed.

The gate opened and shut again.

"I guess they'll let anyone swim in this pool," Avery said.

"Yeah. Look who just walked in," Wyatt tossed back.

"Hey there, Avery." Dani kicked her feet toward her niece's voice.

"And Emma." Emma's voice was so tentative, so sweet.

"Dani," Ellie called over. "Luke just texted. They want us inside for the meeting."

"I thought it was just the guys." Dani stroked across the water until she bumped against the rail at the steps.

"He says we were supposed to be there too."

"But I don't have time to get ready. My hair. I need lipstick." She held the rail and climbed the steps, nearly running into a fluffy towel.

"Here. You look fine. And I brought you a pretty cover-up. We need to go right away. The attorney is there, but he needs to leave soon," Ellie explained.

"Attorney?" Her brows drew together.

"What?" Wyatt asked, alarmed. "Why the lawyer? Is—"

"This has nothing to do with you," Ellie answered Wyatt.

Wyatt had been in town to speak with a detective several times. As part of a deal, he was now on call in case they needed him to assist with their ongoing investigation. They were working with the FBI and DEA to find and identify the criminals involved in the crime ring. At least OD was behind bars.

"He wants to talk to us," Ellie said softly.

"But why?" She'd been questioned up one side and down the other. There was nothing more to say, and they'd said she wasn't in trouble. She had been the victim and had acted in self-defense. But it put her on edge. Why did she need a lawyer?

Dani toweled off and slipped into the soft dress her sister had brought, then held Ellie's arm as they walked over to the main ranch house.

"Have you decided on a venue for the wedding yet?" asked Ellie. "Because if we're using the pole barn again, it'll take some work to clean it up."

"No. We settled on having the ceremony at the little church in Pine Crossing and the reception at Lone Star Pete's."

"You can do that? What about Wyatt and Avery and them?"

"Pete said he'd close for the afternoon and drinks are on the house. That's our wedding gift. But I strongly suspect he worked out some kind of deal. They were talking about Pete getting a side of beef."

"Sounds like Jack to figure out a workaround."

"Garrick thought of it. He's good at coming up with out of the box ideas." They climbed the steps to the ranch house where she'd be living until they figured out how to make all this work. In some ways, it'd be a relief to move in with Jack and his dad and brother, even though it would be crowded.

Bud sat tall, at the head of the table, like a king holding court. Beside him, Hiram Goldsmith, the attorney, shuffled through a file of paperwork. Jack exchanged a glance with Garrick, then Luke, who shrugged. When their dad asked for a meeting with the attorney, they hadn't expected it to include Striker, the only non-family member present.

The door opened, and Jack sprung from his chair to greet Dani and walk her to her seat.

"What's going on?" Dani whispered.

"The attorney wants to go over some paperwork." He kissed the side of her head. She smelled like the pool and shampoo. "You got a little pink on your nose."

She touched her face. "Should I be nervous?"

"Nah." Jack pulled up a chair for Dani, and an empty one beside it for Ellie.

Striker shifted his gaze around the room, looking uncomfortable.

Once everyone was seated, Hiram cleared his throat.

Jack drummed his fingers on his thigh.

Bud's eyes crinkled as he offered Striker a lopsided grin.

Jack fought back the sense of surrealism and reached under the table for Dani's hand. When he rubbed the ring she'd been wearing for the past ten weeks, the corner of her mouth curled up. If he'd had it his way, they'd have been married at the courthouse in Heron Park two months ago. But she wanted a traditional event, and that's what they were doing.

He wanted Dani happy. Plans had recently been finalized to build an additional barn and turn the miniature horses into a certified equine therapy program. He and Dani had enrolled in online training, and she was in touch with the regional center for the blind to organize their first clients.

Hiram began talking, "Your father is divesting and dividing his shares among you brothers. Bringing your shares even. With the provision, he continues to occupy the position of management advisor. And there's a right of survivorship on the property, so he'll always have a home here."

Jack met Garrick's gaze and nodded.

"You didn't need to put that in writing, Dad." Luke sounded affronted. "You'll always have a home with me."

"What about Maryann?" Jack asked. His sister wasn't here, but she'd always been a part of the ranch before she'd married.

"That's a different financial arrangement. And Luke," Hiram continued, "you're not getting any additional shares. But the others ...."

Hiram pushed papers across the table.

"Hold up." Jack's brows drew together. "This brings me to thirty. The math is wrong. You're keeping ten, Dad?"

"No," Bud said.

"Last time I checked three times thirty is ninety." Jack shook his head. This made no sense.

"Striker Powell is granted the remaining ten shares along

with a substantial raise, increased entitlements, and an indefinite contract." Hiram slid a document toward the foreman.

Striker's eyes rounded.

Luke gaped.

Garrick stood and paced.

"What?" Jack swung his gaze from his Dad to Striker, hardly able to contain his shock.

Dani laid a hand on his arm. "It's okay, Jack."

Bud spoke, "You need to know Striker's—"

"Don't tell me Striker's—" Jack shifted away from Dani, too upset to accept her comfort. If this was related to another one of his dad's affairs ....

"No." Bud waved his hand. "He's not related to you. But his father ...." A shadow crossed Bud's face.

"You knew my dad?" Striker studied Bud with open curiosity.

"I did. From the rodeo. He was a damn good bullfighter. I owe him. He mighta saved my life. That ...." Bud's face screwed up like he might be losing control.

"Was that the night of the ...?" Striker stared out the window, his gaze unfocused like he was remembering something.

"Would someone explain what in hell is going on?" Garrick stood away from the group, hands jammed in his pockets.

"Striker's father, God rest his soul, was hurt on account of me," Bud said glumly. "Ended his career. I heard, well ... he never fully recovered. I broke a few ribs. His injuries were more severe."

Striker huffed. "You're ...."

"It was me." Bud nodded. "I lost touch, got busy." Bud glanced at Luke. "I swore I'd make it up to him somehow. When I found out you were the foreman here ...." Bud slumped back, exhausted from the conversation. "Now you own a share of the ranch. Too little, too late, but it's something."

"And this paperwork is for Dani." Hiram took control of the meeting. "Ellie, I understand you signed a prenup when you married Luke."

Ellie leaned forward. "Well, yes, but it was—"

"Legitimate, as far as I can tell," Hiram continued. "And Bud wants to make sure Dani is taken care of, so I've had this agreement drawn up."

"No." Dani frowned, folding her arms across her stomach and leaning back.

"Seriously?" Jack asked.

"I don't need some piece of paper," Dani said.

"Let me look at it." Ellie and Luke read it over.

After a long moment, Ellie leaned toward her sister. "Dani, you have nothing to lose. This guarantees you money if the marriage ends for any reason. You're taken care of. This guarantees it. I don't see a downside."

"Just take it, Dani," Jack whispered. "My dad and I talked. We want you to have it. He can afford it."

"But that's if we divorce, right? Isn't that betting against our marriage?" Dani asked.

"It's a substantial sum," Hiram replied. "And since Ellie was provided for, Bud wanted to do the same."

"Sign it." Jack squeezed her hand. "But you'll never need it if I have anything to say about it. Because I'm in this forever." He leaned forward and kissed her right there, in front of everyone.

"Aw," Ellie said.

Jack grinned at Ellie.

The corner of Luke's mouth edged up, and he nodded.

Jack dipped his chin in return. They might not be as close as some, but they were brothers. It was better than it had been. He'd take it.

They handled all the paperwork and stood. "Welcome to the family business." Luke shook Striker's hand and glanced at Jack.

He was expected to shake, but he paused. He wasn't convinced Bud hadn't had an affair with Striker's mother.

Garrick stepped forward and shook Striker's hand. "Welcome to the business." Then he checked his phone. "Gotta go. See you later." Garrick was consistent. You had to give him that.

Jack met Striker's gaze and then looked away. Dani nudged him.

He nudged her back. He would've gotten around to it on his own. "Congratulations Strike. Looks like we'll be continuing to work together when your contract runs out."

"Guess so." Striker shook his hand and exited, saying something about Brick.

Luke was across the room talking to the attorney. It was time to leave.

"Jack." Bud approached, leaning on his cane. "Can I have a word with you?"

Jack laced his fingers through Dani's. "Whatever you have to say, you can tell me in front of Dani."

"Alright." Bud's brow furrowed. He looked Jack squarely in the eyes but spoke haltingly, "Son. I'm sorry how things went down."

"With Striker?"

"No. When you were a kid. I know...Well, I could've done it better."

Jack's chest tightened and tension crept into his face. "It?" He released Dani's hand and folded his arms across his chest.

"I was shocked," Bud continued. "I felt guilty. The whole thing with your mom, and Luke being injured, being...abused." That last part was almost a whisper. "I always loved you son. But you were strong." Bud huffed. "You were born tough. I knew you'd be okay. Luke was broken. He needed me. But that didn't mean I didn't love my firstborn son. I always loved you. Admired your grit."

Tears pricked at the corners of Jack's eyes. He blinked hard.

The edge of Bud's mouth curved into a small smile. "That's why I wanted you to be the one to help me. To make things..." Bud turned up a palm as if searching for the words. "to connect with you. But you kept hiring all those women to help."

Jack gaped. "You fired all them women because you wanted me to take care of you?"

"Nah. Maybe." Bud chuckled. "I'm proud of you, son. You deserve to manage the Tall Pines. I love you."

Something in Jack's chest broke open.

Bud raised his arm, love and hope shining in his eyes.

Jack stepped forward and gave his dad a hug. "I love you too, Dad."

Luke strolled over from across the room. "Dad, Hiram wants to talk to you before he leaves."

"Alright." Bud straightened, then addressed the two brothers. "You boys are gonna be okay." He ran a gnarled hand through his thin hair. "Now we need to work on Garrick. I'm worried about him."

Hiram approached. "I just received a message on the matter you asked me to look into."

Jack and Luke both swung their gazes to the attorney. "What matter?" they asked almost simultaneously.

"Go ahead." Bud dipped his chin.

"Your father asked me to check into McClure's property." Hiram said.

"You've been working on this without telling us?" Jack asked.

"Your old man still has a trick or two up his sleeve." Bud grinned.

Jack perked up. "More acreage would be great. We could tear down that old house and barn. Use that land—"

"Are you still interested in purchasing the property? I think we've located the owner," Hiram said.

"Good." Bud leaned both hands on his cane. He was getting tired.

"No." Hiram's brows drew down. "The owner is an old woman living outside Chattanooga. And she isn't interested in your offer."

"Why?" Bud asked.

"It's steady income, and the value is appreciating." Hiram shrugged as though it was obvious.

Bud's forehead wrinkled. "There must be some way to convince her. If the price is right."

Hiram shook his head. "The management company didn't think so."

"You hoo." Thea had let herself in.

"I need to leave. We can talk on the phone." Hiram gathered his things and left.

"Jack," Bud said. "Thea's bringing me dinner. She insists we watch another one of those awful nature programs. So, you and Dani ...." Bud grumbled, but his face radiated happiness.

"Right. Good. Later, Dad."

"Jack," Dani said. "I want to go home, change clothes, and feed the kitty."

He huffed. He'd broken down and gotten her the kitten— the soft, tiger-striped monster with needle-sharp claws and a V6 motor in his chest. For the first time in his life, he owned a cat that lived indoors, of all things.

Jack took Dani's hand and led her down the path toward her cottage. Well, his cottage, too. He pretty much had a foot in both houses now, and so did Dani. His bride-to-be. He pulled her closer and kissed her there, in the shade of the oak tree.

In the distance, Wyatt and the girls were laughing in the pool. Warmth washed through him. This was good. Nothing like he'd thought his life would turn out.

Maybe better.

Keep Reading for a peek at the next book

Born Brave: Garrick

Garrick Stone stared in the direction the trauma team had taken his patient. Double doors closed behind the gurney. Beeping and murmuring voices, the usual late-night hospital sounds, faded into the background as he fought back the images escaping the vault inside him. He finished typing his report and wrapped up his conversation with Janie, the ER nurse.

"I hope that's it for tonight," Janie said, drawing down her brows. "You look how I feel." Despite being busy and hardened, as you had to be to survive in this environment, she noticed the details and showed empathy. She was good people.

"Yeah." He huffed. In the months he'd worked for the Pine Crossing Fire and Rescue District, he'd witnessed a lot—and years working as a combat medic should have prepared him. He'd seen worse. But tonight, it got to him. Tonight, it was a young girl. "Call when you know something?"

"Seriously?"

"If you don't mind." Following up on the sick and injured people he'd transported to Heron Park Mercy wasn't part of the job. Unless he caught the gossip at the feed store or diner, he never even knew if his efforts had paid off.

"Okay." She shrugged. "But it might be a while."

"Thanks." The automatic doors of the emergency room

entrance whooshed as he strode through them and over to his rig. His driver, the EMT, had their rescue cleaned and was restocking the cervical collar.

"You ready to heat up the bricks?" Levi drawled.

The corner of his mouth lifted at another one of Levi's odd expressions. "All set." They climbed in, and Levi started it up.

He squeezed his forehead between his thumb and fingers, relieving the tension.

It's not your emergency. It's not your emergency.

His chief had told him to remember that when he'd taken the job. It was true. What might be the absolute worst day for that family wasn't his emergency. But he'd seen a kid like that before, back in Afghanistan.

And he'd seen her again. Last night, in his dream.

A wave of guilt and regret pressed on his chest, and he brought his attention to the city lights giving way to dark landscape outside the window. Long ago, he'd learned to compartmentalize. There were more vaults and catacombs inside him than under Rome and Paris put together. But lately, the hinges on those doors seemed rusty, and memories were slipping out, affecting him more than usual.

Like other veterans, he'd been offered various services when he'd separated from the Army. And like most guys he knew, he'd barely taken advantage of them. He didn't need to talk. He was good. Tough. And he'd wanted to get back to real life. Normal. What was that, exactly? If normal was a place, he couldn't find it if you handed him a map.

It might be time to go back to that group at the Vet Center.

"Did you get a chance to talk to Janie?" Levi asked.

"Not much."

"But you talked to her. How'd she look? Did she ask about me?"

He snorted. Levi had it bad. "She was busy." What was this,

grade school? He wouldn't play middleman for Levi and Janie. If Levi wanted to go out with the woman, he'd have to figure it out.

"Did you see Kelsey?" Levi asked.

"I didn't notice."

Levi gave him a skeptical glance.

Kelsey, an ER tech, was Janie's friend, and Levi had it in his head that they should all four go out. They'd run into Janie and Kelsey when they'd stopped for a beer at Turner's Tap, and Levi had fallen hard and fast.

He didn't have that problem.

A quick scan of the ER had revealed no sign of Kelsey, and Garrick had breathed a little easier. After breaking his rule and going out with Kelsey a second time, he'd decided to make a list. Rule number one. Only date tourists. Rule number two. Don't forget rule number one.

Levi continued, "I was thinkin' we'd go to Pete's and dance. Janie likes to dance."

"You're on your own. Things are good the way they are. I'd rather go to Turner's. Less complicated."

True, he'd been agitated lately, not because he needed a woman—something else was happening. When he'd earned his paramedic certification and taken the job offering high-stakes work with a solid team, a legitimate way to help, he'd figured that would do the trick. The job should be a perfect fit. What was wrong with him?

Darkness blanketed the road as their rescue headed toward the independent volunteer fire station in the small town of Pine Crossing, about an hour in from the SW Florida coast. They pulled into the firehouse and unloaded their gear.

Zeke, the fire chief, appeared in the doorway. "I got a call from the ER. Janie wanted me to tell you the girl's still critical but holding on. Same with the mom. And the adult male will be released soon."

"That's what I'm talking about." Levi fist-bumped Zeke. "I need me some coffee." He headed into the lounge.

"Good to hear." Garrick turned away. It'd been a miracle the girl had made it to the ER alive. She'd lost so much blood, and he'd only been able to give her isotonic IV fluid. There was likely internal bleeding, and her spleen was probably involved. Her small arms and face were cut up from glass and metal. The woman was worse, but she'd arrived in a different rig.

Dead on his feet after being up thirty-six hours, dealing with bad news would've been rough, but it was too soon to celebrate. Still, his shoulders relaxed, and he shut the door on the memory of the girl in that village, back in Kandahar.

"Are you staying?" Zeke nodded toward the bunk room.

It was supposed to be his day off, and ranch chores came early. He'd been playing poker when the call came in requesting additional support. As the paramedic on staff, Garrick had stepped up. It had been a bad wreck, and three other rigs had transported injured to Heron Park South.

An image of his own bed came to mind. "I'll stay if you need me."

Zeke waved a hand, dismissing him. "Cody and Walt will be here in a few hours. Levi and I will handle anything else that comes in." Molly, their female firefighter, often worked with Levi, but she was out sick.

The chief lived in the house behind the fire station, supposedly a perk of the job, but it meant Zeke was never entirely off duty. The firehouse had a crew of seven, with two paid staff members on-site at any given time. Others were officially on call, and the others off duty, but along with their fifty or so volunteers, wore pagers in case they were needed. Apps on their phones gave them more details when they got the page, but some of them lived in areas where cell service was spotty.

Zeke cocked his head. "Are you safe to drive? You look..."

He raised his palm. "I've been worse."

His friend nodded slowly. "Okay then." A few years older, Zeke was his friend and his boss and knew a bit about Garrick's time in the Army.

Garrick hit the john and splashed cold water on his face, then climbed into his Jeep. Before he put it in drive, his phone buzzed with a text.

Avery: *Garrick?*

Avery? Why would his nineteen-year-old niece be texting him at this hour? A lump formed in his throat as he wrote back. His dad had been recovering from a stroke but was almost back to normal—and now pushed himself too hard. But if anything would've happened, wouldn't he have heard the 911 call on the radio? And Zeke would've told him if he'd missed it.

Garrick: *Everything okay?*

He studied the screen, drumming his fingers on his thigh, waiting for the reply. The phone vibrated in his hand. Avery was calling.

"Garrick. Good," Avery slurred her words a little. "I figured you might still be up."

She didn't sound upset. Was she...had she been drinking?

"Where are you?" he demanded. "Are you okay?"

"I'm sleeping over at Emma's and ...well. We just got in from a party."

He ground his teeth. At three-thirty? There'd likely been alcohol there, but he had little room to talk. He'd raised hell when he'd been her age. "I might've been sleeping."

"And I wouldn't have called if you hadn't texted back."

"Fair enough. What's up?"

"Uncle Garrick," Avery's Georgia accent became more pronounced, and her voice filled with honey. "I need a favor." She always used that sweet tone to get what she wanted from his brothers or the other cowboys on the ranch. It wouldn't work on him.

"What?"

"I need you to feed Bambi and Snowy."

"Come again?"

"They still need bottles."

She wasn't seriously asking him to bottle-feed her baby goats. Was she? The first-time mama goat didn't have enough milk for her babies. He knew that, but until now, hadn't seen that intel as relevant.

"They still need to be fed four times a day, and well," Avery's tone lowered, "I shouldn't drive home because...."

"You went to a party and got wasted?"

"Not exactly wasted. But...please. I'll owe you. I fed them early last night. They need to be fed extra early this morning."

He snorted.

"Don't tell my dad or Jack. I promised I'd be responsible."

"I didn't say yes." The vision of his bed was breaking into pieces.

"Please. I'll make you cookies. Peanut butter-oatmeal."

He would've done it anyway, but he wouldn't turn down homemade cookies. "I'm not lying to my brothers for you." His half-brother, Luke, had adopted Avery when he'd married her mom. It still boggled his mind. And Avery called Luke "Dad". How strange was that?

Avery continued, "If you get the goats fed soon, they might never know."

"I'll handle it. And you shouldn't be out there drinking until all hours." He winced hearing himself, sounding so parental, feeling older than his thirty-nine years. But he'd seen the carnage resulting from those back-pasture parties.

"I'm tired, Uncle Gare. I need to get off now."

The call ended, and he stared at the phone. She was tired? He hadn't had eight hours of sleep in years.

He drove the dark seven-mile stretch to Tall Pines and pulled in front of the cottage he called home. Several months ago, his oldest brother married a woman who lived at the ranch. She'd moved in, and Garrick had moved out and taken her empty house.

It's the damnedest thing. When he returned from overseas, he hated staying at the house with his father and brother. Their bickering brought back all kinds of bad memories. Living with family again was strange enough, but settling in on a different ranch from the one in Montana where he'd been raised was like slipping into someone else's life. It made him feel like some kind of alien body snatcher. Only this body, so achy and scarred, had to be his.

Before setting up a hideout in the abandoned farmhouse next door, he'd enjoyed solitude sleeping outside in a hammock, listening to the birds. Now that he lived in his own house, with as much alone time as he wanted, the quiet got to him, made him miss the camaraderie of Army life.

He changed his clothes and headed over to the small barn he'd helped his brothers build for the goats—an Avery project. One step inside, and the smell engulfed him. Images flooded his mind, taking him back to the outskirts of that village in the desert.

He anchored himself in the present moment. He stared at the hay, the new fridge, the microwave—the orderly system Avery had created. This was new, shiny, and state-of-the-art, thanks to Luke subsidizing Avery's venture. Nothing like the dusty images fighting for space in his head. He focused on the texture of the bottle in his hand and checked the time. Zero four hundred. He was here. Florida. It was early morning. February. Family was nearby. No threats.

He prepared the formula, scooped up the first kid, and leaned back on a bale of hay holding the small creature. It bleated as he positioned the nipple, and the goat greedily drank. Soft and warm, it nestled into him. It was kind of ... nice. Ten percent of his tension drained away. He'd never admit it to anyone else, but goat-feeding didn't suck. When the first goat finished, he moved on to the next one, alert for the sounds of his brothers.

Boots thudded in his direction. His senses sharpened. Who else would be working this early?

Find Born Brave: Garrick on Amazon

JULIET BRILEE BOOKS

Scan the QR code above using the camera on your smartphone and get a free e-book, an e-book cookbook, author updates, bad jokes, and more in my newsletter.

Find Juliet Brilee books on Amazon.

The Sea Stars and Second Chances series

Beachside Bakery a second chance, single father romance with suspense
    Tea Leaves and the Texan a romance with suspense
    Bayside Cottage a later in life, suspenseful romance
    Sugar Star Christmas a second chance romance
    Peppermint Cocoa Christmas a single dad sweet romance

The Pine Crossing Cowboys Series

Born Ready: Luke a fake marriage ranch romance with suspense
    Born Tough: Jack an off-limits romance with suspense

Born Brave: Garrick romantic suspense at the ranch

Born Strong: Striker a friends to lovers romantic suspense

The Valencia Cove Series

Salt Bay Sunrise: a brother's best friend, wounded veteran, tropical romantic adventure

Second Chance Rescue: Tender Hearts Get a Second Chance at South Paws Dog Rescue, an opposites attract suspense romance

Christmas Cake Day a heartwarming holiday romance full of traditions, family, and holiday baking

Shell Point Secrets: a tropical romance with a dash of mystery.

Salt Bay Summer Dance: a friends to lovers romance

Salt Bay Sanctuary: a friends to lovers second chance romance with suspense

Lemon Cookie Christmas a second chance for love, clean and wholesome holiday romance

ABOUT THE AUTHOR

Juliet Brilee has a master's degree in math and science education and has been writing, making art, and teaching for most of her life. Inspired by her tech nerd husband who gardens, and her son who's blind, Brilee creates brainy characters who often work outdoors, in the arts, technology, or science fields. The people in her books overcome challenging obstacles, deal with the unexpected, find love, and create the life they want.

Her visually impaired son, and his friends who are blind or have other disabilities, help her portray individuals with disabilities more accurately. It is her intention to be respectful and compassionate.

Take a virtual vacation through stories at the intersection of romance, women's fiction and suspense.

When she's not writing, making art, or coaching, she's enjoying the beaches and woods of Florida, or hiking in the forests in North Carolina with her bossy dog.

Join my newsletter and get a free novella: A Second Chance for Bronson and other freebies and updates.

Made in the USA
Las Vegas, NV
01 February 2025

17340448R00184